FOR THE LOVE OF PARVATI

AN ANITA RAY MYSTERY

SUSAN OLEKSIW

D1265273

Hale Street Press ◊ Prides Crossing ◊ MA ◊ 01965

Hale Street Press
P.O.Box 161
Prides Crossing, MA 01965

First published by Five Star Publishing, a part of Gale,
Cengage
Learning, in 2014.

Cover design by Kathleen Valentine

Photograph by Susan Oleksiw

ISBN 978-0-9912082-9-6

Dedication Page

For Usha Ramachandran

Acknowledgments

Dr. Charlene Allison and Eleanor Lodge kindly read the manuscript in an earlier form and made valuable suggestions. The Malayalam kinship system is complex, and I have attempted to identify characters correctly by kinship terms where appropriate or important to the story. Any errors in this and any other aspect of the story are mine alone.

For the Love of Parvati

One

The wooden footbridge was a proud achievement when it was first constructed in 1924, thanks to the Maharajah of Travancore. The two dressed stone pillars, one on either side of the narrow stream, tapered ten feet to the top where metal plates secured three wooden planks, which carried villagers across the water to the other side. Almost ninety years later the pillars remained, but the planks had been replaced a number of times until now they were merely scraps of wood held in place by large rocks on either pillar. Crossing safely required the balance of a mountain goat and the faith of a good Hindu.

The man underneath the eastern pillar, his back pushed hard up against the stone, was at first grateful for the haphazardly placed pieces above him but as the monsoon rains intensified, the wooden boards did little to protect him. The force of this year's northeast monsoon in Southern India, and in central Kerala especially, made a mockery of roofs and shelters of all sorts. The rain pummeled the planks and the wind lifted each one, dropping it again and again onto the now useless metal plate, shifting each board this way or that. The boulders had long ago been moved to the edge, by human hands or storm, the man below couldn't say. He cringed each time a board came crashing down onto the pillar. The first time, he started and jerked aside, but the rope around his neck pulled taut and he slid back down in the mud, his back

1

scraping against the stone pillar. He gasped for breath.

Torn between fear and rage, fear the pillars and boards would collapse and crush him and rage that he had let himself get caught, he kept a wary eye on the action above. He kept an equally wary eye on the sapling at the far corner of the stone pillar he leaned against. There, whipping in the wind, folding low over the stream and snapping erect again and again, was a thin mango sapling, the anchor for one end of the tether around his neck. From his neck to the sapling. Every time he moved, he felt the cord around his neck tighten. If he tried to pull away, it would strangle him. But he couldn't get closer to the tree. He'd tried that. The other end of the rope was looped through an iron ring set into the pillar.

At first he thought the crumbling stone around the iron ring was a weakness he could exploit. Even though his hands were tied behind his back, he thought if he could loosen the ropes on his wrists he could pull the ring out. He could get the ropes up to the base of his thumb, but he could work them no further off his hands. Even in the rain he could feel the blood seeping onto his wrists from the flesh rubbed raw by the rough coir fiber; his hands stung with thin sharp cuts.

For two days he had waited, tied to the pillar and the sapling, soaked and cold, his world shrinking to the boards above and the roiling stream at his feet. He didn't know where it came from—somewhere higher up in the mountains, he assumed—but he knew where it went, into the Pamba River, which twisted and churned all the way to the valley floor and from there to Vembanad Lake on the coast. He had begun there, at the edge of the broad, still lake that shimmered in the sun, its surface a soft warm white, like an old man's silvery hair. The directions had been to follow the river to reach his destination, so he had.

When he thought about how close he had come to his goal, the rage burned inside him. He didn't mind dying, but not like this. He had promised to join his sister, to find her and protect her. But with every passing hour, he knew his chances of keeping that promise grew slimmer. He had been stupid enough to trust another, and this was the result—tied to a pillar and left to die here. Despite his careful planning, he had come to this. The hours passed, and he sank deeper into rage and fear, more fear than he would have ever admitted to himself was possible.

His captor said he would return, and he had—once. But that was two days ago. And now the rain was so much worse. With each passing hour, the jungle seemed to grow thicker and more threatening. It was not safe for a man here. But perhaps this was the point. The man tugged at the rope tied around his wrists. He wouldn't dwell on what might happen to him here—he knew about jungles and how to live in them—he wouldn't let fear overcome him.

There was one good thing about the monsoon and the decrepit bridge above him—it drove away the creatures curious about a human being resting here at this time. A bandicoot had nibbled at his ankle when he'd nodded off; his sudden awakening startled the animal and it jumped away. But only the clatter of the boards above drove the creature into seeking shelter elsewhere.

The man thought about that warm body skittering away as he pressed his arms close against his body, trying to shut out the cold. He'd never been so cold. Even when he pulled his legs up, kept his knees close, every part of him shivered. The rain was cold, the ground, every part of his body. If he nodded off from exhaustion, his head bobbed, and the rope caught, and he was awake again. The rope chafed and cut into his skin, and he winced at the slightest touch. The rain stung his open sores. That too kept him awake. Oh, how he needed rest, if only for a moment, to curl up and be warm, to be out of the cold and wet. He ached to sleep, to feel warmth and a night's ease.

Bright shiny eyes pierced the blackness, and he

forgot he was tired. He watched for the eyes but they disappeared. Had he imagined them? The wind swooped through again, lifting the leaves and branches, and the eyes shone and blinked again, closer this time. The man watched, calculating where the animal was, how far away, as the shining eyes appeared and disappeared behind the waving branches.

The animal crept closer, closer, placing its paws carefully in the muck, seemingly sensitive to the precariousness of the rain-soaked soil. The man made out the snout, then the ears—maybe a dog. No, not a dog. He had been warned about such an animal—a chennaya, the wild doglike animal of Periyar Wildlife Sanctuary. If he saw many of these, he had been told, he'd gone too far, too far into the mountains, perhaps even into the park. But he hadn't gone so far. He knew by the steepness of the climb, the number of houses he had passed, though there were fewer as he climbed, that he had not left the villages in the foothills of this part of Kerala. No, he had not gone too far. It had to be the rain, driving animals out of their usual habitat, confusing them, pushing them down the mountain into strange territory in their hunt for food.

The man searched the darkness for other shining eyes—these wild dogs didn't travel alone. He'd been warned. The animal drew closer, the wind clattered the boards above, the animal lifted its head, shifted its gaze left, right, then backed away. Overcome, the man closed his eyes in relief, praising Shiva the Protector, Shiva All Powerful, Shiva All Seeing.

The sky darkened for the third time as the man stared up at the boards clattering and trembling in the wind—they were both his safety and his threat. How could this have happened to him, a sharp-eyed soldier who had never fallen into a trap before? He had been trained well. He had proven it time and again. Yet, here he was. The irony of failing in this, his last clandestine journey and the only one that truly mattered to him, cut out his very soul.

The wind whipped the sapling back and forth, its roots increasingly exposed as rain washed the dirt down the riverbank and currents carried it away. On the opposite shore whole sections of the bank had caved in and been sucked away by the churning water—coconut palms shifted and fell on top of other trees and shrubs; saplings slid like children into the stream.

The man watched his own sapling, his anchor to death, and calculated what might happen and how he could use it if it did. If the sapling fell, and its roots dislodged, he could pull it to him without the tether tightening on his throat. The man had practiced the quick movement he might need to catch the rope with his teeth and pull the sapling to him. Once he had the tree within reach, he could use his feet to work himself loose of the rope. He had been a laborer, a man used to doing for himself and his family. He could build his own palm-leaf house, roof and walls, braiding the fronds with his own feet. His toes were as supple as most people's fingers. He could catch the sapling, pull it to him, and escape this imprisonment.

As the night darkened, the rain continued steadily, insistently, as though Shiva had determined to destroy the world this time not with fire but with water, all the water of the cosmos. The man scanned the riverbank, recited mantras to keep himself awake. He had to be alert to catch that sapling before it slid down the bank and fell into the stream, where the rushing water would pull the rope taut.

He heard the animal first. It was there, out of sight, but there. He didn't doubt his ears. The wind rested, gathering strength for its next onslaught. He heard the animal. He knew that sound. The intermittent guttural purr pierced the wind and rain and stabbed at him like a jolt of electricity. It couldn't be—no, it couldn't. He looked deep into the forest. These were the Cardamom Hills, on the slopes west of Periyar Wildlife Sanctuary, where all sorts of wildlife had been left to live in their own ways. The leopard shouldn't be down here, so far from the park. Perhaps it was stalking the chennaya, or maybe the bandicoot, looking for food. The man strained to hear.

The animal couldn't smell him—he was sure of that. As frightened as he was, he was covered in mud and soaked to the skin—no odor of fear could leak from his body. He looked down at his lungi, the wrapped lower cloth that looked like it had been painted onto his limbs, so heavy was the rain. Oh. There, yes, there it was. He had betrayed himself. His captor had left him so long he was now sitting in his own excrement. The animal roared again—low, a warning, unsure of what kind of being hid unmoving beneath the bridge. A paw began to probe the ground.

The man instinctively pulled away, but this time the rope did not grow taut—the sapling had loosened and tilted in his direction. He had room to maneuver—not much; a little. Mud slid in chunks down the riverbank, the roar grew louder; water surged down the stream. Waves churned up the bank, scraping the undergrowth from the shore. The man saw it coming at him, a wall of water almost level with his line of sight. It was certain death unless he could do something. He pulled against the rope tying his wrists together and felt a sharp pain. But the rope tore and his hands flew apart. One thumb wouldn't move, but he had one good hand. He could smell the leopard. Out of the corner of his eye he saw a muddy, spotted paw reach out. The surge of water hit the sapling; a gust of wind lifted the planks; the water ripped the man from his manacle and knocked the leopard from its hiding place.

Two

"Oh how I envy Lalita Amma!" The middle-aged woman curled her fingers around the pleats in her light cotton sari as she leaned toward the window; the paddy fields stretched all the way to the foothills, the sharp slope of a hillside at the end of a flat expanse. She seemed oblivious to the gray sky and mud.

"You are romanticizing, Auntie Meena," Anita said. She liked the landscape too, but she had no illusions about what it meant to live in the central part of Kerala and how hard it was to grow paddy or any other crop. She liked good food, but she didn't want to grow it. Right now the farmers were struggling not only with an overwhelming monsoon but also with the loss of farm workers, the loss of markets, and a decline in prices. Farming was not an easy life.

"Ach! You are cynical." Meena swung toward her. "And that is why I wanted you to come. You need to have . . . get . . . ."

Anita studied her aunt as she stumbled through her list of random excuses. "I thought I was keeping you company."

"Exactly!" Meena patted her sari skirt.

"So what exactly is it you think I need?" Anita's eyes narrowed as Meena began to fumble her words again.

"Why, ah, fresh air!"

"We live on the ocean with unremitting breezes."

"And new perspectives of . . ."

"Of what?" Anita's eyebrows flattened.

"All that is out in the wide world."

"You're going to have to accept Anand at some time, Auntie Meena."

"But I do, I do." Meena shook her head. "You misjudge me. You are unkind."

"You are sneaky, Auntie, sneaky."

"You must not talk like that. I need you to be cheerful and kind. We are taking this little trip for the sake of your aunt Lalita. She is troubled, sad. Now she is a widow—all her life is changing." Meena gave a little gasp, and drew back from the chasm that opened before her—she too was a widow, a woman who had lost her husband when they were both relatively young. Even now she was known to burst into tears at the sight of the widow's traditional white garment. Anita softened—it was rare that her aunt revealed true feeling. She was most often given to histrionics over things others considered trivial.

"Auntie, she has been a widow for over a year now." Anita patted her aunt's knee.

"Ah! Even so. But still, there is great change going on. Moving to the old estate, now, that is not to be disregarded." Meena leaned back in her seat as the car rounded a curve, scattering sand and pebbles into the yard of a house sitting close to the edge of the road.

"And I don't see what good I can do her." Anita frowned. She had capitulated to her aunt's repeated requests that she come along on this visit, but she was beginning to have second thoughts.

"You will be so good for her." Meena clapped her hand on the back of the driver's seat. "Joseph! Too fast! You are going too fast!"

"Shari, shari." The driver slowed, and Anita noticed his shoulders relax. "Very bad driving in all this wet weather," he said.

"We are soon there," Meena said.

"Perhaps I can say hello and leave you and Auntie Lalita to enjoy each other's company. I can return to the hotel with Joseph," Anita said. It was the middle of November and Hotel Delite was open for the season, but few foreign guests would appear before the end of the month. Meena felt safe leaving the hotel in others' hands.

"No, no, you must stay." Meena grabbed Anita's hand.

"Auntie?" Anita waited but Meena continued to stare out the window. "Meena Elayamma?" Anita knew the more traditional title for a mother's younger sister would break through Meena's reserve. Meena's lower lip trembled and she squeezed Anita's hand. "So, what haven't you told me?"

"Why do you always accuse me of such things?" Meena did her best to sulk.

"Do I not know you as well I know my own mother?"

"Ah! Your mother! What will she say when you are thirty and not yet married?" This was entirely rhetorical, and Anita knew it, but she still felt the compulsion to correct her aunt.

"She won't say a thing. She is happy in America, and she understands I am to be allowed to make up my own mind."

Meena flinched. "Don't say such things. Lalita Amma will be shocked." She nodded to Joseph in the front seat to let Anita know she should be more discreet. "It would be most inappropriate at this time."

"Why at this time?"

"Valli is there." It was barely a whisper but Anita heard, and she noticed that Joseph in the front seat did too. The car slowed.

"Why is that something to whisper about? And why

9

didn't you tell me? I haven't seen her since her wedding two years ago. This is wonderful news." Anita smiled at the prospect of a visit with her cousin. "It is good news, isn't it?"

Meena shrugged. "What is good news, what is bad news? Who knows?"

And that, thought Anita, means you are not telling me everything. Anita looked out at the soaked landscape. She ignored Meena's melodramatic sighs and stared at the road ahead, gearing herself for whatever Meena was up to.

Joseph swung the car around a pothole and slowed to take a sharp curve; when the road straightened out Anita saw a line of vehicles stopped ahead at a roadblock. She tried to count the number of policemen as the car came to a stop at the end of the line of automobiles and motorcycles. At first she thought they were stuck at a puddle too deep to cross. The northeast monsoon was turning out to be heavier and more intense than anticipated, with the usual intermittent showers turning into unrelenting downpours, and puddles merging into streams that flooded village squares and washed out homes and shops. Families forced to flee with their belongings to higher ground watched pots and bedding and odd bits of furniture float by. But it wasn't a puddle that had brought the cars to a halt. Two police officers in their starched khaki uniforms leaned against a portable wooden barrier while four more officers peered into cars and read papers clutched in their hands.

Farther ahead, near the next bend in the road, an old bus with the letters KSRTC emblazoned across the front was slowing down. When it pulled to a halt, a policeman climbed aboard.

"Hmm," Joseph said. "They are searching for contraband again. Rice, perhaps alcohol."

"No, no, not now." Meena peered through the windshield. As a hotelier, she felt she knew what was worth smuggling into the state and what could easily be left elsewhere.

"Maybe they're collecting bribes," Anita said.

Joseph inched the car forward as the driver of the car stopped at the portable barrier took his documents, got into the car, and drove away. A stout officer waved a small red car forward, then thrust out his hand, ordering it to stop. A second policeman ordered the driver, a man, and a woman passenger out of the car and motioned them to stand to the side of the road. He took the driver's documents and read them slowly, glancing up at the driver every now and then. With a wag of his head, the officer waved the man to the back of the car and ordered him to open the boot.

"Now this is very curious," Anita said. "Not small, large enough to be hidden in a car's boot." Anita clucked while she considered the possibilities. "Could be drugs, but probably not. These people do not look like they are drug couriers." When it was their turn, Joseph drove forward to the temporary wooden barrier. Anita and Meena immediately handed over their papers.

"What are you looking for?" Anita asked the policeman. He must have been close to Meena's age, with a sour, dull look that warned people away, a man who had been passed over year after year for promotion and now had the unenviable job of searching cars on back roads for contraband while his senior officer, a much younger man, stood by, giving the orders to raise the portable barrier, lower it, search this car more carefully, look here, look there.

The officer gave Anita a careful, regarding look before taking her papers and studying them at his leisure. The two women stood by the back door, while Joseph stood at the front.

"Where are you going?" the officer asked.

"To visit a friend, outside Chengannur. In the hills." Anita noted that he didn't even start to look up at her as she spoke.

"What place?"

Anita named the small village.

"What family?"

Anita named Lalita Amma's family.

"Hmm." His head began to swing in affirmation, but then he stiffened and Anita wondered if he would be warned for breaking the blank wall of official duty, or if he had noticed something in her papers. He began to flip through the documents one more time, though almost casually.

"And you are only going for visit?"

"Yes, yes. Lalita Amma is a relation." Meena pressed up against Anita.

The policeman looked at Meena beneath his eyebrows, pursing his lips and studying her as though she were speaking a foreign tongue and he found the flexing of her facial muscles of great interest. He sighed. "Boot. Open." He tipped his head toward the back of the car as he walked around it. Anita popped the latch on the boot. "Remove." He pointed to the luggage. Anita pulled out two suitcases and a cloth bag of gifts for the family.

"What are you looking for?" she asked. "Drugs?"

The policeman paid no attention to her; instead, he leaned into the boot and with his lathi lifted up the edge of an old rug covering the floor, moved his hand over the rough surface without actually touching it, careful to keep his fingers and palm clean, and again used the lathi to push the rug to the side. He poked deeper into the dark space. He wrapped a clean handkerchief around his hand before pulling out the spare tire and looking into the well. With a sigh of sheer boredom, he motioned Anita to open the luggage.

"Here?"

"Here."

"Shari, shari." Anita knelt down and unzipped the

two bags, laying them open on a blue plastic tarp the police had spread out on the ground. The officer knelt and began looking through her things, poking, probing, pressing, even squeezing the clothing. He picked up the cloth bag containing gifts and set it in the well of the boot, then pushed his hand in and moved it around. Anita had the awful feeling she was going to be asked to unwrap the two gifts she had tied up in silk fabric. She avoided looking at Meena—and had no trouble imagining her aunt's stricken look of insult.

A coolish breeze lifted the end of Anita's dupatta and she glanced up at the blackening sky. It looked like it was about to throw a month's worth of rain right at them. Rainwater glistened on tree branches and tall blades of grass; muddy puddles covered the shoulders along the roads; cows and goats nudged each other on narrower and narrower paths; lanes were impassible. And it was cool. There was so much rain that the sun barely shone through the clouds long enough to dry up the puddles, leaving the people of Kerala with the odd sensation of feeling a slight chill. Most who lived along the coast had never experienced a temperature below twenty degrees Celsius, and Anita found herself pulling her dupatta tighter around her shoulders and wishing she had kept out a shawl for the drive.

"Done."

"Of course it is done." Meena lifted her chin. "Do we look like criminals?"

The officer glanced at her before calling out, "Hari? Okay?"

Anita turned to see whom he was calling to, and found another officer crawling out of the backseat of their car, dusting himself off. Joseph stood to the side, a look of resignation on his face. He seemed to be taking the whole thing philosophically.

"Okay." Hari nodded and walked back to the officer

who seemed to be in charge; the two men studied the front of the car, and the officer wrote something down.

"Are you recording our registration plate?" Anita asked.

"It is all right. Go." The policeman ignored her question and waved them to drive on. He walked back to the next car, a bright-green foreign auto driven by a young man wearing dark spectacles.

Anita repacked the boot and got into the car as the barrier was raised. She glanced back to see the constable leaning over the back of her car, his left hand resting on the fender. As Joseph drove slowly away from the roadblock, Anita heard her aunt's mutterings about the police search but didn't think to reply; she was too caught up in going over the encounter, the way the policemen searched, the notes they had taken of the various registration plates, the questions asked and those not asked. It all seemed typical of an area search for, perhaps, a suspected criminal, smugglers or drug runners, or political operatives. But it wasn't typical.

"These things are becoming so annoying," Meena said. "Government is intrusive." She crossed her arms and pouted.

"Too much of this," Joseph agreed. "Typical."

"No," Anita said. "This was not typical. The man in black hiding in the trees and pointing his rifle straight at us was not typical."

"What?" Both Meena and Joseph spoke at once.

"The man among the trees. He was the one in charge, not the man at the barrier with the clipboard. The man in black was the one who signaled to the officer that we could leave."

A man with a rifle, thought Anita, in Kerala.

* * * * *

Joseph maneuvered the car through the narrow streets of Chengannur. This was the last stop on the train line for

anyone heading deeper into the hills, and in general, the
only ones heading deeper into the mountains were the few
villagers who lived there or devotees going to Sabarimala, a
mountain where a holy site held an annual festival that was
famous throughout India. Beyond Sabarimala was Periyar
Wildlife Sanctuary, but tourists did not take this route to
get there. The car began a slow ascent, weaving through
villages, past the great temple town Arunmula. After a
while the car turned off onto a narrow paved lane.

This was one of the ways Anita measured the
modernization of Kerala—the old dirt lane had turned into
a one-lane paved road during her mother's childhood, and
now was a newly paved two-lane road, with wider dirt
shoulders to aid cars in passing each other. The car entered
a small village.

"We are collecting Lalita Amma's son, Prakash. He
is working here." Meena smiled, relaxed now that they
were climbing into the hills and would soon reach their
destination. "He is a priest here, very successful—a rising
star."

So that's what this is all about, Anita thought. This
was more than Anita usually managed to get when Auntie
Meena brought up someone she considered a suitable
prospect for her niece. Anita was beginning to think Meena
was hopeless—after coming to admit that perhaps Anand,
Anita's friend, was not such a bad sort, she seemed to have
reverted to her earlier state—the older female relative on
the hunt for a suitable spouse for a young woman in the
family. Anita pulled out her mobile phone.

"Such a fine young man," Meena said, starting to
preen as though she were his mother and not a distant
relation. Unlike most of the men Anita's age, Prakash had
turned away from high-tech work, the booming
construction sector, and almost everything else that came
his way. After dropping out of engineering college, Prakash
sought and obtained his current assignment as an assistant

15

priest and was marvelously content. Anita knew all this because Meena had suffered through his various career vicissitudes as though she were his mother. Aside from all this, Anita thought Prakash was a nice sort, very much the younger brother she'd never had.

"What are you doing?" Meena asked, eyeing Anita's mobile phone.

Joseph swung the car wide to avoid another puddle.

"I thought I'd call Anand, and let him know where I am." Anita wiggled the phone in a futile effort to improve the reception.

"Maybe it will work later," Meena said.

Joseph grunted and glanced at the two women in his rearview mirror.

"It will be nice to see Valli and her mother—and Prakash, yes?" Meena smiled and tapped Anita's knee.

Anita agreed, and tried to fix in her memory exactly where Valli's mother fit in the family tree, which right now had so many branches that on some days Anita feared she was related to every other Nayar in Kerala. Valli was sitting on a branch somewhere, but despite their many wonderful childhood summers together, Anita couldn't quite grasp why Valli and her mother, Lalita Amma, had suddenly become so important to Auntie Meena. Unless . . .

"Don't look at me like that," Meena said.

Joseph swerved around a busload of men dressed in black lungis and black shirts. "Sabarimala returning," he said. "Just finishing their pilgrimage."

Despite the heavy rains, the pilgrim traffic up to and from the holy site in the hills was unabated, and Anita enjoyed seeing the truckloads of devotees going or coming—they gave a festive quality to the journey. The trucks of those returning also told others the roads were still passable up ahead. The men gathered in their villages all over Kerala and set out in large and small groups for the temple at Sabarimala. The roads were filled with men on pilgrimage.

"We will collect Prakash and be on our way," Meena said. She moved closer to Anita and lowered her voice. "And with all this rain you and Valli will be confined to the house." She glanced at Joseph to make sure he was not listening. "And then you can learn the things we need to learn."

Anita scowled at her aunt. "What things?"

"She is only one." Meena gave Anita a knowing smile.

"Only one? Oh, yes, I see. Valli has no child yet."

"And you as her friend are able to learn why this is so." Meena flicked her head in satisfaction with handing over this task and moved back to the window.

Anita considered her aunt's words. Perhaps she'd been wrong about her aunt. Perhaps this trip wasn't about introducing Anita to the idea of Prakash as a prospective husband. Perhaps it really was about comforting Lalita Amma after her husband's death, and finding out if things were all right with Valli.

But even so, Anita wasn't sure she wanted this assignment. Valli had been married for almost two years and so far there had been no child—this was unusual for an Indian marriage—but Anita knew there could be nothing to it. Valli was known to be of an independent mind.

Joseph steered around a cow rummaging through a pile of refuse; he drove into a sandy lot in front of a temple compound wall, and parked under a banyan tree.

The Thiruvadnagar Devi Temple was modest by most standards—a high compound wall enclosed five shrines. The central shrine was the largest, about the size of an average village house, and the shrines at the four cardinal points were the size of dollhouses. Each shrine at a cardinal point was painted in bright colors. The back and sides of the main shrine were also painted in bright colors, and two voluptuous women were carved on pilasters to serve as door guardians at the front. Because it was midday, and the morning puja long finished, the compound was empty of devotees; a sweeper woman passed in front of the main gate with a basket of leaves under her arm, her free hand carrying a broom.

"Now to find Prakash." Meena and Anita climbed out of the car, slipped off their sandals at the main gate, and walked in. The door to the office was open, and Meena strolled over, but Anita decided to circumambulate the main shrine. She set off, passing shrines to Ganesha, Karttikeya, Bhairava, and Parvati, Siva's consort. When she returned to the front gate, she saw Prakash waving to her from the office.

"You have come! You have come!" He loped over to her, pressing his hands together in anjali, his face one large smile, making him look much younger than his years. "I am so happy to see you, Anita Chechi, so happy." Anita began to laugh—his exuberance was that of a small child. "Meena Amma has told me—we shall have such a good visit—all of us together. You and Valli and me—like old times."

"I did not realize Valli would be here too," Anita said. "Wonderful news. I haven't had a real visit with your mother in donkeys' years and I can't wait to see everyone," Anita said, wondering what else her auntie Meena had failed to tell her. "The car is outside."

"Yes, I am almost ready. One delay only," Prakash said. "First, we have a passenger. I have promised a devotee we can give him a ride to the village." Prakash lowered his voice. "He is very poor. A laborer. Work is scarce and travel is costly."

"Of course," Anita agreed, though it was a bit awkward. Another passenger meant that Joseph would have to share the front seat with two men while Anita and Meena sat in the back. "And the delay?"

"A small matter. The priest wants a few quick

words with me before I leave. Just now. It is some technical matter, since I am going only for a short visit." Prakash loped back to the office, turning to wave to her before he disappeared inside.

Anita decided to use the extra time to get to know the temple better. She strolled over to one of the smaller shrines, walked around it, and strolled back to the gate. The tiles covering the compound wall were thick with mold from the heavy rain but otherwise most were in good condition; the wood doors to the small cells that served as storage or rooms for traveling monks were old but also in good condition. The dirt ground, though damp, was tidy and smooth; door metalware was shiny but, again, old. A small temple, thought Anita, but well cared for. There might be no money for the newer embellishments—brass door decorations, new oil lamps, new doors for shrines— but the temple was not neglected. It obviously had sufficient devotees to keep it going. As evidence of this, a woman came through a side entrance with a bundle of battered aluminum pots still dripping from washing. When Anita heard the prayerful greeting to a priest, she turned.

"Ah, Prakash." Anita smiled and started to walk toward him, but she paused when she saw his face. Something was different now. He glanced almost furtively at the old woman with the pots as he passed her.

"We can go now." He managed to smile, but Anita wondered at how hard it seemed to be.

"No passenger? I haven't seen anyone, so I was wondering . . ."

"What? Oh, yes, he's waiting outside. This way." Prakash led the way to the car, and stood, his arms hanging at his side, by the back door. Meena sat in the car chatting with Joseph.

"Prakash?"

"What? Oh, Anita Chechi, I am so sorry." He seemed to remember where he was and once again became the professional, the new assistant priest. He waved to a man sitting under a tree, who immediately rose and trotted over to the car.

Yes, this man is poor, thought Anita as she watched the stranger. His clothes were worn and faded, and he carried a small bundle over his shoulder; the rubber chappals on his feet looked like they were ready to fall apart. She ushered Prakash and his friend into the front seat and climbed into the back. Joseph turned around to glare at Anita and Meena. But Anita ignored him, and Meena clucked at him. She was not one to take criticism from her driver.

"Do you need directions, Joseph?" Prakash asked. "Anita Chechi? Have you given directions?"

Joseph headed into the hills. The car had not gone far before they were halted at a second roadblock. Anita steeled herself for another delay but to her surprise, the police officers only walked around the car, peered into the front seat and backseat, then motioned Joseph to drive on. When they later arrived at the estate and Anita went around to the boot to supervise unloading the luggage, she understood why the car had not been searched a second time—two thin red pieces of nylon twine marked the seam between boot and body. If anyone had opened the boot between roadblocks, the police would have known—and searched a second time.

* * * * *

The drive into the mountains was not as Anita remembered it. Joseph navigated the ever-narrowing roads, Prakash reassuring her they were on the right track, and Meena chirped that it all looked so familiar, changed but familiar. Anita doubted that anything looked familiar in this year's rains—old mud walls lay collapsed along the shoulder, shrubs sprawled in ditches, their roots rainwashed clean of soil, and every now and then a solitary and soaked rag waved from a tree branch. When she turned to comment to

Prakash about all this, she found him staring abstractedly out the window and his friend lying slumped down, apparently asleep.

"He's tired," Prakash replied the first time Anita noticed this. "Construction work in Goa. Very hard. So now he is doing day labor in this area. Very hard." He delivered this news in a flat monotone and Anita resigned herself to a silent drive. She had started out with pleasurable anticipation and had been quickly deflated. Whatever had gotten to Prakash seemed to be getting to her too.

"Mind the goat!" Prakash called out.

A black-and-white goat jumped across the road, slipped in the mud, and stumbled into a nearby yard. Anita could hear the animal bleating as Joseph drove on. The little houses became sparser as they rode higher into the hills, and the rivulets of rainwater running along the road thickened into small streams in deep gulleys.

Three

The old family house sat in a cleft in the hillside, surrounded by the thick trees and bushes of the region—a few cardamom trees, mango and papaya trees, pepper vines, and more that Anita couldn't distinguish in the graying afternoon light and thickening mist of a monsoon season. But it was, she was certain, as beautiful as always.

This was a place she loved. Here she'd spent month after month in her childhood with Valli, a distant cousin but also a dear friend. In the early-morning hours they fled the house and the ayah and followed a mahout and his elephant down to the river where he washed his beloved animal. If the mahout was in a good mood, he commanded the elephant to shower the girls with water, which drove them giggling up and down the bank. Sometimes he pretended not to notice them, and the girls crept up close to the other side of the animal before the mahout slapped his hand down on the water and sent them fleeing to the riverbank. Sometimes he scowled at them, and they hunkered down to watch, tossing pebbles into the lapping waves and wondering what they had done to anger him.

The old feelings of blissful freedom from responsibility rose up in Anita—here she had always been a girl set free from whatever ills beset her relatives or their village, her ship loosened from the anchor of duties that held her at home under her mother's watchful eye. She could drift on a breeze, find a quiet harbor of solitude, a sail for a storm. Joseph drove the car up to the gateway now standing in solitary splendor, time and weather having crushed the baked brick compound wall that used to extend on either side.

"Oh, Prakash! I am so glad to be here. It has been too long! Your home in the North may be grand, but this will always hold my heart." Anita waited for him to turn around and acknowledge her enthusiasm.

"Ah, yes," Meena said. "The old ways are the best."

Prakash glanced at the house, tipped his head to one side, and seemed to think about Anita's comment. "Yes, it is an old house of memories." He offered her a ruminative look. "My mother will be glad to see you, Chechi. She has missed you. She often says so and Valli promises you will come." He tried to smile, but his smile seemed to flag just as it got going. "And so you have. You are here."

* * * * *

An hour later, Anita unlatched the louvered doors that opened onto a small upper veranda and stood on the sill while the rain fell in sheets. The only sound was the sound of rain. No birds sang or cawed indignantly, no cows mooed, no goats brayed. No car horns honked, no lorries squealed around corners. The rain was a wall enclosing the family in its own private world, as though nothing else existed outside this rambling old house. And crumbling gardens, Anita added to herself as she caught sight of the low walls and potted plants at the far end of the courtyard. Sad, she thought, and went back inside to change her clothes before joining the others for tea.

"Come!" Anita called at the sound of someone knocking on her door.

"Luggage is here." Prakash pushed open the door and slid a suitcase into the room.

"Prakash?" Anita tried to conceal her surprise. "Where is Thampi?"

"Ah! Going to Sabarimala!" Prakash waved away the question about the old family servant who managed the garden, maintained the house, chased after the animals, and ran whatever errands anyone came up with. Making the pilgrimage to Sabarimala had been Thampi's dream for years. "His first trip, so he is most particular in his preparations—he is adhering to his austerity vows for almost two months now. Very hard."

Anita could imagine how difficult this might be for the elderly man—no meat, no fish, no sex, no alcohol, and no abusive words. "Does he come at all to work?"

Prakash shook his head. "He came one day all in black, the pilgrim clothing, and we knew. He is not needing to speak." He shrugged. "The first group from this village leaves in a few days, I am thinking, and he will be gone with them."

Anita thanked him and began to unpack. She would miss seeing Thampi, but she was happy for him, and she hummed to herself as she arranged her clothing in the closet. She loved this room. This one had always been Anita's after both sets of parents decided the girls, Anita and Valli, were old enough to sleep in their own rooms during visits—not so long ago, it seemed to Anita. Her room faced the front, looking out over part of the veranda, and giving her a view of the wing that jutted out to her right. This was called the new wing, though it had been added decades ago. To her left and behind the house were the hills and jungle. The room was the same, the view was the same; only the people were different.

Except for the laborer who had hitched a ride with them and gotten out at the village crossroads, Anita didn't see anyone as they passed through the village—the rain was keeping everyone inside. When Joseph stopped the car for the passenger to alight, the laborer slipped from the car with barely a word and no acknowledgment of the others at all—merely a perfunctory nod to Prakash. The stranger

melted into the mist as though he had been an illusion, a
figment of Anita's imagination. His departure added to her
feeling of isolation and even estrangement, of having
entered a separate world defined by the rain, created by the
rain, at the mercy of ceaseless rain, cut off from the rest of
the world on the plains below.

"Come, come. Tea is here." Valli's mother saw
Anita coming down the stairs and waved her into a large
sitting room, with finely carved mahogany chairs and
settees covered with brightly colored cushions. Meena
plumped a pillow behind her, and smiled the smile of one
who feels so comfortable that she sees no need to conduct
conversation.

"Lalita Amma, my room is the same!" Anita took a
chair close to Valli's mother.

"Why should it be different? When we moved
North, we took so little, so everything is as we left it."
Lalita paused. "I am glad you are pleased."

"You don't like the North?" Anita ran her hand over
the old fabric, shabby with age but still beautiful. She
meant the question kindly, the way she had always teased
her aunts when they grew nostalgic or sentimental, but
Lalita Amma seemed to take it literally.

"This is my home. But my husband—he found
success in the North."

Anita couldn't miss the wistful note in the old
woman's voice, and found herself thinking it matched
Lalita's condition—the plain white sari, no gold or colored
border, no colored choli, no jewelry, the dress of a widow.
Somehow success didn't seem to glow for her anymore.

"But you must take tea." Lalita Amma nodded to
the maidservant standing nearby. The woman was so quiet
and unobtrusive that Anita hadn't really noticed her. The
maidservant picked up a metal cup and its flat-bottomed
bowl, and began pouring the hot tea from cup to bowl and
back again, to cool it off. The wide arc of chocolaty tea

whooshed again and again, until the maidservant deemed it ready, when she handed the cup in its bowl to Anita.

"Now, the news. I must have news." Lalita settled into her chair, her hands resting in her lap. "First, your mother. How is she?"

Anita searched her memory for news about her mother, which was mostly of the variety of vacation travels or the like.

"Meena, you have told me none of this. You are not confiding in me?" Lalita said.

"Ah." Meena smiled. "I am tired of hearing of her travels and the ease of her life. I sit in my little office with the accounts books in front of me and my sister's life is like a fantasy."

Lalita Amma chuckled. "Perhaps you should tell her, and she will come back to help you. Family duty, isn't it?"

"Ayoo! Do you think she would give up so much easy living to come back here? My sister has all the conveniences and also a housekeeper. Why would she come here, where she has to argue with servants and do so much of the work herself because no one wants to be a maidservant anymore? No, she is quite satisfied to be an NRI—all the advantages of being an Indian and none of the disadvantages."

"NRI is it? Nonresident Indian, eh? More likely Never Return to India." Lalita lifted her hand to forestall any protests.

"It is no matter, Lalita Amma," Anita said. "She would not be happy here, and besides, Meena Elayamma would then be the younger daughter even in her own home. She would lose status. No, better my mother stays away, where she is happy." Anita leaned back on the settee and stretched out her feet. "Let things remain as they are."

"I do not see how she can live there," Meena said, more to herself than the others. She had been listening to

Anita and Lalita bantering, and instead of joining in had grown quiet. "She will always be a stranger, always be foreign. She can never belong. No one knows who she is, not really. They only see the name of her husband. Who is she to them? She is not a woman with a family going back four hundred years, yes, four hundred years with all the documents to prove it. She is only a woman with a strange accent from a strange country with a lot of poor people." Meena shook her head, looking down at her bare feet peeking out from beneath her sari hem. "No, we should not leave our homelands. Better we stay where we belong, where people know us and recognize us. It is much better."

The two other women stared at Meena, their mouths agape. Anita hardly knew what to say. She had never heard her aunt talk like this. Coming into an old family home seemed to have unsettled her.

Anita gave Lalita Amma a careful smile, and said, "But shouldn't Valli be telling me about her new life?" Anita signaled the maidservant for more tea, and the young woman padded across the floor to pour another cup and cool it before handing it to Anita. "Where has Valli got to? She showed me to my room, and then disappeared."

"She is with her brother."

For a moment Anita thought she might be imagining it but she knew she wasn't. The warmth had dimmed in Lalita Amma's eyes. Her initial enthusiasm while welcoming her guests had been eclipsed by darker feelings. Anita had known Lalita Amma for too long to miss the signs of trouble. Something was definitely wrong.

* * * * *

The cook listened with her head tipped to the side. Vengamma was as old as Lalita, perhaps older, a fixture in the household for as long as Anita could remember. Her earliest memory of the cook was watching her standing in the old cooking annex, now long gone, on the hard-packed dirt floor tending her cooking fires, ordering the helpers without turning around to watch them, putting out her hand for what she wanted when she wanted it, knowing her palm would be filled.

"Hmmm." Vengamma unfolded the sheet of paper and studied it, then waved it in the air, calling to the maidservant in the farther room. "Parvati! Va!" Vengamma handed her the slip of paper without even looking at her.

"Stupid girl," Vengamma said returning to Anita. "She is so shy, she would hide in a latrine. But what am I to do? Who will work today? No one will work. They want fancy jobs in big hotels, big tips from the foreigners and money to buy their own televisions. I am lucky I have anyone." Vengamma continued the litany of complaints that Anita was used to hearing whenever she visited the friends of her parents, an older generation confused and sometimes stunned into silence by the changes going on around them.

The maidservant Parvati withdrew deeper into the cooking rooms, and Anita wondered what the servant thought of all this lamentation. Anita got the feeling Parvati wasn't from this area; if she were, she'd ignore Vengamma's complaints or give as well as she got. But instead Parvati seemed to crawl inside herself, staying as quiet and as unobtrusive as possible. Hers was the mentality of the ill-used servant, Anita knew, and one of the worst legacies of centuries of repression. Anita wondered how far the young maidservant had traveled before fetching up here, isolated in the hills from any of her own people, far from her own village. How desperate did you have to be to wander so far for work?

"But she can cook and she is not bothering me with idle chatter about film stars and Bollywood." Vengamma reached for a plate on the stone counter behind her, and showed it to Anita. "Now, come. Fried banana."

Vengamma led the way into the family library, where Valli was peering into the bottom drawer of an old wooden desk.

"Ah, there you are." Anita leaned over the desk and tapped her cousin on the shoulder. Valli sat up and smiled at Anita.

"You eat!" Vengamma plopped the plate down on the desk and left.

"She hasn't changed," Anita said, "nor has this room."

"You talk as though it has been years." Valli pushed the drawer shut and reached for the plate, pulling it closer to her and examining the offerings.

"Almost two years, I think. Not since you were married." Anita walked along the periphery of the room, fingering the books on the bookshelves, the odd china cup kept for its delicate painted decoration regardless of the chip in the rim, the baked clay figure of Krishna in bright paint now flaking and fading, and the stack of wooden coin counters pushed into the corner of a near-empty shelf. "What are these doing here?" Anita pulled out one of the counters—a thin piece of mahogany about eight inches long by five inches wide, with a carved handle at the top; the body featured ten rows, each with ten shallow round pockets; each pocket, about the size of the impression of a little finger, could be filled with a small gold coin. The coins of the time were so small and thin that they became impossible to handle individually—spreading them over the board, to fill in the pockets, proved to be a much easier way to calculate the required quantity.

Valli looked up as she finished eating one of the fried banana slices and licked her fingers. "I'm looking for something for Prakash, but not having much luck. What have you got there?" She peered at the wooden counter in Anita's hand. "Oh that." Valli leaned back in her chair. "Have you tried one of these?" She tipped the plate toward her friend. "So good. I get so fat here."

The wooden coin counter was light, the wood

29

smooth from years of use. In the stack on the shelf Anita noted about a dozen in different sizes, and imagined the bags of gold coins, some as thin as paper, carried by property owners to make purchases. Anita wasn't surprised that Valli's family had a pile of the counters, but Anita was mildly surprised at seeing them stacked all together on a shelf in the library; the family had a business office elsewhere in the house where such things were kept. She replaced the small counter on the stack and continued her walk around the room. When she had made a complete circuit of the room, she curled up on an old settee, stuffing cushions behind her back.

Valli watched the rain pouring down outside, its roar filling the room. After a moment, she rose and closed the doors to the veranda.

"It's too bad you got here so late. We could have had a walk to the neighbors. But the rain comes on early and lasts and lasts. This year is very bad, very hard for the farmers."

"I am sorry we are late. A roadblock delayed us. Our car was searched."

"Really? A search? This happened to you?" Valli seemed concerned and pulled a chair up close to the settee. "And why are they searching?"

"The police didn't say, but I was not convinced it was drugs. I saw a man with a rifle hiding out of sight."

"Oh." Valli's eyes widened and she stared at Anita as though she were a complete stranger. Oddly enough, Anita felt like one, too.

"Then we stopped at the temple to collect Prakash." Anita leaned forward. "Something is wrong there, I am sure of it. He was so happy to see us and we started to plan, but he had to go back to the office; then, after a final word with the priest, he was quite different. He went away happy and came back sad. Something is wrong, isn't it?"

"Oh, really, Anita." Valli huffed and flounced back

in her chair. "Can't you be like other people and ignore these little things in the name of etiquette?"

"What rule of etiquette is that? To ignore someone's distress?"

"Oh . . ." Valli looked around her, her lips turning down into a pout. "I didn't think it would be so obvious so soon." Valli picked at the folds of her sari, pulling them into alignment. "I am hoping a visit with us will cheer him up. You are like his elder sister too, yes?"

"Yes, yes," Anita agreed. Prakash had always addressed her as Chechi, elder sister, and tagged along with her and Valli whenever they went off into the jungle to explore. He was dear to her.

"Why does he need cheering up?" Anita asked.

Valli looked around at the old family library, as though the answer lay hidden somewhere among the books long undusted and even longer unread. Her father had spent his evening hours in here playing chess by postcard with dozens of friends around the world, his miniature chess sets covering a long table and his favorite chess set sitting on its own table by his desk.

Missing, thought Anita. She looked around the room for all the little chess sets, but they were missing too. She waited for Valli to answer but instead the other woman grew gloomier and gloomier. "Did Auntie Meena know Prakash needed cheering up?" Anita was becoming increasingly suspicious of her aunt, but Valli shook her head.

"No, no, of course not."

Anita nodded, only partly convinced. She had the feeling Valli wasn't telling her the whole truth.

"It is the temple," Valli said. She pulled herself up in her chair, trying to get more comfortable, pushing a pillow behind her. "They say they are not satisfied with his performance."

"Not satisfied?" Anita tried to grasp what this

31

meant. "How can he not be adequate in his performance as a priest? Does he forget the ritual? Is he careless with the offerings?" Anita forced herself to halt the onslaught of questions—she knew that throwing them at someone feeling as low as Valli obviously did would only make her feel worse. But Valli's news was upsetting. Anita had attended some of Prakash's pujas and they seemed as perfect and as correct as anyone else's. He was never rushed, nor careless, nor sloppy, nor forgetful. His recitation was sweet and melodic, an offering all by itself. "What does that mean?"

"It means his future is uncertain." Valli rested her elbows on the table and her chin on her clasped hands. "And my mother is unhappy all over again."

Four

Parvati spread the sari blouse across her lap and reached for
the scissors. She slipped the blade beneath the black thread
holding the plastic hook and eye onto its cardboard plate,
snipped, and let the two pieces of plastic fall into her lap.
With small delicate fingers she picked up the eye and held
it in place on the blouse placket, matching its openings with
the holes made by thread and needle. She poked the needle
and thread in and drew the needle through on the other side,
pulling the thread taut.

She liked sewing. She enjoyed the stillness required
to do a good job. Sewing took concentration, a steady hand
and a keen eye. Sometimes, while working on a choli
blouse or repairing the embroidery on a tablecloth or
handkerchief, she forgot where she was, and lost herself in
the rhythm of the needle. She had learned to sew at her first
job as a maidservant, and it seemed a marvelous skill that
made her someone special. When she was finished sewing
one part and needed to rethread her needle, she'd look up
and wonder at the furniture around her and the room in
which she sat. Then it would come back to her—where she
was, who she was. In that moment, a great rush of sorrow
that threatened to rise up and overwhelm her—a sorrow as
dense as the monsoon rain, as pervasive as the wind, as
devastating as the mud slides, sweeping away all her

rational thoughts and all her promises to herself, and her discipline, especially her discipline, the iron will that had brought her this far. Parvati looked down at the blouse resting on her lap and poked the needle through the cloth. She watched the shiny steel tip rise up towards her chin.

It was cold here—colder than she had ever known. At night she wrapped herself in the thin blanket Lalita Amma had given her and curled up on the floor; the lumpy mattress she unrolled onto the cement was better than anything else she had slept on in years. Vengamma clucked over the blanket and Parvati feared the cook begrudged the gift from Lalita Amma, but the next day the cook appeared in the doorway, before leaving for her own home in the late afternoon. She held a small blanket, its pink silk binding falling from its worn edges. "A little better," the cook said, handing over the blanket. Parvati draped it over her shoulders and torso and lay down to sleep, staying awake to smell the fragrance that spurted into the air every time she moved. She couldn't identify it, and after a while she didn't care. She twitched her shoulder, shifted her hips, rolled her head, and little bursts of beauty shimmered in the atmosphere above her.

This place was a wonderland. The old woman, Amma as they all called her whether she was their mother or not, except for the new one, who sometimes called her auntie—the old woman was brusque and warm, aloof and kind, careful with a rupee but generous with her own property. And Vengamma, who wailed at her troubles running the household, watched over Parvati surreptitiously. And always there was good food.

The food was the people. That's something Parvati had learned since coming here. She had worked in many homes in India since crossing over the Gulf of Mannar, from Sri Lanka, and she knew the food, or so she thought. She cooked many things, learned many things, and in each home, she learned how the owners felt about their own,

their family members, their workers and their servants. She
expected the poor rice and dhal that made up most of her
meals in the cities, and she liked the chilies that always
came with her meal in the family household outside Kochi.
The master liked his food hot, and gave everyone the
hottest dishes to try. It was his joke—he was the only one
who could tolerate them. He was proud of that. Parvati saw
his joke, and when he offered her the hottest chilies—"Bite
into that, only a taste"—she was ready. "Too hot," she
cried out. He laughed; he was pleased. She kept her job.

That was an easy place, with easy work. But it
didn't last. Too much turmoil in the family, too much greed
and envy, and too much time to be angry and to bicker. It
wasn't safe for her. But once she knew she had to move on,
there was no stalling. A few things in a sack were all she
needed, along with the little money she received and saved.
Saving was easy for her. A trip to the market, to purchase
any foolish thing, could be her downfall. But she needn't
fear. She had lost the desire to possess the pretty things that
sparkled in the sun, and in the part of her mind that she
refused to hear, she knew it meant there was something
wrong with her, that she had let some part of her die.

But this place.

"It is chicken. You don't eat chicken?" Vengamma
had stood over her with the pot in her hand. "The meal is
over. Vengamma no throwing it." The housekeeper was
angry. She didn't realize that Parvati was not rejecting the
offer but only trying to understand it. Vengamma's
expression softened when Parvati reached for the pot.

The blanket. The chicken. The hours of sleep. It was
as though each one in the household acted out their need to
offer comfort and compassion, the gloomier Lalita Amma
became. For she was increasingly gloomy, and Parvati
could see no reason for her mood. The son, Prakash, visited
her weekly, taking the long bus ride into the hills to stay
with her. The daughter had now also come, and guests too.

At first, Parvati did not dare think about anything more than her work, but over the weeks she began to worry about Amma—the old woman seemed to be failing right before Parvati's eyes but without any medical reason. Parvati stood apart and watched, until she could no longer control herself. Pushing fear from her mind, she made a special tea—something she had avoided doing wherever she was. To make a special food was the same as announcing your origins, your native place, your most dangerous secret. But Amma was suffering, and by then Parvati had grown fond of the old woman and trusted her. That was perhaps the deepest reason. Parvati trusted Amma to say nothing if she understood what the tea concoction meant.

The tea made the old woman feel well again, and in subsequent months if Amma felt unwell, she would lie on her bed and call out, "Priya? Dear one?" And Parvati would go to her with a concoction specially made for the ailment. The old woman would drink it, then lie back and stare at her maidservant, then up at the ceiling. Sometimes Parvati wondered if the old woman knew where she was and who was with her. Sometimes in the nighttime, if Amma was especially unsettled and called out, Parvati would go to her with her blanket and lie down on the floor beside her. Only then would Amma fall back on her bed and eventually fall into the fragile sleep of the old. Parvati listened for the sounds of even breathing before falling asleep herself.

Valli and Prakash thanked Parvati for her care. "Amma appreciates this," Prakash said one afternoon. "My sister also appreciates this. It is a big change for Amma, coming back here. We want her to be happy." His eyes lingered on Parvati as he said the last, and after a few months she was not afraid to look at the other members of the household.

Five

"Come. Let us eat." Valli stood up, switching off the
reading lamp and leading her guest into the dining room.
Two large banana leaves were arranged on the floor, and
Anita and Valli sat down, cross-legged.

"What about the others?" Anita said.

"Amma and Meena Amma will take their food later.
You are too modern for them," Vengamma said as she bent
over and ladled rice onto the leaves.

"I suppose it is early for them." Valli began to
inspect her meal. "Amma never ate before ten o'clock,
even when we are living in the North."

"Meena Elayamma won't eat at the hotel until the
evening meal is finished and she is confident the guests
have dispersed." Anita smiled at the familiar image of her
aunt crossing the dining terrace, to ensure all was well.

"And what about Prakash?" Valli said, looking up.

"Ah, Prakash announced he has taken a vow."
Vengamma sighed as she straightened up. "Only kunji
water and a little fruit will he take for a week." She paused.
"The kunji water has so few grains of rice—it cannot be
enough." She returned to the kitchen. In the doorway stood
Parvati, the maidservant, who took the rice bowl and
handed the cook a smaller bowl of vegetables. In this way,
Vengamma walked back and forth between kitchen and
banana leaves till the two women, Valli and Anita, had

been served with a full thali—avial, fried fish, curried vegetables, lime pickle, curd, and a bowl of rasam. Anita rested her left elbow on her knee, and began to eat with her right hand, working the food into small balls with the tips of her fingers, careful not to let the food reach higher than her second knuckle. Valli was less fastidious, thereby telling Anita she was quite relaxed—or very distracted.

Anita was glad of the quiet; she could enjoy the texture of the meal, its tastes and fragrances, without her mind being elsewhere. Since her arrival she had been accompanied by some member of the household at every turn—Lalita Amma, Valli, Meena, Vengamma—and felt the need of solitude, or at least quiet. The undercurrents and the sense of information being withheld disturbed Anita, and she wanted time to absorb it all. Plus, she knew, when Auntie Meena got Anita alone again, the conversation would turn to Valli and her unorthodox visit to her mother. For Meena, any young wife's untraditional visit to her mother hinted at marital discord. Anita might scoff at this, but watching her cousin with her aunt's words ringing in her ears, Anita had to admit that this time her aunt might be right.

The meal finished, Vengamma gave each woman a glass of patimukham and disappeared into the kitchen with Parvati. Anita rose and went outside to wash her hands at the spigot rather than use the sink inside. Valli followed her. Anita returned to her place in the dining room, and reached for the glass of pink-tinted water with the small brown stick of Himalayan wild cherry. Valli, the good hostess, dutifully sat beside her.

"May I ask you a question?" Anita began.

"You are a sister to me." Valli smiled but Anita heard the note of caution in her cousin's voice.

"I think it is wonderful that you came all this way to be a comfort to Prakash." Anita sipped her water. "You're fortunate to have a younger brother."

Valli murmured her agreement. "You have always wanted one, I know, but you have Prakash and so many other cousin brothers, isn't it?"

Yes, thought Anita, refusing to let Valli derail her thoughts. "It is fortunate you are here now, especially when Prakash was so obviously upset after he spoke to the priest. He was so happy and carefree when we arrived at the temple and I first spoke with him, as he has always been."

"Yes, trouble can take our mood, like a monkey steals our shiny bracelet carelessly left out." Valli patted Anita's knee.

"Yes, but how is it, Valli, that you arrived here to comfort your brother before he even knew he would need comforting?" Valli blanched. The only sound was the rain slashing against the trees outside.

"Is that the kind of question a sister asks?"

"If she really cares about her family, yes." Anita put the glass down on the polished cement floor and leaned closer to Valli. "What is the real reason Auntie Meena has asked me to come? It doesn't matter to me what it is, but I want to know the truth. Tell me now."

Valli seemed to relax, her shoulders sinking, her head tipped to one side. "You are right. I deceived you because I deceived Auntie Meena, but I knew you wouldn't mind." She rubbed her hand along the polished floor. "I heard a rumor."

The way Valli shifted away again was not lost on Anita. Another lie, she thought.

"I heard someone at the temple does not like him, my one brother only, my dear Prakash."

Truth, thought Anita, is so easily shredded. The mix of lie and truth was beginning to disturb her because the one that a sister might understandably try to conceal was the one being revealed, and the statement that hardly mattered was being concealed.

"So you think someone at the temple has tried to get

Prakash fired for personal reasons?"

"It is a small temple—there is so little to fight over. So they fight with greater passion over nothing."

"What is the nothing they are fighting over?"

"It is nothing, something about the price of prasadam and other foods."

Anita frowned. Temples posted their prices for pujas and offerings, and prasadam was part of a puja—cooked food was offered to the deity, and what the deity did not take was redistributed to the devotees. It was part of the puja, taking the prasadam a sign of submission to the deity. "I don't understand."

"The price of puja with prasadam was raised, and Prakash asked about this."

"This seems a small matter," Anita said, still wondering if this could be all there was to the situation.

"Exactly." Valli's fierce agreement surprised Anita.

"Temples raise their prices all the time—they are subject to the same costs as anyone else—the electricity and gas, the dhobis and sweepers and carpenters and all the people it takes to maintain so much," Anita said.

"Exactly, exactly. You understand perfectly." Valli sat up straighter. "And there are simple ways to do these things."

"I don't think I understand what the argument is," Anita said. "The temple has raised some fees and Prakash questions something about it."

Valli looked as confused as Anita felt.

"Perhaps your husband can help. He also is from this place, isn't—"

"No! Kumar cannot help."

"Have you asked him?" Anita was surprised at Valli's vehemence. When Valli was first married, she delighted in her new husband's attentions; she was proud to be the woman of the house. But her attitude seemed to have changed.

Valli rose and carried her glass to the kitchen.
"Parvati! Va!" The maidservant appeared in the doorway
and took the glass; she noticed Anita's still on the floor and
hurried to collect it. She moved quietly, placing her bare
feet soundlessly on the floor, and lowering herself to the
glass like a dancer moving effortlessly to music only she
can hear. Her face was a mask of concentration, and she
never looked either of the other women in the eye. When
she spun around to go back to the kitchen, a long black
braid flew out behind her.

* * * * *

Anita pulled a thin green blanket from the bed and wrapped
it around her, drawing it tight against the chill. This was the
coldest, wettest monsoon she had ever experienced, and she
didn't like it at all. She had never really been cold before, at
least not in India, not even during visits to the North,
though she was careful to avoid that part of the country
during the coldest months. It was scary to feel the cold and
not be able to find a spot where warm air enveloped her or
the sun-heated floor warmed her feet.

A single flame in a glass-enclosed lantern cast a
shaky light over Anita's room, the light's golden edges
fading into darkness as if the black night were an
encroaching wave that would soon drown the lantern and
Anita. This was the only light available since the power had
shut down soon after the evening meal.

An hour earlier the wind had died down as though it
had given up the fight and the rain had won, pouring down
with not so much as a breath of resistance from the cosmos.
The ocean had come alive above them, around them,
everywhere. Anita pushed open the venetian doors and
stepped onto the sill, feeling the rain spray from her toes to
her forehead. Little patches of mist struggled to rise but
were beaten into the ground. Anita stared into the darkness.
There was someone out there.

Anita walked along the balcony parapet, trying to

41

discern the figure more clearly. She was sure she had seen someone passing from tree to tree, concealed first by large shrubs and then by thick tree trunks. The undergrowth was so dense here that even in daylight it would be easy to miss someone moving around the house.

There, and there. Among the trees. Going away from the house. Someone in a dark lungi, molded to the body by rain.

Anita watched as long as she could, but the figure disappeared into the dark and the rain. She lost track of time standing there, wondering: Who would be out on such a night? Someone from this house? A villager passing by? Anita leaned over to get a glimpse of the windows below, but no light shone. Everything was dark. If anyone else was up, they weren't giving any sign of it.

Drenched and cold, Anita went back into her room and pushed the doors shut against the rain. She knew the house was locked up—she had chatted with Valli as she made the rounds, checking with Vengamma and Parvati, tugging at the windows to test them, pushing on a door, wiggling a latch. Whoever it was outside, they would not get in without help.

* * * * *

Anita made her way down the stairs, reminded of their age by the worn-smooth treads. At the last step she waited for the sound of someone knocking or working a door to get in, but there was nothing to hear but the rain.

You should call Prakash, she thought, or at least Valli. It was a rational thought, a reasonable reaction, and she made note of it as she felt her way through the darkness, reaching for the doorway, running her hand along a wooden jamb, trying the light switch—the power was still out—reaching for the table she knew was there inside the door. She made her way to the windows and followed along the wall, then on into the next room. She knew she was probably being absurd in searching through the house at this hour because a villager walked past in the dark—but she couldn't stop herself. The door to the kitchen rooms was latched, and Anita felt her way past it, then stopped.

She paused. Something. There was something more than rain.

Yes, now I should call Prakash, she thought, as she lifted the kitchen latch and pushed open the door. At once the monsoon was upon her, blowing in through an open back door, the rain washing over the stone floor and reaching for the locked cupboards.

"Parvati!" Anita called out.

The young maidservant turned, soaked by the rain, a length of rope in her hands. "Amma."

Yes, still respectful, thought Anita.

As the maidservant spoke, she averted her eyes and moved backward into the kitchen storeroom, clutching the rope to her chest. "A goat. A goat has escaped. The goat is valuable—Amma prefers the goat milk only." She looked to one side and then the other, seemingly disoriented by Anita's sudden arrival.

"And did you find it?" Anita asked, hurrying across the slippery floor to the back door. She leaned hard on the thick plank door, pushing it shut. She had forgotten how heavy doors in these old houses could be. When she at last got it safely latched, she turned to Parvati. They were both drenched. Anita pulled the blanket from her shoulders and draped it over the stone counter, which was also soaked.

"Did you catch it?" Anita asked again.

"What?"

"The goat? Did you catch the goat?"

"Yes, yes, caught, caught." As Parvati spoke, she looked again and again at the closed and locked door.

"Good. I did not know Amma only took goat milk."

"Only goat milk. That is all we are serving, at her request."

"Is there no longer her cow here?"

43

"No cow, Amma. No cow."

Odd, thought Anita. The goat was always the poor man's cow. She pressed the door one more time, to make sure it was fully closed, and wiped the rain from her forehead.

"You are thirsty, Amma? Take tea?" Parvati huddled near the door, making the obligatory offering, but Anita declined.

"It is late and you are cold and wet. Go." Anita sent the maidservant away to sleep and pulled the inside kitchen door shut behind her. She wanted to go back outside but knew it would be futile. Whoever had been out there was gone now—it hadn't been Parvati, she was sure of that. Even in this dark and wet, Anita could tell the difference between a woman's white mundu and a man's plaid lungi.

Six

In the stillness of the early morning, during a lull in the rains, Anita could hear the family moving about the house in preparation for the day. In the distance music blared; the priests were awakening the gods and calling the faithful to worship. She supposed the priest or a committee picked the music—certainly not the deity—and she wished the committee would consult with Shiva or Bhagavati or whoever it was; she was sure the choices would be much more congenial to those who liked to awake and arise gradually.

Resigned, Anita sat up in bed and pulled out her mobile phone; she had punched in half the numbers for Anand before she realized there was still no reception. She had promised to call him when she arrived, to set up an evening together for when she got back to Hotel Delite. Even as she felt the tightness in her chest and the little bubbling of annoyance, she knew she was falling into the trap of wanting everything faster and faster. It hardly mattered if she called him today or two days from now, but she missed him and wanted to hear his voice. She flipped the phone shut and made a mental note to ask Valli for the best spot in the area for mobile reception.

In deference to Lalita Amma, her hostess, Anita tied on a sari and went down for early-morning coffee. It was barely five o'clock, and she was still tired from the aborted

45

adventure of the night before; she had lain awake shivering for some time, before falling into an exhausted sleep. She still felt clammy and cold, and pulled a shawl tight around her shoulders. She found Lalita Amma and Valli in the eating room. Valli leaned back against the wall, her legs stretched out in front of her. A coffee cup rested in the palm of her hand. She welcomed Anita with a smile.

"Such a lotta noise," Lalita Amma said. "It is almost too much noise to sleep. You are rested?"

"Yes. And now hungry." Anita sat down cross-legged on the floor. "By the way, Valli, I tried to use my mobile this morning and couldn't get any reception. Where is the best spot?"

"The best spot?" Valli looked confused. "Didn't Auntie Meena tell you?"

"Tell me what?" Anita had a sinking feeling she wasn't going to like the answer.

"We have no reception up here—very erratic in good weather and almost none in this sort of weather. And the landline isn't any better. It's gone now, at least for a few days." Valli sighed. "All that rain."

"No," Anita said, more to herself than her hostess. "She didn't tell me." Anita paused so long that Valli called her name softly. "Sorry, Valli. I was thinking. Perhaps I'll go up and make sure Auntie Meena has everything she needs this morning."

"No, no, Anita." Valli placed her hand on Anita's knee. "This is not necessary."

"Not necessary at all," Lalita Amma repeated. "I have ensured that Meena will sleep, and she will have coffee sent to her room." The old woman waved to Parvati in the kitchen doorway. "Meena told me last night she is tired, and I have promised her a visit of rest. She will have it no matter what."

Considering how murderous I feel right now, thought Anita, Meena could end up sleeping into all eternity, but aloud she said, "Yes, we must see to it she gets all the rest she desires. She works very hard at Hotel Delite."

Parvati hurried in with a bowl of idlies and placed three on a plate in front of Anita. The maidservant returned with a bowl of coconut chutney and another bowl of tomato vegetable sambar.

"Forgive the plates, Anita. With such rain we cannot get to the market and the market cannot come to us. We reserve our leaves for a meal." Lalita Amma gave Anita a weak smile.

Anita settled to her breakfast. In the background she could hear Prakash moving about the puja room. Outside, the barest hint of daylight pushed against the rain clouds and the waning night.

"Is your goat all right?" Anita asked.

"My goat? Why should my goat not be all right? Shivayashivoo! Am I to lose that too?"

"Amma!" Valli whispered, glancing at Anita.

Lalita Amma rose, pushing her stiff body off the ground with effort, and padded into the kitchen, calling for Parvati. Anita could hear the old woman questioning the maidservant about the goat but could not hear Parvati's answers. Apparently satisfied, Lalita Amma reappeared. "Forgive me! I am old and foolish." She smiled at the young women, then walked through the eating room and on into the rest of the house.

"I hope I didn't upset her," Anita said.

"No, no. It is nothing."

"Parvati said the goat got loose last night." Anita waited for Valli's reaction.

"Got loose?" Valli paled, but recovered. "The goat is here—quite well. Oh, Anita. It is our shame, but at least it is not visible to all." Valli shook her head. "Or so I like to think. But this is a village. There are no secrets here."

"Perhaps you will tell me the truth now," Anita

said. "Your mother has come here to live, not only to visit, isn't it?" Anita looked hard at Valli—it was not a question. "She has sold her cow, lost her home in the North. Has she sold off some of her land?"

"No, no, the land is still ours. But yes, the house in Kochi is gone, the cow is gone." Valli looked up at the ceiling and around the room. "This is our wealth now."

"Our wealth? You are a married woman, Valli. Are you including yourself in this household? Has something gone wrong that I don't know about?" Anita sighed as she read the look on Valli's face. "So, this is more than a visit for you."

"No, no, Anita. I do not mean you to think that. I wanted your comfort and your counsel, that's all." Valli pushed the remnants of her breakfast around on her plate. "There is nothing to be done, but I thought you might have wise counsel. And, truly, I suppose I hoped I would find again some good feeling in my life. Things are not going well all round."

"I think you had better tell me," Anita said. She leaned back and waited while Parvati cleared the breakfast things and brought more coffee.

"Thank you, Parvati." Valli dismissed the maidservant, and the two women waited until the maidservant closed the door to the kitchen. Elsewhere in the house, Prakash's recitations continued.

* * * * *

Anita knew herself well enough to know that she could be very impatient, even intolerant sometimes, if she thought someone was wasting her time. For those she loved, she offered infinite patience; for those whose burden was great, she felt only compassion; but for those who lied or refused to be honest, she felt only contempt and annoyance. As she listened to Valli tell the tale of woe that was her young marriage of barely two years, Anita couldn't decide if Valli was telling her the truth, having trouble facing the truth, or avoiding telling her the real story.

"I was naive, wasn't I?" Valli said.

"Lots of people don't get along with their husband's relatives. How does it matter? You are not living with them—are you?"

Valli pulled a face, then shook her head.

"Then tell me what this is all about?" Anita was teetering on the edge of impatience—and disappointment that her cousin Valli would misuse a friend in this way.

"I have come to live here with my mother. This is my home." Valli jutted out her chin, then turned to rubbing her hand over the polished floor, worrying the tiny imperfections that sometimes made the floor look like a seabed.

"And your wealth," Anita added; she was startled by the shock in Valli's eyes.

"Yes, of course." Valli gave an awkward laugh, and returned to rubbing the floor.

"It is money trouble?"

"We are poor but we have enough."

This was a simple sentence spoken without emotion or inflection, and yet it was perhaps the single most important statement Valli had ever made. For Valli came from a family that had always had wealth enough to enjoy life and not have to worry; they did not have enough to fritter away, but enough to feel secure and do what they wanted. It sounded like a sad tale, this loss of money and status. Anita was heartened that Valli seemed to be facing the change with such emotional maturity, but wondered that she seemed to have accepted without challenge something that should never have happened.

"You went to your husband with great wealth," Anita pointed out.

"So I did."

"Kumar, your husband, he is successful. Didn't he own his own company, or is that too lost?"

"No, no. He is very successful, very successful indeed."

"Then how can you be poor, Valli?" Anita softened her voice, urging her friend to explain the inexplicable.

Valli sat up and looked straight at Anita. "Do you know what my mother is doing now? She is doing a family history—yes, a family history. She is tracing our lineage to the distant past—she is doing this to comfort herself. We are not a negligible family, are we? No." Valli shook her head in short sudden bursts. "No. This is a family of some reckoning, no matter who says otherwise." Valli stood up, shaking out her sari and tugging the pallu, the decorated end of the sari, into place over her shoulder. She looked down on Anita, still sitting on the floor.

"You are speaking in riddles and puzzles, Valli."

"The representatives of the temple trustees will be here soon. I must prepare myself—and Prakash."

Anita stood up. "Why are they coming here?"

"They want to question Prakash about his . . . his— there are accusations." Valli opened her mouth to say something more, but seemed to think better of it; instead, she nodded and hurried from the room.

* * * * *

Anita knocked on Meena Elayamma's door before opening it. Anita remembered this room from her childhood, for this is where she slept with her parents when she was too young to sleep alone. The two mattresses tied together on the floor kept them all close through the night; she liked waking up in the dark and hearing her father's cough and raspy breathing and her mother's light sighs and nasal whistle. The two mattresses were gone, replaced by a low wooden bed frame with a stack of three mattresses on it, and Meena Elayamma sound asleep on top. She opened her eyes at the sound of the door closing.

"Ahh?" Meena sat up and shook her head. "Is it morning?" She looked around the room, apparently disoriented. She sat up and reached for the cup and saucer in Anita's hands. "Such a pleasure."

Anita sat down at the foot of the bed and folded her legs under her. "Did you have a nice visit with Lalita Amma last night?"

"Wonderful visit." Meena sipped her coffee, closing her eyes to better enjoy the fragrance. "I do not see my loving family often enough."

"You saw her a couple of months ago at a family wedding," Anita said.

"Ah, so I did." Meena smiled, then frowned. "Why didn't you go?"

"I had flu."

"Oh, yes, so you did." Meena took another sip of her coffee.

"Which means, I missed out on all the gossip, so I'm a bit behind."

"Behind?" Meena gave her a suspicious look. "Behind what?"

Anita glared at her.

"You are looking hostile, Anita. You mustn't look at me like that. It is unsettling, and you are a dear child to me." Meena wiggled deeper into the pillows.

"Which explains why you probably forgot to tell me certain things."

Meena eyed Anita warily. "Now we should plan our day, yes? A pleasant visit."

"As long as we don't need to make any reservations anywhere, since there's no phone service—no mobile and no landline." Anita moved closer and closer as her voice grew quieter.

"Oh, is that so?"

"Auntie Meena, you have been lying to me."

"I have said nothing about the telephone service, nothing."

"Technically, that's true. But every time I told you I

would go but I had to continue arrangements for other events—with Anand—you simply agreed. But you knew that would be impossible."

"It is only a few days!"

"And why? Why lie to me? Why keep me from telling Anand exactly where I am?"

Meena leaned forward with a glint in her eye. "But isn't it wonderful to be able to spend so much time with our family. Lalita Amma, Valli, and Prakash. Yes?"

"No, it is not wonderful. Lalita Amma will soon be depressed over her new state of poverty. Valli is already depressed over her failing marriage. And Prakash is heading into serious trouble from the hints I'm getting from his sister and mother."

"But such a nice boy."

"What?" Anita pulled back. "A nice boy?"

"Very suitable, yes?"

"Oh, Auntie Meena!" Anita drew up her legs and rested her forehead on her knees. "Shivayashivoo! Save me! Amma, he is from the wrong family line and he is younger than I am!" Anita took a deep breath. "You are so far off the mark, Auntie, that I will not even bother arguing with you about this. No one can be as desperate as you are to have such an idea!"

"You are not going to argue with me?"

"I have more important concerns. Namely, Valli. What has Lalita Amma told you about Valli's marriage?"

"What makes you think she— Don't look at me like that, Anita."

"Tell me."

"This is very good coffee. No—"

Anita took the cup from her. "Tell me."

"A shameful thing. I cannot tell you." Meena closed her eyes and rubbed her hand across her face. "It is too terrible."

"Meena Elayamma!"

Meena sighed heavily and pulled the sheet up to her face. "Oh, I will tell you, but you must not let Valli know that I have told you. I don't think she understands."

"I will say nothing." Anita agreed in a nanosecond, thinking Valli was a lot shrewder than anyone was giving her credit for.

"Very well. It is shameful—and painful to speak of. And embarrassing."

"Okay, Auntie, I get it. Please tell me."

"The gold saris displayed at the wedding? The saris, the jewelry, the auto, the fridge—all of it."

"Yes?" Anita said when Meena fell silent.

"It wasn't from the groom. It was a sham."

"What? What do you mean a sham?"

"Kumar said he would give dowry or he would give job for Prakash, but not both. So Lalita arranged for the items to be purchased and she paid for them, but no one was to know. Now, he has taken both Lalita's money and Prakash's job." Meena closed her eyes and moaned.

"Prakash owes his job to Kumar?" Anita tried to take this in. The position of pujari or priest in a family or community temple was supposed to go to a member of the founding family of the temple, and Prakash was a member. How could he owe his job to someone else's efforts?

"He would not have gotten the position otherwise. Another laid claim to it." Meena shook her head sadly. "And Lalita Amma has beggared herself."

Anita stared at her aunt. "Do you really think Valli hasn't figured out what happened with Kumar? She's not stupid, Auntie; she must have figured it out."

"No, Lalita has told Valli her father's business went bad and there wasn't as much money as they thought. Valli believes her mother; the girl is naive."

"Is it her husband who has ended the marriage?"

Meena nodded, and covered her face with her hands.

Seven

Anita found Lalita Amma in the old office, sitting at a plain wooden table in the middle of the room, stacks of books and sheaves of paper tied in red ribbon teetering on other tables nearby.

"May I join you, Amma?"

"Always, always." The old woman nodded to a chair placed along the wall, and Anita removed the piles of books and placed them on the floor before dragging the chair closer to the old woman.

"Valli told me you are researching your family."

"Yes, it is a simple way to occupy my time, and I think the results will please other relatives when I present a little booklet about our family to them."

"Meena Elayamma will certainly be pleased."

Lalita Amma smiled and chuckled. "Yes, the one of us who loves the old ways most is also the one of us who lives the most modern life, surrounded by foreigners in a village that seems foreign to me."

"All those tourists," Anita said.

The old woman copied down a name, her tiny neat handwriting crossing the page in a perfect, straight line. When she was done, she laid down the pen and leaned back in her chair. "Is it interesting to watch me work?"

"I used to watch other people work in their offices when I was a little girl."

"So you did. And now?"

"Valli tells me she has come here to live."

"Ah! Yes, so she has." Lalita Amma rearranged the pen, lining it up with the top of the paper. "And did she tell you why she has come?"

"No, not yet. She has told me many stories about her in-laws, her husband's temper and some other bad qualities. She has told me about the loss of her dowry, but she has not told me the real reason she has come." Anita drew up her legs, resting her heels on the edge of the chair, draping the sari over her knees, and wrapping her arms around her legs.

"Why do you think those are not the real reasons?" The older woman studied her, and Anita studied the floor. "Did you know he was educated in the North?"

Anita shook her head.

"Yes. Delhi University. A good student. We checked, of course."

"Of course."

"A promising future. We checked."

"Yes, of course."

"His family is quite remote from our branch, but still there is a distant connection. We checked."

"Of course." When Lalita Amma did not continue, and the silence lengthened, Anita decided she had to ask, and now was as good a time as she would ever have. "He beats her?"

"Oh! No! No, no, no." Lalita Amma looked shocked at the very idea, and Anita was surprised at how relieved she felt.

"I am very glad to hear that." So, what is it, thought Anita, that brought Valli home? Despite all the trials of being a new member in an established family, she fled the family for a deeper reason.

"I can hear you wondering, if the choice was good and the man well vetted, what has gone wrong?" Lalita said.

"I am at a loss to discern this, Amma." It was prying but, Anita hoped, of a civilized sort. Despite all that Meena had told her, Anita wasn't ready to accept the loss of a dowry as the real reason; something more was going on here.

"He picked up some bad habits. And he appears to have the upper hand now. We must accept." Lalita Amma reached for her pen. "They will be here soon, the temple trustees, to question Prakash." She gave Anita a weak smile. "You may have questions yourself. I am not certain they will be permitted, but I will not object."

Anita thanked her, wondering what sorts of questions she could possibly have, since she hardly knew what was going on.

"It is so much better when there is complete understanding. Don't you agree?"

"Of course." Anita peered more closely at the old woman.

"I hope you will spend time with Prakash," she said. "He always trusted you. You were good for him. You always got along so well."

Anita couldn't bring herself to reply, not after her earlier conversation with her aunt Meena. Despite everything she and Anand had done to get Meena to accept him, Auntie Meena was still beating the bushes for the perfect son-in-law—not the perfect mate for Anita, but the perfect young man to welcome into the family. She couldn't believe Auntie Meena disliked Anand so much that she would stoop to such a poor prospect as Prakash. Anita forced a tight smile and said, "He was always a very sweet boy."

* * * * *

It was pretty easy to guess where Prakash was in the household at any one time, Anita had learned. You stood still in a hallway and listened. You were sure to hear him

chanting, reciting mantras, working in or near the puja
room, or on his way there or from there. Anita paused to
listen, and guessed he was still in the puja room. She trotted
along and settled herself in the hallway outside, to wait
until he was finished. Her intent was a conversation that
would only become more awkward with time. Better not to
wait.

The sound of Prakash's voice rose and fell, and as
she listened she got another insight into his personality. She
hadn't thought about it before, but he had his own distinct
style. While some pujaris fell into a quiet recitation, their
hands moving in fluid motions in concordance with their
prayers, Prakash used his voice as a musical instrument.
She listened as his voice rose and fell.

At one point, she heard a foot stamp and hands clap.
It sounded so vital and assertive, and so unlike the Prakash
she had always known—the little boy tagging along behind
her and Valli, the young man excited at his first position in
his vocation. Anita imagined this was how parents felt
when they catch sight of their child acting like an adult
with other adults, someone to be proud of but someone who
has hidden the child they loved.

"You could have come in." Prakash stood over her.

Anita stood up. "I didn't realize you were finished."

"Only now." He smiled at her. Anita was at a loss to
begin the conversation she didn't really want to have. "You
want to talk, yes?"

She nodded, and he led the way to a back sitting
room where desks were set out. Anita recalled that this
room had been reserved for the tutors years ago, when one
or another came at six in the morning to tutor the children.
Prakash took a chair at one desk and Anita pulled out a
chair at another.

"I am glad you have come for a visit." Prakash
smiled.

"So am I." Anita smiled, wishing she were

anywhere but here. How did one say, My relatives are meddling fools and I would like to strangle them all, even though you are a nice guy but definitely not for me, without hurting anyone's feelings?

"My mother has missed seeing you. She has missed having the house full of laughter."

"We did make a lot of noise back then." Anita waited for him to add something, but as the silence lengthened she noticed she was probably more uncomfortable than he was. Prakash sat with his hands clasped, resting on the desk. "So different now, yes?"

"So different," he agreed.

"I was talking with Valli." Anita wished she could call back the words the minute they were out.

"You must not fret, Chechi. She is not as unhappy with Kumar as she lets on."

"Really? I'm very glad you are saying this." Anita felt enormously relieved. She hated the mess of disintegrating marriages—far too many people were hurt in the process. Civility and decency seemed to go out the window the minute a divorce loomed.

"She will be happy again."

"And what about you?" Anita shut her eyes again, wishing she would stop saying stupid things. Why couldn't she simply blurt out what she had to say, that Auntie Meena was way out of line and Anita was not, simply not, in the market for a husband.

"What about me? I am happy." His smiled faded. "Ah, you mean the temple." He sighed. "This is a problem to be worked out. But besides that, I have all I want in life. My mother would not want to know that, but it is so."

Anita studied him as he repeated this, and she believed he was telling her the truth. He really did seem to be genuinely satisfied with where he was in life—unhappy about the temple difficulties but on a personal level, quite happy. "This is very good news."

"I hope you are not disappointed." He gave her such a patronizing smile that she almost slapped him. The custom of centuries prevented her from speaking freely. Instead, she smiled and waited before speaking.

"Auntie Meena, and perhaps your mother, will be disappointed—and they should be for coming up with such an absurd idea—but I am not." She noted the flicker of surprise in his eyes. "I see Auntie Meena's intent is not unknown to you. But I assure you, she acts on her own volition. My parents have told me to be polite but otherwise ignore her efforts on my behalf. And I assure you, I take their advice—on this."

Prakash chuckled. "On this," he repeated, apparently savoring the words. "One must find contentment in doing one's duty, and today we have greater understanding of how duty is defined. You agree?"

Anita nodded, but she wasn't at all sure she knew what she was agreeing to.

* * * * *

When Prakash wandered off to collect materials for the evening's puja, Anita was relieved. She hadn't understood much of the conversation; it felt as though he had been speaking to his own self of things about which Anita knew nothing. But at least the confrontation was over, and it had ended well. Or at least, it seemed to have. Prakash had no interest in an arranged marriage with her, and he was not at all interested in her feelings on the matter. Both were a relief.

Anita went over the conversation several times in the privacy of the old school room, reassuring herself that it had ended the way she thought it had. Relief grew into conviction, and she felt confident she could now persuade Auntie Meena that Prakash was definitely a no and to leave the question of Anita's marriage alone.

Anita didn't know when it happened, but as she sat in the schoolroom plotting her conversation with Auntie

Meena, Anita suddenly realized something was different. She sat up, looked around, and then it came to her. It was quiet. The rain that had been relentless since her arrival, the wind that had driven the water into every crevice, the sheer noise of the monsoon, had ceased. Anita went to the front door and pulled it open. The veranda was pockmarked with puddles, rain dripped from every branch, but a golden glow above told her there was a real chance that the clouds would clear and the sun would shine. She went to get her camera and smiled in spite of herself.

"Valli!" Anita called out as she hurried down the stairs. "Look, it's clearing." She rushed through the house, looking for her cousin. "Valli! We must go out for a walk—visit the neighbors, go to the village. Oh, here you are." Anita burst into the library, startling Valli and Prakash as they sat opposite each other at the desk.

"What?" Valli looked up.

"The rain—it has stopped. Come with me!" Anita peered from one face to the other. The siblings looked at each other, both serious and frowning. She knew she must have looked ridiculous standing there like a child with her camera in her hands and the excitement of going outside written all over her face. "Oh dear, you have no time to go for a walk right now. I'm sorry. I shall go alone."

"Not at all, Anita." Prakash stood up. "We shall go, too."

"No, we can't, Prakash. We have too much to discuss." Valli turned to Anita, begged her forgiveness, and whispered something only her brother could hear.

Anita closed the door behind her. Whatever was tying them into knots, she didn't want to know right now—maybe later, but not now. She headed for the door, slipped her feet into her sandals, and stepped out onto the front veranda. She felt she could grow to fill the entire world. She hadn't realized how cramped she'd felt cooped up inside.

Anita pushed the frizzing strands of hair away from her face and stretched her arms up. She had never been one to stay inside when she could be out moving around, talking to people and planning things to do, and that was especially true of a household where she had spent so many happy months of her childhood. Anita checked her sari.

She liked to tie it so the pallu was long and draped down her back, which meant wrapping less fabric around her waist and making smaller pleats, which draped down in the front. She pulled the pallu from the back, draped it across her chest and tucked the end into her waist. Satisfied, she rolled her sari skirt at the waist and picked her way around the puddles to the lane leading to the village. The village was small but it had two or three nice shops, with shop owners she had known for years. She was eager to see them again. Anita jumped puddles and slid in the mud as she went along.

About halfway down the slope the lane came to an end—washed away by the stream that normally was little more than a trickle. Anita pondered this problem, trying to recall the nearest secondary path she could take. She backtracked and turned onto a spur leading to another house. She followed this to what she knew was a footbridge recently constructed to accommodate residents in new houses being built along the edge of the village.

The path twisted beneath trees snapped in half by the wind; branches slapped at her face. After a while she emerged at the foot of the steel-and-iron bridge. It was a modest effort compared to the footbridges she was used to in Trivandrum, but it had a certain charm. Unfortunately, trees and other debris were lodged across the walkway, making it impossible to cross without clambering over dangerously slippery ground. One misstep would toss her into the stream.

Frustrated, Anita turned back and picked up a lesser-known path down to the village. She trudged through muck and over torn branches, followed what she thought were streambeds until she realized they were gulleys gouged out by the recent flooding. When she passed a house she tried to decide if she recognized it, but houses became fewer and fewer, and after a couple of hours she had to admit that it wasn't the monsoon damage that was slowing down her trip to the village. She was lost.

Whatever path Anita had been following had petered out. She stopped to listen, hoping for some familiar sound to orient herself. Into the quiet came the sound of rushing water. She began to walk toward it, thinking that this would at least run closer to a village or a home.

Anita walked on until she emerged into a clearing. Up ahead was a small house and in the courtyard a woman was lighting a cooking fire. If nothing else, Anita could find out where she was.

"And there is the bus station," the village woman said at the end of her long and careful directions.

"I've gone that far off?" Anita said. It was a rhetorical question. The old woman explained that Anita had walked around the small village, her intended target, and missed the crossroads. If she kept going in the same direction she would start descending onto the plains of paddy fields and other crops. She should have known. She had been so eager to get out for a walk that she had missed all the signs that she was overshooting her mark. It would be some time before Anita would come to a road and have an easy walk up to the village. She set out again.

The path veered close to and then away from a stream, and sometimes simply disappeared into the roiling muddy water. Anita was careful to avoid the slippery bank. She came to a pile of debris that looked like a lorry had deposited it, and Anita wondered if she dared climb over it or if it were wiser to go around. She went around and once on the other side glanced back.

"Shivayashivoo!"

Anita took a step closer to the pile. Yes, she had seen what she thought she had seen. A twisted and swollen limb, its hand half cut away, stuck out of a mass of twigs and leaves and branches.

Anita found a long stick and prodded the debris enclosing the arm. In a second she threw down the stick and rummaged along the riverbank to get a stronger prod. She removed more clumps of leaves and twigs. The arm was attached to a badly swollen and damaged body tangled up in the refuse of the storm.

She moved around to another vantage point and knelt down, again prodding and moving debris about. She had noticed something odd on the hand, coir rope, but the hand had not been grasping it, as though the dead person had been trying to pull himself to safety. Chunks of debris fell to the side, opening a window on more of the body, and this time the image was unmistakable—a head with a coir rope tied around the neck. The rope had cut deep into the throat. On the shoulder was some sort of tattoo.

Anita paused for a moment to hope the dead man had moved on according to good karma. She studied the man, wondering how he had died with rope caught around his throat and rope tied to his wrist so tightly it had almost severed his hand. Battered as the body was, it could not have been in the water for very long. As she looked it over, she noted one more thing odd about this body. She moved closer to the other arm, attached but damaged. It looked like a huge chunk of flesh had been torn away from near the shoulder. I need to remember this, Anita thought, and she lifted her camera to her eye. She couldn't feel a lot for this corpse—he was unknown to her as far as she could tell. But still, it was a horrible thing to look upon someone who had been alive a few days before and now was nothing more than limbs and fragments of limbs tenuously held together by entanglement in rotting trees.

Anita stepped away from the corpse. This poor soul,

she thought. However did he come to die in such a way?

Eight

Parvati worked her way along the narrow path, dodging dripping branches above and muddy puddles below. Every few feet she stopped and looked up, listening, turning her head from side to side. With the rain ended, at least for the time being, the jungle was heavy in silence, as though worn out from the daily storm. Satisfied, the woman walked on. The lane twisted one way, then another, and without warning ended in a small clearing. On the top of a gentle rise sat a small wooden temple. The maidservant hurried to the entrance and pushed open the door.

"Aar illa?" Her voice was soft and tentative. She pushed the door open wider and entered. The wood floor was swept clean but still the temple had the air of neglect. No one worshipped here, she knew, but every time she entered she felt a presence, as though the gods who had lived here, been honored and cared for here, had chosen to remain after their *murti*s had been carried away. This was not an empty house, as she had been promised—she knew it; she could feel it.

The maidservant walked to a small bench set along one wall and laid down her bundle—rice she had taken to be ground at the village, a task that had taken far longer than was expected. The latticed windows filtered the dim light that still managed to reach below the deep overhang; the light washed the floor with a dusty gold. At the sound of a twig snapping and footsteps rasping on the wooden steps, she turned.

"Ah! Parvati!" Prakash stood in the doorway, his hands pressed together in anjali. She couldn't help noticing the cloth bag dangling from his wrist, swinging back and forth as he moved his arms. She returned his greeting, bending her head and trying not to let him see her confusion.

"Vengamma is waiting for me," she said.

"She is always waiting for someone she has ordered about. Pay her no mind." He came toward her and stopped a few inches away from her. They were shy in each other's company, both afraid of meeting alone and the silence that demanded honest words freely spoken. "Why are you so afraid, Parvati?"

She took a quick step back from him. "How can I not be afraid? Amma will send me away if she thinks we sneak off to see each other. Maybe Vengamma will beat me."

"No one beats servants anymore." He flicked his hand in dismissal. "Come. Let's sit. We have some time." He moved to the bench and pushed the bag of rice aside. "Please."

She heard the doubt in his voice, and it pained her. She went to him and sat down, turning to face him. "Suppose Vengamma is displeased with me and sends me away? What will I do? I have no place to go. I cannot go farther into the mountains. There is nothing up there, nothing for me."

"She will not send you away. I won't ever let that happen." He grabbed her hand and held it tight, as though squeezing out her terrors and his. "When I first saw you, I felt like the Great God Shiva when he first saw his beloved Parvati. I know how he felt. He saw the world and all that is good standing in front of him. You are my goddess, my Parvati."

Parvati listened and her eyebrow twitched. She had never heard such talk. No one she knew had ever compared her, or anyone else for that matter, to a goddess. She was just a servant girl. Sometimes she wondered at the way Prakash talked.

"Listen to me, Parvati." He smiled and drew closer to her. "We must plan. We should not wait."

"Not wait?" Parvati studied him. "But last time you said . . ."

"I know, I know." Prakash released her hand and turned away. "I thought we had all the time in the world, but now I don't know."

"Has something happened?" Parvati's jaw clenched and unclenched. "It is perhaps time for me to go, just go." She seemed to move beyond fear and worry, and spoke with a calm that belied her earlier words.

"It is not something to fear," Prakash said.

"Your guest said her car was searched. The authorities are looking everywhere." Parvati grew thoughtful. "We cannot be naive, at least I cannot. It is not safe for me here."

"That roadblock had nothing to do with you. They were searching for contraband. This monsoon is so bad that smugglers are bringing goods over the mountains. They are thinking no one will notice and they can sell for outrageous prices. And the drug dealers—the monsoon makes them bold."

"There was a man with a rifle. I heard her tell this to Amma."

"Of course. This is the new India." He dismissed every objection with the same flick of his wrist. "Here. I brought you this. It is what all Malayali women wear. I have taken it from my sister's room—she won't notice. She has so many." He opened the bag to reveal a two-piece sari and its matching choli, or blouse. "Keep it safe." He handed it to her and she held it in her lap. "You could smile." He ran his finger along her chin.

"It is nothing to you if I am caught."

"You cannot say that—you know it isn't true. It is everything to me if you are caught. But you will not be found. Nothing will happen to you."

"I will be sent back. I have no papers, Prakash. I speak like a foreigner if I speak more than three words. They will hear who I am."

"Parvati, you cannot give in to these irrational fears. No one will send you back." His arms stiffened as he spoke, as though he were facing down a man with a gun and a court order.

"I cannot go back, Prakash. I cannot go back to Sri Lanka. I have no future if I am caught." She began to tremble.

"You are frightening yourself for no reason."

"You don't know. No one is safe there. Government will never allow any of the Tamils to survive. Even farmers are not safe. Didn't my father and mother die only because they lived in the wrong place? They were not part of Tamil Eelam, but only farmers in the wrong part of the country."

He reached for her hands again. This time he didn't try to soothe her fears with words. He held onto her hands, moved closer to her, and let his body envelop hers. This was not passion, though he had no lack of that; he would do anything to comfort her, reassure her, even if it meant denying everything he felt or believed. "I have promised to keep you safe, and I will. Soon we will leave here. I have saved most of my salary and income from the temple. I have told you this before. I promise you we will leave here. But we cannot be hasty. We must plan carefully."

She wanted to believe him. She longed to believe he was right, that he could predict the future because he knew the astrologer and the chief of police and powerful men of his native place. But she was no one, and she had not been safe in Kochi or Goa. Each time she had moved, she had gone farther and farther south, taking the road to the most obscure place.

When she had crossed from Sri Lanka some time ago, landing in Tamilnad, leaving behind a lifetime of war, she had headed north, working her way inland and along the mountains. She had not thought when she fled Goa and Mangalore and then Kochi that she was moving closer to her misery, not farther away. Here she understood the language and easily found work, but here her accent was noticed and questioned if she spoke freely, so she spoke little. Her fear grew, and with it her loneliness. And now Prakash made promise after promise, telling her she didn't have to fear. She struggled to believe him.

"Please, Parvati. I will keep you safe." Again he reached for her hand, and this time, with the gentleness of a lover, he held it in both of his and murmured his promises again.

Nine

Anita followed the men carrying the corpse, its swollen, bruised and broken limbs wrapped in a woven mat, as the bearers made their way down the narrow path to a road meant for carts and perhaps an intrepid autorickshaw driver. Here, the men loaded the corpse onto a cart and stepped back to gossip among themselves. The cart driver hit the bullock's thin bony hindquarters with a switch. The animal started, its eyes widening in fear, then heaved itself forward, jostling the cart into motion. The cart swayed, the corpse wobbled, the men stepped onto another path that would lead them through the jungle to the village center below. Anita fell into step behind the cart.

"I was out walking," Anita said when she arrived at the police substation. The constable sat behind his desk, which was no more than a table with a single drawer, studying her as though he wasn't really interested in her words but in discovering what sort of alien being this was—someone who went out walking for no apparent reason. Anita knew he was deciding whether or not to believe her, or if he had decided, he was mulling over how long he might keep her here and how many times he might make her tell her story—until he grew bored. She was getting restless waiting for him to finish with her. Her feet hurt and she was tired of standing.

"The rain, you know. So bad this year," she said.

"We end up sitting inside all day, all night. Very tedious. So, the first chance I had, I went out for a walk." She waited. She had no idea what this constable was like because she was in a village she had only driven through a few times over the years. She'd overshot her target, the little village near Lalita Amma's estate, by a good distance. "I was so glad to be out walking, so I kept going. And there he was."

In moments like these, her sense of invincibility evaporated. It took almost nothing to smash a bone, to tear off a limb, to stop a heart. It was better not to think about that, for who could live freely with such knowledge ever present in her thoughts? It would be crippling, terrifying. Better not to think about it.

"You know this man?"

Anita shook her head. "I have never seen him before. This one is a total stranger. Perhaps he is known to you? Someone who lived in the village?" As soon as Anita had knelt down to get a better look at the corpse and saw the damage to its neck and hand, she knew what she was looking at—this was not an accidental death. But that was all she could tell by looking at the body. A man tied up and strangled might well be a criminal known to the police, but this constable was telling her nothing. The men who came at her urgent call from a nearby farmhouse didn't seem to know the man either, at first speculating he was a devotee going to Sabarimala who got lost, but then changing their minds as they worked to free his damaged body.

No, not a devotee who got lost in the jungle.

No, not a criminal known to the police.

No, not a recent visitor to the village who ran afoul of local gangs.

Anita stared back at the constable. Really, this was getting annoying. She looked around for a chair. She walked to the corner and grabbed a plastic chair, dragging it across the room and dropping it in front of the constable's desk. She was cold, wet, tired, and frustrated. She had to sit down.

"When is CID sending someone?" she asked.

"He is coming."

"Yes, soon?"

"Yes, soon."

"If no one knows the dead man, and he has no papers on him to identify him, where will you take him?"

The constable seemed to consider this over several minutes, looking down at the single sheet of paper in his hand on which was written a brief description of the cart driver's work and the names of the men who had brought the body out of the jungle. "The body will go to Chengannur. After that . . ." He shrugged and put the paper on his desk.

"They will want to know exactly how he was found," Anita said, not yet ready to give up. "When the others came to collect the body, they weren't careful to note how things were arranged."

"Arranged?" The constable's eyebrows seemed to grow denser.

"Yes. Take the coir rope around his wrist and his neck, for instance."

The constable flicked his hand in dismissal, as though he was talking to a pesky beggar. "Laborers become entangled—they become careless. He slipped in the mud and injured himself and then he drowned. It is not complicated."

"It did not look like an accident."

But the constable was practiced at ignoring the inconvenient. "Ah." He nodded to the open doorway. "There is rain again, very hard." He stood up. "Are you wanting umbrella for walking home?"

* * * * *

When Anita returned to Lalita Amma's house, three men lounged in the front sitting room, cups of tea on little tables in front of them. Anita passed the open doorway and went in search of Auntie Meena.

"They are trustees from the temple," Meena said when Anita found her aunt in one of the cooking rooms. Wherever she went, Meena managed to find her way to the kitchen and interrogate the cook, always looking for something new to introduce to her hotel clientele. Although she had known Vengamma for years, Meena looked forward to commiserating with her on the cost of onions and ginger and the difficulty in getting capable workers to harvest coconuts.

"They have been here for almost an hour already," Vengamma said when she noticed Anita. "Have you taken good photos?" The cook smiled and nodded at the camera.

"She is hopeless," Meena said, folding her arms across her chest.

"One very good one—of a dead man." Anita pulled the camera strap from around her neck and began to punch the buttons that would bring up her recent shots while both women gasped and threw startled questions at her. "There. Look." Anita showed them the first shot. Meena blanched and turned away, but Vengamma peered at it, turning her head this way and that to get a better look.

"Hmm." The cook pulled the camera closer.

"Do you know him?"

"Hard to say. He is not looking himself, is he?"

"These marks," Anita said as the cook squinted at the screen. "And this."

"Yes, they are singular, are they not? I can't quite make them out." Vengamma frowned and clucked, but in the end she pushed the camera away. "There are animals about, forced out of the hills by the rains. Some are coming far down." She shook her head and turned away. "There is much to be done. We are having a main meal this evening. These guests have disrupted everything." She returned to her cooking, but not before she paused to look over her

73

shoulder at the camera resting in Anita's hands.

"It is gruesome, Anita." Meena held her hand over her mouth. She might disapprove of what her niece had done, but she would not let her distress at that override her stronger feelings of sorrow and compassion for a person who had died in such a way. As flighty as Meena seemed to the rest of the world, Anita knew that, beneath all her flutter, her aunt was a sensible and kindly woman who felt deeply for the sorrows of others.

"The constable thinks he is a laborer who got caught up in his own ropes and then drowned." Anita pushed another button and the screen went blank. "But I think he is wrong. The man's hand was almost severed, and his neck had a deep gash."

"Those marks on his arm and shoulder," Meena said. "Vengamma is right. There must be animals about. We must be cautious."

"None of the workers who came to help me seemed to know him." Anita placed the camera on the table and pulled out a stool. "If he was someone who did ordinary labor around here, wouldn't other laborers have recognized him? At least six came to help and the usual crowd of villagers followed to see what was happening. But no one knew him."

"Then he is not of this place." Meena relaxed as the conversation veered into the mundane and away from the grotesque. "And it is not our concern." All of a sudden, Meena grew rigid, a look of alarm spreading across her face. "It is not our concern, Anita. Not our concern." If Meena were a woman who shouted, she would be shouting now.

"It is possible he is new to this area," Anita continued, apparently oblivious to her aunt's intensifying panic.

"Not our concern. We are guests. We must have nothing to do with any of this. Nothing."

"It is possible he was brought here by someone else, tied up and left. Then it was perhaps an accident that he drowned, that he was not meant to drown, only to be restrained." Anita rested her elbow on the table and fell into thought.

"The body and any questions have moved into the capable hands of the local authorities, Anita. We are to show our respect. And Lalita Amma needs your support now. Turn your thoughts to her and Valli and Prakash. That is your duty."

Anita leaned back and gave Meena the same blank look the constable had given her, Anita, barely an hour earlier. Behind her blank, disengaged eyes, however, Anita was wondering why the body was so quickly whisked away, and in a very nice new ambulance, too. Why was an ordinary laborer given such treatment? For any other laborer found drowned during the monsoon, no matter how badly mangled his corpse, a cursory look and quick burial or cremation would have sufficed. It might be hard to hold a cremation in this weather, but Anita knew there was bound to be a village cremation ground nearby, a small plot of land enclosed with a brick wall and devoid of trees or flowering bushes—a plot of land unkempt with only a few straggly weeds and piles of ashes. But this body was not taken to a cremation ground. Instead it was taken down to Chengannur.

"Anita!" Meena shook Anita's shoulder. "If you must have something to occupy your mind, what about Lalita's predicament? The trustees are here this very minute challenging Prakash, and no one is able to dispute them. We are barely understanding the charge, or if there is a charge. Perhaps here you could help."

Poor Auntie Meena, Anita thought. She so dislikes dead bodies. "Trustees?" Anita stood up. "Valli has told me some things that are confusing. Perhaps I should learn more about this situation."

"Exactly." Meena gave a deep sigh. "Forget these dead bodies."

"Oh, no," Anita said as she left the room. "I could never do that."

* * * * *

Introduced as she came into the room, Anita was not surprised that the conversation came to an awkward pause. She smiled properly and took an unobtrusive seat, noting that the conversation picked up again as soon as she was mostly out of sight and definitely out of mind.

It was one thing for Anita to say, only partly truthfully, that she had gone for a walk to get out of the house during an oppressive monsoon season; it was quite another for three businessmen to say the same. A car was parked in front of the house, its driver napping behind the wheel. Anita had passed dripping umbrellas and mud-soaked sandals stored on the veranda after she climbed out of an autorickshaw on her return from the police station. For these men to come this far on such an afternoon meant this was no ordinary visit. Sitting as still as she could, not looking at Lalita Amma or Prakash or Valli, who sat in a row on a single settee, Anita avoided catching anyone's eye; she must be invisible if she was to learn anything.

"So many troubles these days." A tall, stout man smiled, showing irregular teeth stained yellow from betel juice, his pressed white shirt and dhoti growing soft in the heavy humidity. "I myself am seeing this in Kochi." He leaned forward, as if about to reveal something private. "I have many relatives there, you know. Most informative they are. One has business in Ernakulam—such different ways of seeing in the city mind, isn't it?"

The man sitting to his left nodded, pulling his mouth down in a frown meant to suggest the profundity of his colleague's statement. The third man, small and birdlike, murmured agreement and shifted in his chair. His legs were crossed at the ankles, the ends of his dhoti covering most of his feet, but his large toes stuck out and wiggled back and forth, giving away his anxiety.

"Yes, indeed, sar," the middle man said, "we are a mere backwater compared to Kochi and Ernakulam."

"These things that we learn," the first man said, his smile growing oily, "are a caution for us. We are so naive, isn't it? We are not having to deal with such evil. We are such a small place." He nodded, to encourage agreement.

"Yes, a small place." Lalita Amma repeated his words. She looked worried, sitting up straight at the end of the settee, with Prakash beside her, but Anita noted a stony look in her eyes. Only Valli leaned back into the cushions, slipping her hands between her thighs, a sad frown on her face. She was almost scowling at the men, but she was also listening intently.

"A large temple in Kochi has so much more experience than we do out here in our little village. We are learning from them, isn't it?" The first man turned to the other two men to his left, and they nodded, their heads bobbing in syncopation.

"Now the Sri Ram Temple near the train station south of one of the big Ernakulam markets," the third man said. "Very careful in its dealings, it is." He pursed his lips. "From much experience they have learned, great care is important. And how have they established this care?"

"Ah," the second man said. He smiled, nodded to Prakash, and urged his friend to continue, underscoring again in his soft speech how important this was. "Yes, continue; we are all listening, isn't it?"

"Hierarchy! Yes, it is hierarchy." The third man nodded once, rearranged his shoulders, and set both hands onto the chair arms as though about to launch himself into the center of the group, where he could stand as he harangued them. "Chain of command, hierarchy, communications. This is how they are becoming so well run."

"Yes, this is so. Hierarchy." The second man closed his eyes and repeated this potent word.

"Decision is made, order is given, action is taken. Simple!" The first man threw up his hands as though the entire universe could be explained in those few words. "Three steps only."

Prakash's face had gone from pale to ashen, and he began to study the floor in front of his bare feet. Whatever he had done to earn the displeasure of the temple authorities, he would not be given any leeway. He had disobeyed a direct order of some sort, but even so, something didn't feel right about the way the trustees were presenting their position.

Anita looked over each man again. There was nothing distinctive about them except their air of self-satisfaction, their obvious power over Prakash, and their indirect approach to what was essentially an announcement of a decision of a discipline hearing that may or may not have already taken place. None wore expensive jewelry, or spoke of anything other than temple regulations and practice. Anita couldn't figure out if Prakash had stolen or misused funds, insulted another temple officer, offended a devotee, or failed to show up for work. There was nothing in their conversation that pointed in any particular direction, and yet there was an ominousness to it all that Prakash clearly felt, and Valli also. Lalita Amma seemed more and more confused, as though a safe path existed somewhere if she could just find it.

"You see our predicament?" The first man leaned forward, claiming the stage from his partners. "What are we to do? Hierarchy! It is all the hierarchy! We cannot disobey. We are sworn to serve Devi. What would happen if we disobeyed hierarchy? What would her devotees say? Her servants look to us to carry out her wishes."

At this Prakash sat up. "She has not expressed her wishes." The first speech from Prakash was like a hammer on a mirror, shattering the clearly balanced image of the three on one side and the three on the other. There was nothing obsequious in his tone either, which Anita would have expected if he held any regard for his superiors. And as clear as his speech had been, Anita had no idea what he meant by his words. Devi has not expressed her wishes? What did that mean? Whatever it meant, the three visitors seemed to understand exactly what Prakash meant. Each one stiffened.

"You are not understanding." The third man leaned forward, fixing his sharp eyes on Prakash. "Trustees have met. Decision is made. Devi is satisfied."

The transformation in Prakash was nothing short of amazing. He straightened up as though every muscle in his body was stretched and tensed. His arms flew out from his sides and he loomed over the trustees.

"I am the priest. I am the devotee. I am the one Devi speaks to. Only in the inner sanctum does she speak, and you do not go there." He pulled his arms to his side and straightened his back. "Devi has not spoken to you. It is not for Devi you do this." His face getting redder and redder, he turned and left the room.

* * * * *

The house went eerily quiet after the three visitors had made their way down the muddy slope to their car and driven away. Anita stood in the doorway and watched them go, then turned around, her lips parting, ready for speech. She looked down the hall, then back into the sitting room. She was alone. A light breeze forcing its way in through the open door told her the rains were about to start up again.

"Kashtam," she murmured to herself.

Arguments and conflicts could arise so suddenly, without warning, among temple workers and trustees. Certainly the trustees weren't chosen for their piety or engagement. They were mostly prominent men in the village or town, respected members of the community who knew how to run a temple according to proper business principles. They might never participate in a puja, or sponsor a homa for themselves, but they oversaw the festival finances and arrangements, and for the most part left the worship side of the temple to the priests. After listening to these three trustees, Anita knew Prakash had violated something important, but what? The one person who should understand enough to explain it to her was Valli, but she too had evaporated, it seemed, as soon as the men stepped out onto the veranda.

Anita went from room to room, checking on Auntie Meena, who turned out to be asleep, sprawled across her bed without a care in the world. Anita left her there and wandered through the downstairs rooms, finding Vengamma in the kitchen and Lalita Amma poring over shopping lists—the monsoon was keeping everyone from essential work, including shopping. When Anita tried to speak, the old woman waved her off.

"They are the same as dalits," Lalita Amma spoke so coldly that Anita was doubly shocked. Dalits were the lowest of the low, still untouchable in the view of many Indians despite all the changes the country had tried to make, and Lalita Amma spoke with a calmness that belied how extreme the insult was.

"Perhaps it can be resolved if—" Anita went no further. She had never seen such contempt in Lalita Amma's eyes. The old woman made no effort to mask her opinion of Anita's more temperate view.

"It is settled in their eyes," the old woman said. "And my opinion of them is just as fixed."

This new view of Lalita Amma was something for Anita to consider in private. She filed away the old woman's words, and went in search of Valli.

"So here you are!" Anita leaned into the main entrance of the new wing. She had never fully explored this wing. For years it remained mysterious and off-limits, and then she forgot about it. Now it seemed to be open—at least to Valli. Anita walked around the room, taking it all in. "Musty." She sniffed and scanned the floor for signs of the animals that probably took up residence after the humans were gone. "What are you doing in here?" Anita dusted off a chair and sat down, knowing that Valli was probably hiding out in here while trying to recover from the shocking experience of the visit just ended.

"What? Oh, I am so sorry, Anita." Valli shifted in her chair and looked around the room.

"You're unsettled, isn't it?" Anita pulled her feet up onto the edge of the chair and wrapped her arms around her knees. "Yes, I am too. It was a disturbing encounter." Anita waited, hoping her friend would jump in and explain it all to her. "Valli?"

"It's so shameful, isn't it?" Valli moved to a daybed; the wood gave a little squeak and the rolled-up mattress slid toward her. She pushed it away with a slap, and a little puff of dust rose into the air in protest.

"I don't know if it is or not. I don't know what it was all about." Anita waited. She didn't want to ask outright—that would be rude—but she wasn't going to let her friend put her off. "Were those all the trustees?"

"Those three?" Valli shook her head. "No, no. They were the officers, the ones who make the announcements." She leaned against the mattress. It barely gave under the weight of her body and a quiet tearing sound told Anita it was older than it looked, dry and neglected and left to rot years ago.

"How many trustees are there?"

"Seven."

"Who are the others? People you know?"

Valli laughed, a sound that was not warm or humorous. "Yes, I know them. I know them well."

"So, who are they?" Anita asked when Valli fell silent again.

"They are different businessmen from this area," Valli said, adding in a voice barely audible, "even if they don't live here anymore."

"What do you mean they don't live here anymore?" Anita put her feet down and leaned forward. "What's going on here, Valli?"

"It is very shameful, Anita. Very shameful." Valli rubbed her hand across her eyes and looked up at the ceiling, then at Anita. "One of the trustees you know, too. It is Kumar."

"Kumar? Your husband Kumar?" Anita sat up straight. Anita hardly knew what to say. If Valli's husband was part of the group criticizing Prakash, he could have no chance at all to save his job or his reputation. If what Auntie Meena had told her was correct, that Prakash owed his job to Kumar, it seemed Kumar had turned on his protégé, and as a result Prakash would have no chance of saving his position. But for Kumar to turn against his brother-in-law was inconceivable—yet he apparently had done that.

So what had Prakash done to earn the displeasure of the trustees? If it was a major crime, the police would be involved soon, and the trustees would have no role in Prakash's future. But no one was talking about his having committed a crime. It was all this talk about hierarchy— Prakash had disobeyed a direct order of some sort.

"Are you sure Kumar is involved?"

Anita knew the answer before she finished asking the question. She didn't need to see Valli's tears begin to flow, nor the expression on her face. Valli had been here before the trustees came to visit, before the priest told Prakash that he was in trouble. Valli had known days earlier, time enough to make plans to visit, Anita thought.

"What can we do, Anita? If he loses his position, what will happen to him?"

"He'll get another."

Valli shook his head. "No, he will be finished. He will never work as a priest again." She took a deep breath, the air shuddering into her lungs. "The trustees will see to it."

"Valli, Kumar wouldn't let things go that far."

But Valli's look said he would, and Anita feared that Prakash was caught in an avalanche that would carry him to a bad end.

* * * * *

Anita let Valli's tears flow, believing her cousin would be no good in thinking through a problem until she had spent her anger and sorrow over the day's events. When she was at last calmer, Valli stood up and tried to smile. She fussed with the pleats of her sari, and rearranged her pallu over her shoulder.

"I come here sometimes when I want to be alone and quiet." Valli smiled again, this time a real one. She looked around at the neglected room. "Surprised? Yes, I am too. I never wanted to be alone when I was a girl—always I am asking Amma, 'Who can come to visit us? Who will you invite?' But I'm not that girl anymore."

The rain began again, quieter this time, sliding down the outside walls, washing the windows, filling the tanks to overflowing.

"Does no one use this wing anymore?" Anita asked.

Valli shook her head. "We closed it up some years ago, even during long family visits. It is too much work now—there are so few of us." She rearranged a large white sheet covering a settee, pulling it over an exposed carved wooden arm. "No one comes here now. Only mice."

In the dust Anita saw little paths made by small feet running from doorway to settee and chair and bed, proof of Valli's words. Anita slipped her arm through Valli's and led her out of the room and back into the main part of the house.

"You should rest, Valli." Anita led her to the main

stairs and up to her room. "This has been a difficult day, and after you rest, we can talk. I can't help you if I don't understand everything that is going on."

"Yes, yes, of course," Valli agreed. Her distress was turning to sad acceptance, and even resignation. It made Anita wonder what else had transpired between Valli and her husband, and if the trouble with Prakash was only one incident among many.

"We'll talk later." Anita made sure that Valli lay down for a nap. Anita wanted to return to the closed wing for a more careful examination. Hers and Valli's weren't the only human footprints in that room.

* * * * *

Anita turned the key and listened to the heavy shifting of metal inside the lock; the door slipped lower on its hinges, and she pulled it open. Valli had insisted that this wing had been closed off for some time, with her being the only one to seek out its quiet and solitude. But Anita was sure this was incorrect. She let herself in and closed the door behind her.

The wing, the newest part of the house, was two stories with one room leading into another. The doors had been left ajar, so Anita could slip from one room to the next soundlessly. Moving through the rooms gave her a sense of discovery and time forgotten, of a world abandoned but also preserved, relinquished without cheer. The signs were everywhere—small statues left on corner tables, prized possessions of an earlier relative, neatly upholstered chairs positioned around a tea table, as though guests were imminent, leather-bound books left in a low stack, their bindings black with mold accumulated over years and pages rotting into a single mass.

Because she lived in a small flat as part of a hotel, Anita often felt rootless, as though she were drifting through life. These rooms, left as though ghostly owners would soon return, reminded her of the need in people to

see around them the things that define them: the art objects
that tell an old man of meager means he is a connoisseur,
no matter what the village elders think of him; the array of
framed photographs that tell a young man at his first job in
Chennai that he is not alone in the world; the silk saris and
matching cholis that tell a matron she was valued, even if
her husband has been dead for years; the new bride who
looks to her jewelry to reassure herself that her husband's
folly need not be hers; the house that tells the world this
family is important. And yet they are only things, easy to
possess and quick to decay.

These were the kinds of rooms that drew some and
repelled others, Anita knew. She had friends who would
take one look at a sitting room with matching Victorian
love seat and chairs, antimacassars turning yellow with age
and neglect, and urge the owner in no uncertain terms to get
rid of it all. And still others would embrace the whole lot
and beg the owner to preserve it until someone came along
who could and would love it as their own.

But to Anita all these things were stories, stories
about the life they helped create, define, and support. Over
the generations one person after another had lived here and
added evidence of individual lives, and even now, someone
was carrying on a life here. These rooms were being used;
she was sure of it.

Anita crept up the stairs to the landing. The sound
of the rain was muted here, locked out by the thick walls
and window shutters, the heavy khadi cloth sheets covering
furniture and carpets. In the central, penultimate room,
Anita found what she was looking for. In the near total
darkness, she swung her torch across chairs, settees, tall
lamps, bookcases and tables, baskets piled in corners.
There, on a daybed positioned along the outer wall, were
the signs of someone sitting—the imprint of a body on the
sheet. The dust on the floor was scuffed into little piles
along the edge of an uneven circle where someone had

nervously rubbed a foot back and forth, back and forth.

Anita walked around the room, wondering why someone would have chosen this spot for a retreat or perhaps a secret meeting, this of all the half dozen or so rooms in the wing. As she examined the room, the choice began to make sense. A light shining here would not be visible from the front of the house to anyone passing by; it might be visible along the side, but there were no other houses close enough to see it on that side. But what about the side perpendicular to the front of the house, including the room where Anita now slept? Along the wall facing the main entrance and the balcony in front of Anita's room stood two tall screens. Each screen concealed a tall shuttered window. This could be, she realized, an added precaution because normally no one used the room she was in now. Everyone else slept in the back of the house; only Anita had a complete view of the front from her balcony. She cast her light over the floor and found the spot where the screens had stood before being dragged across the room to their current positions.

There was no way to know how often someone came here, but it should be easy to see any light if she made small adjustments to the shutters. Anita unlocked the farther shutter, hooked it in place, and rearranged the screen to conceal the change. If anyone came this night or the next, or while she was here, there was a good chance she could see the light from her window.

Ten

"Is it over?" Meena poked her head into her niece's room. Anita was shaking out her saris and arranging them on hangers dangling from the backs of doors and hooks placed around the room. The humidity was so thick that no one dared hang or pile clothes inside a closed almira. As a result, bedrooms were littered with clothes hanging off light fixtures, open doors, backs of chairs, and hastily strung clotheslines.

"If you mean, have the three trustees gone?" Anita shook out a choli and hung it on a doorknob. Meena came into the room and sat down on the bed.

"A terrible thing, terrible. They accuse this poor innocent boy, and his mother is helpless to defend him." Meena shook her head in disbelief.

"And you don't even know what he's accused of, do you?" Anita winked at her aunt.

"Anita! You are speaking of family!"

"Why do you think he is innocent?" Anita pulled up a chair and sat down, resting her feet on the edge of the bed. Everything felt clammy and damp, and she wanted to get away from it all—back to the coast, where at least the sea breezes gave the illusion of dryer weather.

"What could he possibly have done?"

Anita pursed her lips and considered the question. "From the hints the trustees dropped, I'd say he's been managing money in a questionable manner, to put it nicely."

"Anita, you don't mean that. Do you?"

Meena was steadfast and loyal to a fault. She would never think ill of a relative, and if one of them got into trouble, she would assert loudly and repeatedly that it was an injustice. When as a young woman she had watched a beloved cousin brother lose his position in government employ to a man less qualified in her view, her belief in the unfairness and arbitrariness of outside forces had hardened.

Anita sensed that certain experiences coming at crucial moments in one's life could redefine values and vision—the child who is taken to hospital at the age of fifteen months who ever after feels disconnected from the mother he adores, or the young woman whose father disappears when she is a teenager who lives with the inchoate suspicion that men are mercurial and unreliable. Watching a relative's fortunes change for no apparent reason had been the pivotal experience for Meena, and there was no point in trying to get her to see this. Her family could do no wrong, and anything a relative might be accused of was a tricked-up injustice.

"Prakash is a nice boy, Meena Elayamma," Anita said, leaning forward as if to catch her aunt if she succumbed to the shock of Anita's words. "But he is a boy. A boy, not a young man growing into the world."

"What does that mean?" Meena's eyebrows clumped in confusion over her dark eyes. "You are not saying flat out what you mean."

"All right." Anita wondered briefly if she was making a mistake by being so direct. "The trustees don't merely suspect. They have reason to accuse him. Something has gone on. I'm not saying the trustees are all pure and unsullied, but Prakash is not pure and unsullied either. He's a boy making mistakes without appreciating the consequences. And no one is telling anyone else the truth. Right now it's wheels within wheels."

"Ah! Now you sound like your father." Meena flapped her right hand, dismissing him, the comment, and with it Anita's impression of the afternoon visit. "Prakash is your cousin brother, Anita. You must defend him."

Anita watched her aunt as she stood up slowly and with effort, like an old woman. To feel a darkness descend on the family line, no matter who brought the accusation, inevitably aged Meena. She repeated her insistence that Anita support Prakash and left the room. Anita picked up another choli and shook it out, then looked around for somewhere to hang it.

Unfortunately, Anita believed Prakash was guilty. After watching him that afternoon as he faced the three trustees, she was convinced that he was guilty of something, though perhaps not of what the trustees were charging him with. It was a bit confusing to her still, mostly because the trustees didn't seem to want to come out and say exactly what was happening, but both sides understood the exchange. The trustees found Prakash lacking in his role as an underling of the temple trustees, and Prakash was angry at having been thwarted in whatever it was he was doing. It was about money and his arrogance in overreaching his position.

* * * * *

"Are you hiding out or working?" Anita asked from the library door. Valli raised her head at the sound of Anita's voice and gave her an absent smile. "I thought we could play one of our old games." Anita held out the red-and-black board in one hand and a small bag of *manjaati* seeds in the other.

"Oh, Anita! I haven't played *pallankuli* in ages!" Valli perked right up when she saw what Anita was carrying, and quickly dropped the papers she had been going through. "Come, we'll play here." Valli moved to a settee near a window, pushed aside a stack of newspapers

89

and waited for Anita to join her. Anita set up the board and distributed the seeds. Both women grew serious as they started play.

"*Pasu.*" Valli called out her move. She collected the pile of four seeds and grinned at Anita.

"You always liked beating me." Anita took her turn.

"You have to concentrate. Don't think about anything else." Valli was proof of her advice, turning the simple game into a different sort of contest.

"I like doing something like this to relax." Anita took her turn. "After some of the days we have at Hotel Delite, I need to do something completely different. Sometimes I play with Ravi." When Valli looked blank, Anita reminded her that Ravi worked at the hotel, one of the desk managers.

"Ah, yes, nice boy." Valli took her turn. "It is good for the mind, to concentrate on other things."

"Perhaps we should invite Prakash to join us. Ah, *pasu.*" Anita collected the four seeds. "He must be very upset after today's meeting."

Valli took her turn after giving Anita's words careful thought. "Yes, I guess so." She began to count the seeds she had collected and those Anita had, and waited for Anita to take her turn. As the silence lengthened, Valli said, "I can't see this would make him feel any better. That meeting was far too serious."

"Yes, I suppose you're right." Anita tapped the table as her seeds piled up. "Did you understand what it was all about? I know Kumar is one of the trustees. Did he tell you what exactly the temple authorities are upset about?" Anita noticed that Valli's game was slipping—she missed making a *pasu.*

"It is enough. This is a child's game." Valli pushed away from the table and pressed her hands to her face. "I can't settle, Anita."

"You're worried about Prakash and Kumar, isn't

it?"

Valli nodded, looking more miserable than ever.

"Tell me, Valli. I can't help if I don't understand what is going on."

Valli gave her a plaintive look. "You can't help at all. It is the trustees—they are all against him."

"But why?"

"It is the sweets. The trustees ordered Prakash to change the price of the sweets, and he said no. He said Devi has not agreed to that."

"Oh." Anita leaned back and thought about this. After a moment, she said, "How does he know this? How does he know Devi does not agree? Does he believe that Devi speaks to him alone?"

"No, no, nothing like that." Valli swung her head back and forth. "It is much simpler than that. In this temple, there is a special puja to seek permission from the Goddess to raise prices for her devotees. If the puja is successful, the prices can go up; if it is not, there is no change. Prakash says they have not conducted the puja, so no change can be made."

"And for this they are going to fire him?" Anita frowned. She knew the managers of any organization could become possessive and proprietary and bossy, but this seemed such a silly disagreement, and one so easily resolved—with a single, simple puja. "Why don't they do the puja?"

"Prakash was asked to do it."

"And?"

"He refused."

"Oops!" Anita didn't like the sound of that.

"How about a game of cribbage. I always beat everyone at that game." Valli rushed to a cupboard and pulled out a board.

* * * * *

Later that evening Anita opened the door to her room and

felt the weight of a sleeping house.

The evening meal had been an awkward affair, with the two aunts carrying on a stilted conversation about far-flung relatives, and Valli adding the occasional commentary to Anita. Prakash was nowhere to be seen or heard, his prayers and vows having taken him to bed much earlier.

Anita wondered about that, about the way he had so far managed to avoid his family and her, instead of popping up in every doorway, asking what she and Valli were doing and had they thought about this or that. He had been for years the stereotypical younger brother in a large family in a remote area, hanging around looking for something to do, wanting to go with his sister and her friend.

Anita waited, expecting to hear someone moving around, perhaps getting a glass of water or a blanket—it was cold at this hour in the hills, with the rain relentlessly beating against the walls and windows—but the house remained silent and still. After another few minutes, Anita moved to the window. There was no sign yet that anyone had visited the new wing after her last visit. She closed the shutters and headed to the new wing. She unlocked the door and entered, then closed and locked the door behind her.

Anita stepped gingerly in her bare feet, trying to remember where the furniture was placed, where the carpeting began, where screens and tables were situated through the rooms like obstacles for the unwary. The antiques that had been so interesting and evocative in the thin daylight were now clumsy-looking and obstructive. She wondered why Lalita Amma had kept this wing unchanged, its old furniture unmoved, even untouched. It made her think Lalita had been less willing to move than she let on, keeping the wing unchanged so that she could return to what must have been for her the real world, her real home.

Anita worked her way up the stairs, stopping every few seconds to reassure herself that she was moving silently, giving no one any sign of her approach. When she reached the room with the daybed that had shown signs of visitors, she thought about obvious hiding places and chose a spot behind a double screen. Even if someone turned on all the lights, no one was likely to notice her here. She settled in to wait. After what seemed an hour, Anita heard the sound of cloth rustling nearby; she hoped she hadn't fallen asleep and taken to snoring.

The sound of fabric rustling came again, and Anita thought someone had moved across the room to the other side. She peered through the reticulated lower half of the screen into the darkness, but one black shape was much like another. Wood scraped across wood and the sound of the rain grew louder. Someone had opened a window. A shutter creaked and the rain roared into the room. Whoever it was leaned out the window and called out in a voice barely audible. Anita couldn't make out the words. The unknown person seemed to shrink down to the floor and become still, the rain spattering in, the wind picking up and dying and picking up again. Anita felt cramped but didn't dare move lest she give herself away.

Anita and the stranger waited in the dark, minute after minute; rain lashed the house before settling into the steady fall most typical of the monsoon. After some time, well over an hour, maybe two, Anita heard the shutter being drawn in and latched. The unknown person quietly left the room. Anita uncoiled herself and followed, wanting only to know who this other person might be. Anita crept along until she could see the stairs and a small figure descending in the darkness. Uncertain, Anita knelt down and watched. When the figure opened the door to the main house and turned back to reassure herself that all was well behind her, Anita saw the troubled face of Parvati; she held a small parcel wrapped in newspaper in one hand. Parvati closed the door, and Anita stood alone in the dark. She walked to the top of the stairs, and sat down on the landing.

* * * * *

Anita struggled to understand what she had seen in the new wing. Her first thought was that Parvati truly trusted in whoever she expected to meet. She must know whoever it was well to believe that person would come no matter how great the difficulty in getting here. Who did Parvati know in this area who could be expected to show up on such a night? Whoever it was had to be important to her, more important than her job and security. Parvati had purloined a key and risked everything by using it.

Anita made her way back to the room of the vigil, closed the doors and shutters tighter and lit a lamp. With this minimal light, she searched the area where Parvati had been waiting—the floor was soaked, as were the hems of the sheets covering a nearby table and chairs. Anita carried the lamp as she walked along the wall, studying the floor and furniture. At one end of the room, near a window, was a small clump of cooked rice, only a few grains, but enough to tell Anita that someone had recently brought cooked food up here. Recent because ants didn't have any tracks through here, so the rice had lain uneaten for a while, but it wouldn't last much longer. She recalled the parcel in Parvati's hands.

Had Parvati previously delivered food to someone through the window, inadvertently spilling some of it? Had someone else arrived here, through the window or another way, and eaten a meal here?

Whoever Parvati was expecting, that person had not shown up. Who could she know here who could only be met clandestinely at this hour? And for a meal?

Anita opened the window again and leaned out. Even without a lantern, she could see a vine climbing up the side of the building, something easily reached by an agile man or woman from this window. Because the window was clearly visible from only one side, two people could hope to meet here undiscovered. But that again forced Anita to ask, who? Who did Parvati know that she could meet only in this manner? Why would she meet someone like this?

Parvati was a maidservant, Anita reminded herself, and as an employee she could make numerous trips into the village on errands for the household. As shy as Parvati seemed to be, more willing to stay in than go out, these trips would give her ample opportunity to meet someone and carry on a clandestine affair. There was no need to go climbing about at night in the rain.

Anita closed and latched the windows and descended the stairs, but at the doorway she pulled out a ring of keys and double locked the door. No one was going to get back inside without her. She tested the door and left the wing. At the stairs to the second floor of the main part of the house and her own room, she paused. She felt the need of a cup of tea.

* * * * *

Anita padded through the lower rooms, glanced up at the wooden wind-up clock in the dining room, and headed into the kitchen. She made a point of making a little noise—humming, pushing aside a chair—as she opened another door to another cooking room and flipped on the light. The matches sat on a shelf above the stone sink and she reached for the box, pulled it open, and extracted a wooden match. She turned on the gas and lit the gas burner. As she adjusted the flame, she heard another door open, and Parvati appeared behind her.

"I find I must have something soothing, Parvati." Anita smiled at her. "I couldn't sleep, so here I am."

"Yes, yes. Am I sitting here?" Parvati immediately grabbed a pot and filled it with water, setting it on the burner.

"You don't have to help me. You shouldn't be up.

You have to get up very early anyway, isn't it?" Anita crossed her arms over her chest and waited.

"It is no matter." Parvati opened a packet of loose tea, and began making tea with milk and sugar. When it was ready, she poured it into a metal tumbler and cooled the hot liquid by pouring it back and forth between tumbler and bowl. "Done," she said as she handed the tumbler to Anita.

"What is that sound?" Anita held the tumbler and listened.

"The goat. It is crying."

"At this hour?" Anita put down the tea and went to the back door. She pulled it open and stared into the darkness. There was no mistaking the sounds of the goat mewling and struggling against its tether. She turned to Parvati for an explanation.

"The shed came down last night, so we are keeping the animal here on the veranda under a lean-to. It is tied so it doesn't run off again." Parvati began to push the heavy door shut.

"That's not what I heard." Anita moved into the doorway as the goat continued to struggle. "Give me a knife." She felt the heft fall into her open palm and at once grabbed the rope holding the goat and cut it with three swipes. She dragged the goat into the kitchen and pushed the door shut.

"Why, Amma?" Parvati looked genuinely perplexed.

"Large green eyes." Anita wiped the rain from her face.

"What?

"Some animal was stalking the goat—much too close." Anita looked down at the goat, which was looking around the room with dull, incurious eyes, no longer agitated or frightened. The animal lifted its head, its large golden-yellow eyes gazing up at Anita. Such animals were so different from human beings, she thought. Once the danger has passed or been removed, they return to their state of calm, unlike humans, who remain agitated and distressed for hours afterwards. A human being rescued from a stalking animal would be trembling, sweating, choking with relief and ebbing fear. Anita cupped her hand on the goat's snout and gave it a rub.

"A wild animal is out there?" Parvati began to shake, dropping the rope, and pressing her hands against her chest. "No, no, no."

Anita rested a hand on her shoulder. "You are worried because you went to meet someone and they didn't show up, and now you're worried this wild animal outside could be the reason. Yes?"

"I have done nothing wrong. Please, Amma. I am honest worker."

"Who did you go to meet?"

Parvati stared at her, then took the goat into a corner of another kitchen room, arranged a number of empty canvas sacks, and left the animal to lie down and sleep. Her face a mask of the perfect servant, she returned to Anita. "More tea, Amma?"

* * * * *

"I went through the closed wing earlier today," Anita said to Parvati, "to see the rooms I used to play in. I knew they'd been closed up, so I walked around until I got to the second floor and the room in the center. I could see someone had been there recently, but from what Valli had told me, the wing was closed off for any kind of normal use." Anita accepted another cup of tea from Parvati. "So I wondered: who is coming here, to this place that is supposed to be all closed up?"

In the silence that followed, Parvati stood motionless, the dutiful servant waiting for instructions. But there were no instructions, only an opportunity to speak. A draft from the back door reached the hem of Parvati's mundu and ruffled it. Anita felt the cool air on her toes.

"I saw you come up this evening. You opened the window and you called to someone. You brought food." Anita held the warm cup in both hands.

Parvati's breath quickened, but she maintained remarkable control otherwise. "I did not steal the food. It was my share of the evening meal."

"And?"

"Will you tell Lalita Amma?" Parvati's shoulders tensed as she drew her arms closer to her body, as though anticipating blows.

"Who did you expect to meet?" Anita waited for a reply. "You have taken a key to enter an area that is considered closed off. You should not have done this. I have no desire to cause you harm, Parvati, but you must tell me what you are doing. You have no fear from us. This is a family you can trust. Does not Lalita Amma treat you well?"

"This is true. She does this."

"Well, then?"

Parvati's head began to swivel back and forth, as if she were looking for an escape, but there was none. "These are things I cannot say."

"You cannot conduct secret business here, Parvati. You tell me now or you will be gone in the morning."

"Oh, no! I cannot be gone from here." Parvati clenched her hands to her chest and fell to her knees pleading. She touched her fingertips to Anita's feet and then to her own eyelids. "Please, Amma. Let me stay."

Anita motioned for her to stop. After a moment, she said, "You will tell me now."

Parvati nodded and sat back on her heels. In the flickering candlelight Anita knelt down to listen.

"I am illegal." That was all Parvati said.

"Who were you meeting?"

"My brother. He too is illegal."

"How does he know you are here?"

"I sent him a letter. I went to the post office a month ago and wrote him to come to me here."

"Why? Are you unhappy here?"

Parvati seemed uncertain of her own feelings and frowned as she cast about in her own mind for an answer. "I am afraid, Amma."

"Of what?"

"I am illegal. If something happens to me, there is no one to speak for me."

"But you said your brother is also illegal. How can he help you?"

"He is my brother. My only family."

"You should have told Lalita Amma. She would take you under her wing and help you get papers."

Parvati squinted at Anita through thick eyebrows. "Does Amma not have many other things on her mind? She will not want to think about a maidservant."

"You think it is easier for your brother, then?"

"He is a laborer, and they don't ask questions because he is Tamil and they only want workers. It is harder for me. I am Tamil, but there is plenty of work for maidservants in Tamilnad, so there is no reason for me to come here, and then maidservants must go into the village and conduct business. Vengamma does much of this work—she thinks I am shy and dimwitted."

Anita smiled. She'd heard Vengamma on Parvati's shortcomings. "We gave a ride to a laborer yesterday, when we collected Prakash at the temple. I don't know if he was Tamil or not—he said barely a word; he fell asleep in the car on the drive." Anita paused, remembering the trip.

"Oh, Amma! What did he look like?" There was no mistaking Parvati's excitement. She leaned forward and studied Anita's face, looking for a reason to believe this man was her long-awaited brother.

"I barely noticed him," Anita said, deciding to keep

99

to herself her first impression of the man. "But he did look like a laborer, and Prakash said he was a laborer coming here for work. He didn't say where. Perhaps he hasn't found the house yet."

"Perhaps." Parvati considered Anita's words. "I told him I would be at such and such a window every night, with food, until we met. Then we could plan."

"And what will you plan?" Anita said, thinking only that this young woman had few options to contemplate.

"My future." Parvati smiled at her. "My future."

* * * * *

By the time Anita got back to her bedroom, the rain had settled into a steady, soft waterfall, even but all encompassing. She closed her door and then, without thinking, threw the bolt. She couldn't have said why she did that, but the idea that there was, perhaps, an unknown man wandering along the perimeter of the house made her uneasy. It was foolish, she knew, but she ran her fingers over the iron bar as she turned away. She had already locked the kitchen rooms from the inside, leaving Parvati to the three cooking rooms and the kitchen door to the back garden. She could flee, but she could not break into the main part of the house, nor could she let anyone else in.

Anita's eyes quickly adjusted to the dark as she made her way across the room. She would be glad when the monsoon came to an end—she was sick of the rain. She peered through the shutters out into the darkness, wondering about the goat, Lalita Amma's decline, and Valli's erratic confession and secrecy, affection and distance. This visit was hardly what Anita expected after years of friendship. As girls Valli and Anita had often pulled their mats onto the balcony and curled up together, staring up at the stars and planning what they would do with their lives. Anita opened the door and stood on the sill. With the wind calmer and the rain easing, she could imagine the village down the hill, the neighbors on the other side of the thicket, the lane below.

In the distance an animal squealed, and others followed. Something had disturbed and frightened them. Anita stiffened. Looking into the night, waiting, she saw no large animal creep past with its kill. But it was out there, she knew, and it had caught what it needed. She winced at the thought of the poor creature taken by the wild animal.

The moonlight reflected on something light, and Anita rushed to the parapet and leaned over, but the figure she was sure she had seen had disappeared into the brush. She was certain she had seen someone the night before and here he was again. She hurried back inside and shook off the rain, ready to run downstairs and tell Parvati, but at the last second she checked herself.

If she told Parvati she had seen her brother, or one she thought was her brother, the maidservant would want to go to him at once, and then she would want to bring him inside. That would be wrong. A maidservant could not bring a stranger into Lalita Amma's house without the owner's permission, and certainly not without her knowledge. But suppose it was not Parvati's brother?

Anita closed the doors to the balcony, found a towel and dried herself off, untying her sari and draping it over a chair to dry. She put on a sleeping shift and got into bed. Lying on her back beneath the rough cotton sheets and thin blanket, she kept hearing the cry of the animal caught and slaughtered, the hysterical cries of others fleeing and warning their mates. There was something not quite right about Parvati's story tonight.

Anita rolled over onto her side and got used to the gray light filtering through the venetian doors.

The laborer who had hitched a ride with Prakash could very well be Parvati's brother. But if he was, why did he not know who Prakash was? If the brother communicated enough with Parvati to know where she lived and how to find her, then she must also have told him about the family, about Lalita Amma and Prakash and Valli as well as Vengamma and whoever else came around to help. The groundsman Thampi. That could be why her brother was coming at night, unannounced. He didn't want to meet a man who might question him, recognize he was illegal and make a fuss about it.

No, that wasn't right.

Anita sat up in bed and rearranged the pillows behind her so she could sit up and think. She thought about the man creeping around the house again, and automatically reached out to rest her hand over the tangle of keys sitting on a nearby table. The obvious answer was that Parvati was not at all what she said she was—an illegal immigrant who only wanted a decent job but also wanted to be with her brother, her remaining family. As an employee in a small household made up mostly of women, Parvati was in a position to aid a partner to enter the household and take whatever was valuable. Unfortunately, from what Anita could see, most of the valuables were gone and the rest were on their way out the door. If Parvati had designs on the family wealth, she was two years too late.

Anita had liked Parvati when she first saw her. Liked her modesty, her quiet but steady performance of her duties, her attentiveness to Lalita Amma. Still, Anita knew, such emotions can be feigned by the accomplished con artist, and Lalita Amma was old and tired and easily susceptible to such approaches, especially while Valli was so wrapped up in her own worries.

The rain lessened, its steady beat evolving into an undulating rustling sound. It seemed to give Anita more room for thinking, and she felt her mind expanding. How was it they all seemed to be having such difficulties all at once? Lalita Amma declining into poverty, Valli's marriage falling apart, and Prakash's career and reputation nearly ruined. What horrible karma had descended upon this family?

It occurred to Anita that now was the time for Meena Elayamma to be calling her astrologer. Meena consulted him for almost everything, especially if it wasn't very important. Perhaps she should be calling him now to find out how things were going to turn out for her extended family—at least Meena and Anita could prepare for the worst, because that's certainly what it looked like was going to happen.

Eleven

By midmorning Anita was on her way to the village center. The rain had let up enough to suggest it was safe to venture out for a walk. The village was larger than the population of the area justified, but the town was close to one of the roads pilgrims took to Sabarimala, and over the years the town had attracted a number of businesses catering to the men and older women who made the journey.

Sabarimala was on Anita's list of things to see when she was old enough, since she would never again be young enough. Only females too young or too old to menstruate could enter the temple sacred to Ayyappa, since the Lord was a *brahmachari,* a celibate, and Anita would not be able to make the pilgrimage until she had passed menopause, which was many years in the future.

She vaguely recalled a pair of uncles taking her when she was barely of school age, but all she remembered were the crowds dressed in black, the way her feet hurt, and the sudden bursts of cheering as busloads of pilgrims flew by. Somewhere in all of this she remembered a beautiful hymn sung in the evening, but she couldn't remember the words. And by now she wasn't sure if these were true memories or conflations of what she saw almost every year along the roads heading toward Sabarimala and what she knew must have happened, and her bare feet often hurt on a rough temple path anyway. She was told she had been there, but she couldn't claim that her memories were real, or of that moment.

Anita wasn't the only one leaping at the opportunity to get out of a rain-locked home and back to normal life, which in India meant life on the street, shopping for food and stopping to visit and share news with other shoppers. The crossroads that constituted the village center were already lined with hawkers, the man selling limes laid out on a well-ironed square of plaid cotton, the boy strolling the street with a fistful of hand-carved flutes, the vendor with scores of brightly painted pictures of Ganesha or Rama or Sarasvati and many others.

The growing numbers of shoppers wore an air of expectation and excitement, a sign of their relief at being released from the monsoon-induced confinement. Anita stopped to admire some hand-embroidered CD holders—commenting on the careful depiction of local Malayali actors and singers—but decided not to buy. When she looked up, she caught sight of a man dressed in black lungi and black shirt, the clothing of a Sabarimala pilgrim, heading down a narrow lane. He turned to glance over his shoulder, halted for a second, and hurried on down the lane.

Uncertain of what she had seen, Anita ran to the lane, but when she got there the man was gone. She looked around the busy street, in case he had slipped in among the shoppers, but again she didn't see him. She wasn't sure now of what she had seen. At first glance, she thought she had seen the laborer who had hitched a ride from the temple, but neither Prakash nor the laborer had said anything about his going to Sabarimala. And there was no reason he should have. But still, it felt odd that she should see him here, in the village, dressed as a pilgrim when he had said he was looking for work. And indeed, he had arrived here only the day before yesterday, not enough time to visit Sabarimala and return, though perhaps enough time to plan a visit.

"Is there a group soon going to Sabarimala from here?" Anita stopped a man she knew to be a village elder, the trustee of a small temple nearby. Pilgrims went in groups, packed into lorries or vans.

"Next week going." He paused to study her. "Men only. You know this?"

"Yes, yes, I have gone as a child." She paused, wondering about the schedule, but set that aside. She wanted information, and what did it matter if he didn't know about Thampi's group leaving earlier?

"Yes, very holy place." The man waggled his head, letting his eyes fall shut.

"I thought I saw someone in pilgrim garb just now. So a group is not going now?"

"Not from here." The man looked skeptical. "Perhaps you are mistaken. Perhaps you are only seeing someone passing by." He nodded and left her there.

Perhaps, Anita thought. And perhaps not. She headed for the alley. This led past a row of small houses closely packed together, with small gardens between them and vines growing on sapling fences. The puddles were drying up, and she made her way among them to where the lane ended in a sharp drop down a hillside. Whoever had come this way had vanished, efficiently and quickly. She took another look around, but the only person in sight was a small girl, about ten years old, doing the washing by soaking her clothes in a bucket then beating them on a rock.

"Did you see a man pass by?" Anita asked as she approached the little girl.

"The pilgrim?"

"That's the one." Anita stepped toward the fence. "Did you see him?"

She nodded she had.

"Where did he go?"

"You are knowing this man?"

"Yes, I am knowing." Anita wasn't sure she should

tell the child that she had traveled with him to this village, and that he'd been ostensibly looking for work.

"How are you knowing him?" The little girl came forward, leaving her laundry dripping on the stone. She looked perplexed, and Anita sensed there was definitely something to be learned here.

"My friend's brother knows him, and gave him a ride to this village," Anita said. This was not quite a lie but enough of the truth to satisfy.

"Why did he want to come here?"

That, thought Anita, is what I want to know. Instead, she said, "He said he has work here."

The girl shook her head, turned down her mouth, and flicked her fingers at Anita.

"Why do you do that?"

"This one is not wanting work." The child looked disgusted. "We are having much difficulty with the rains." She pointed to the roof where the leaves had given way in part of the building, probably under the torrents of water and wind of the last few days. "He is taking a sleeping place there." She pointed to a small shed. "But when the roof is coming down, he is not helping. Acchan is offering money, but still he is not helping."

"Not at all?" Anita said. The girl's father must have been mystified by someone turning down work.

The girl shook her head and the look of disgust returned. "Very troubling."

"Yes, I can see it would be." Anita fell into thought. "Has he said when he is leaving for Sabarimala? Do you know what group he is going with?"

She shook her head. "Two days ago he is coming here, then he buys Sabarimala clothes, then he is still here. He knows this village—he has been here before—but he is not going on his pilgrimage and he is not working."

Anita smiled. "You expected him to depart at once with his *irumudi* on his head, yes?"

"He has no *irumudi*," the child said. Anita easily guessed the reason for her disgust. Sabarimala pilgrims were respected and honored while they wore the garments of their pilgrimage. For a man to use the clothing of the pilgrim to gain some sort of advantage was beneath contempt. If he had not purchased the traditional offerings of the pilgrim and the traditional cloth bag, the *irumudi,* for carrying them, then he was indeed suspect. Every pilgrim was expected to carry this bag on his head on the way to the shrine.

"What has he been doing while he's been here?"

The girl shrugged. "He wants to know about the village and who lives here."

"He sounds very particular for a man who is poor."

"He is not poor." The girl was about to return to her laundry but Anita stopped her.

"How do you know he is not poor?" Anita tried to keep the excitement out of her voice. "We thought he was a poor man when we gave him a ride. But now you say he is not. How do you know?"

A guilty smile spread across her face; it was like watching a puppy with a bone in its mouth. "He goes into his shed and closes the door and sleeps in the afternoon."

"And?"

"The chickens like the shed too, so I have to get them and keep them away from pecking at the door." A sly look came over her face.

"And you can see into the shed and you saw him with his money," Anita guessed. "How much was it?"

"The big ones. Many, many, many of them."

"Did you see anything else?" Anita asked.

"Photographs. Many photos, large and small. Many, many." The girl held her thumb and fingers up about an inch apart to show the thickness of the stack of photos.

So he wasn't poor and he wasn't looking for work. He was looking for someone, a particular someone, it seemed. Someone he didn't recognize without a photo to guide him. "You said he slept in the afternoon. When does he get up?"

"At midnight we are all asleep."

"But?"

"But I can see him when he leaves the shed. When all the lights are out and it is quiet, he opens the door and he leaves."

"I see." Anita didn't actually, but she was beginning to think she might. "Do you know what he does?"

The girl shrugged again. "He walks in the rain. What else is there to do?"

* * * * *

Anita retraced her steps down the alley until she reached the village center. She scanned the shoppers and vendors, looking for the man's familiar face and attire. She gave a start when she saw another Sabarimala pilgrim, but when he emerged from the crowd, she knew it wasn't the man she was seeking. This man in front of her now was tall and lanky, and his arms were too long for his shirtsleeves. He collected the items he had purchased and stuffed them into his cloth bag, the *irumudi* all pilgrims are expected to carry. He moved on down the road to the intersection and turned a corner.

If he was purchasing the last few items he might need for his offerings, then he would lead her to the lorry or bus leaving soon with a group of pilgrims. Anita turned the corner, found her new quarry in the crowd, and followed him. After passing through much of the village, past the post office substation and a small gas station, the man turned past a house. Anita followed, and found herself at the edge of a bare patch of ground occupied by a small, brightly painted lorry. The back was open, a tarp tied to the stays arching over the truck bed.

About two dozen men in black were chatting and arranging their possessions, which consisted almost entirely

of the required cloth bags for offerings and the clothes they
wore. Most were in their thirties and forties, and a few in
their fifties. Since all wore beards of similar length, Anita
wondered if they were from the same office, colleagues
used to working together and now making a Sabarimala
pilgrimage together. She spotted her quarry in a group near
the back of the truck.

"You are looking for a relative?" One of the
younger men approached her. No matter how fierce they
might look in their all-black clothing and black beards,
such pilgrims were always unfailingly polite to her, even
when her car backed into their truck, blocked their path or
stalled in traffic. Sabarimala season was a busy time on the
highways.

"Is this the only group going from this village this
week?" Anita asked, trying to remember exactly what
Lalita Amma had said about Thampi's departure.

"This is the first one going. Who are you looking
for?"

"A household friend is going, and we wanted to
give him something for an abhishekham. His name is
Thampi, Rajesh Thampi."

The man shook his head. "He is not in this group."
He turned around as he spoke, surveying the men straggling
across the parking area.

"No, I can see he is not here." Anita scanned the
crowd looking for her original quarry, the laborer who had
cadged a ride from the temple on the day of Anita's arrival,
but he didn't seem to be here either. Anita was increasingly
convinced the man she had met wasn't actually going to
Sabarimala despite his outfit; he was merely finding a more
convenient way to hide in the community. She thanked the
pilgrim and headed back into the village.

Anita had mentioned Thampi as a cover, since she
knew he planned his pilgrimage for this time, but the
pilgrim's answer disturbed her. Thampi was supposed to

have left days ago. If he was not leaving till later, why hadn't he come to work? Why hadn't he let anyone at Lalita Amma's house know his trip had been delayed? And if he wasn't going with this group, the only one leaving from his village, when was he going, and who was he going with? Pilgrims always went in groups. Where was Thampi's group?

Anita's steps slowed until she stood in the middle of the street, trying to get a grip on this unexpected development. She had two disappearing men to wonder about: the elusive hitchhiker and Thampi, Lalita Amma's lifelong servant.

* * * * *

Over the next hour the crowds grew as women came in search of fresh vegetables for the day's meals, and peons unloaded goods for shops. The constable lounged in a red plastic chair in front of his substation, working a toothpick along the bottom row of teeth. He watched Anita approach but made no effort to sit up straight or stand up to greet her.

"Shopping?"

"Looking," Anita said.

"Hmm." He returned to worrying a back tooth and staring lazily at the shoppers filling the village streets.

"I was wondering if you have heard anything about the body that was washed up yesterday. The area where he was found is not far from here, farther to the west. Has anyone come forward about someone missing?"

"No, no one in this village is missing."

"So you have announced that this man has been drowned by the river and perhaps attacked first?"

The constable frowned, looking displeased. He knew he'd somehow been caught out but wasn't sure how to extricate himself. "The peons carrying the man spoke freely. I am not needing to make an announcement."

"What have people been saying? Does anyone have any idea who he is?"

111

"No one knows this man. He is a stranger."

"He was tied up and left to drown or choke to death, and he was injured before he died." Anita paused. "There is no other village between here and where he was found. Well?"

The constable removed the toothpick from his mouth, and turned his head to get a better look at her. In a soft voice, he said, "No one knows this man. This is good news and this is bad news." He began to chew on the toothpick again, and returned to watching the villagers. "But it is not our problem. Only Chengannur can decide what to do."

* * * * *

A sudden burst of rain sent a number of vendors scurrying for cover. The vegetable vendors remained at their stations, an umbrella deftly unfurled and raised aloft, while they waited for the outburst to end. Others folded up their plaid cloths and ran with their arms around their bundles into the nearest doorway. Anita took shelter in a coffee purveyor's shop, a popular choice for many other passersby, since the concrete steps ran the length of the shop, providing lots of room for people to sit out of the rain. Anita stood on the edge of the polished cement floor; two men squatted on the bottom step, sheltered beneath the overhang. Nearby the shop owner continued his work of filling and sealing small plastic bags of ground coffee.

The shop owner poured the ground coffee into a plastic bag, weighed the filled bag, and when he was satisfied, he folded over the top and ran the edge over the flame of a candle, melting the plastic so it formed a tight seal. The rain fell softly and his pile of sealed bags grew. On the step to Anita's right sat a young woman staring out at the rain and holding a cloth bag that dangled between her legs.

They were little islands of life, not talking but known to each other from their years in the village. Since

she was a girl, Anita had known the man who owned the
coffee shop, when he was a middle-aged man working for
his elderly father, probably not thinking that one day he
would be the elderly one. The other two vendors looked
familiar and she would have nodded to them in the street,
but they were caught up in their discussion of the difficulty
of traveling to Sabarimala in this weather, the danger of
mud-slicked roads and speeding lorry drivers. The young
woman was an aide in a nearby clinic, and Anita thought
she recognized her as the daughter of a woman who had
toured the village at the request of Unicef or some other
organization to track down any known cases of polio and
before that smallpox. Anita was about to greet her and ask
after her family and the work of the clinic when the coffee
shop owner interrupted her thoughts.

"Lalita Amma will enjoy this." The shop owner
held out a bag of coffee on which he had attached a bright
green label proclaiming Kerala's finest. "I remember when
Meena Amma always purchased her coffee from our stores,
but"—he shrugged—"that was many years ago when her
husband was alive." Anita reached out for the bag and took
it in both hands.

"I know she'll be pleased."

"We wish your family well in this difficult time."

Anita couldn't imagine what her expression must
have been, so surprised was she at this oblique reference to
the family's current troubles—at least that's what she
thought she was hearing. She glanced at the men studying
the sky for signs of an end to the rain, and the young girl
who had taken out her mobile phone and was scowling at
its blank screen.

"It is a confusing matter," Anita said. "Perhaps I am
not well understanding it." She looked at him for
clarification, and he did not disappoint her.

"Temple trustees must be obeyed. If an order is
given, an order must be followed. The priest is only an

employee. If he is competent, his opinion is sought out, but this comes only after some time as he becomes known to the devotees." The little flame hissed as it licked at another plastic bag.

"Prakash hasn't been there very long, that is true." Anita tossed the bag in her hand, feeling its heft as it settled into her palm again and again. "But he does seem to have a great devotion to Devi at his temple. He speaks most profoundly of her." It was in fact something that had quite surprised her. She had never thought of him as a passionate person, and he had never seemed so adamant before about anything. This was a new Prakash.

"We appreciate his spirit too, his desire to provide service to Devi."

Yes, thought Anita, whatever that means. She turned to the shop owner as he opened another box of labels and pulled out a stack.

"You see a lot sitting here, don't you?" she said.

He looked up at her, seemed to think over her question, then nodded agreement. "People pass by day after day. I see them all. I know their schedules, when they have a little more money and when they have a little less. I know when they are worried or sad—if you watch someone every day, you notice the little things. A man who marches to the post office every morning at noon needs a friendly call when he drags past at one o'clock. I may not know what has occurred, but I know that something has. It is my duty to call to him, neighbor to neighbor."

"You see all the changes in the village, isn't it?"

"Good and bad." He nodded, his eyes fixed on the flame.

"Did you perhaps see a man who came to this village the day before yesterday? We gave him a ride from Prakash's temple—he has work here, I think. I saw him, dressed for Sabarimala, but he wasn't on the lorry just around the corner. It is going soon I think."

"Ah, yes, the first group to depart." The shop owner looked up and scanned the road in front. The rain had ceased and vendors were venturing out to stare up at the sky. One by one they returned to their spots, spreading out newspaper or tarps to protect their goods from the muddy ground.

"Only the first group?"

He nodded.

"Do you know the one I mean?" Anita described the man as best she could.

"Looking for work, you say?" The shop owner frowned. "No, the one I am seeing is not looking for work. He is looking for a friend who works hereabouts. He has come before, looked around and gone away. But then he comes back. He is still looking for his friend, it seems."

"So he is not completely new to the area," Anita said. "Who is the friend?"

"Ah, on that he is vague. Very unclear."

"How was he going to find him, his friend?"

"He thought he knew the house—a large one with land and crops and many cows."

"Is there such a one left in this village?"

"No."

"Then maybe he is lost."

"And today he is the pilgrim, dressed for Sabarimala but not yet ready to depart." The man scowled at the bag sitting on the scale and spooned out some of the coffee, then replaced the bag on the scale. "I doubt he will go on the pilgrimage."

"I too have my doubts." Anita recalled how uncomfortable the man had made her during the drive into the hills. There was something about the way he accepted the ride that made her feel that he was doing them a favor by deigning to ride with them—he seemed to reverse relationships. "Someone told me he walks through the village and hills at night. Where does he go?"

The shop owner looked up. "Does he?" He seemed to find this especially interesting and pursed his lips as his eyes glazed over, as though he were withdrawing deep within himself to ponder this bit of information. Anita looked out through the shop doorway at the crowded street and the hills rising behind the shops. There was nothing beyond the village but a few houses straggling along lanes and pathways used only by those who lived there. But all of a sudden she thought about the figure she had seen late at night during the rain, darting through the darkness, seemingly on his way past the house. Was it a neighbor on his way home, taking a shortcut that took him close by Lalita Amma's house? Was it that man, the pilgrim who wasn't a pilgrim?

"If the person you are looking for does not take a place in the lorry leaving soon, then he is not going to Sabarimala," the shop owner said, putting another bag onto the pile.

"He can go in a second lorry, yes?" Anita turned around suddenly at this pronouncement.

"There is no second lorry. Only the one group from this village."

"But—"

He pushed back his chair, scraping across the cement floor, ending the conversation. He blew out the candle and piled the little bags of coffee into a basket, which he then placed on a shelf at the back of the shop. He walked to the front and began to put away his materials. "You will not forget to tell Meena Amma that I have given you coffee for her."

Twelve

For months Parvati had been weighing up her current
situation against the possibility of something better in
another village. She didn't know where that village might
be, but she had become accustomed to the idea of moving
on, always moving on, in the hope of finding the one place
where she could relax and live out her days, doing her work
mindlessly but safely.

To her surprise, she found she didn't mind the work
of a maidservant, the washing of floors and clothing and
cookware, the sweeping out of the yard every morning, at
least every morning before the rains began. She quite liked
watching the little piles of leaves and debris build up, like
little sentries falling into line behind her as she moved
along the perimeter of the courtyard. When Vengamma
ordered her about, Parvati could hear beneath the cook's
peremptory words and tone a warmth and camaraderie for
another servant. The old cook could be brusque, even harsh
in her review of Parvati's work, scolding her for the tiniest
failure in doing the laundry or making the avial. But that
was only the surface.

The cook would turn to Parvati absentmindedly and
rattle off a list of vegetables for her to collect. Vengamma
trusted the maidservant to take the key for the larder and
retrieve the required items, trusted her to put the key back
where it belonged, trusted her to take grain to be ground

and a few rupees to purchase additional ingredients for the evening meal. This trust caught Parvati off guard, but she came to accept it. Vengamma might be gruff sometimes, but she meant no harm. Nor did Lalita Amma. The old woman was generous and kind, and was a competent chatelaine, or at least she would have been if she had had more of an estate to manage.

Parvati recognized the signs: the distractedness in the old woman's eyes when she thought no one was paying attention, the sighs apropos of nothing, the instinctive gesture of generosity before working out where the donation would come from, the cloak of shabbiness spreading through the house, like an invasive vine strangling the healthy garden of a family's history.

Lalita Amma had taken to her—Parvati sensed that right away—and she wondered if it had something to do with an intuition that recognized someone who had been through a similar loss. Granted, Parvati had never known luxury, never experienced life in a large home with servants and the entitlement that carried one through throngs on the street into the head of a line in a temple or a concert. But she understood the loss of status, the loss of a sense that the world was a safe place for her even if it was a nightmare, cruel and harsh and unforgiving, for others. That too Parvati recognized in Lalita Amma, the implicit belief in a world order that favored her and would protect her from the crass and ugly. Lalita Amma had lost more than money. That was clear to Parvati if not yet to anyone else in the family.

Valli would probably be the next one to figure it out. The guest from the seacoast already knew—Parvati could tell by the way that woman, Anita as she was called, watched others, tapped a finger on a dusty old table, made a quick review of a linen closet or a china cabinet when she thought no one was looking.

Parvati took Valli's laundry up to her this morning,

as soon as it was reasonably dry after two days' effort, and was surprised to find the other woman studying an old horoscope. Valli didn't seem disturbed to be caught with it, and merely regarded Parvati with a vague look and nodded to the bed, where Parvati deposited the stack of laundry. Parvati had noticed that no telephone had rung in the house since Valli's arrival—no phone call from a husband or friend, especially a husband. And after the phone lines went dead, the anticipated letters failed to appear, or if they did so, no mention was made of them.

When Parvati first met Valli, the maidservant cringed when the other woman burst into tears or rage at any offhand remark. But after a while, perhaps after Valli's second visit, she began to calm down, and now she seemed more likely to snap in anger and impatience. Her character was selfish—she wanted things done in a certain way, rarely said if it was well done, and wanted small purchases that were beyond the modest kitchen budget. She rarely expressed appreciation or even approval, using anger to express her feelings. Kindness was not in her nature.

Parvati didn't mind because she didn't really think of herself as being Parvati the maidservant. She found it easy to take this work with the orders and criticisms because it was as though someone else was doing it all and she was looking out through the other person's eyes, living inside a stranger's body. Her entire being now was a mask, and she alone, hidden within, could see into the hearts and minds of others—Lalita Amma, Valli, Vengamma, and . . . Prakash? No, no, she could not see into Prakash.

This was her failing. Prakash and his protestations of love and devotion, his willingness, as he said, to give up everything for her, his eagerness even to depart with her and leave everything else in his life behind him here in this tiny village, and flee with her. His fervor frightened her. She understood passion and daring and persistence, but all this from a man she barely knew seemed to promise catastrophe rather than escape and release.

And yet he was endearing and loving. She could sense that and she wanted to believe him. She would have to make up her mind soon. He might wait forever, but she couldn't. She supposed it should be the other way around—the woman chasing and the man losing interest—but it didn't happen that way. He was like a puppy, lapping at her feet and begging her to notice him, to love him even if only in a small way. His devotion paralyzed her. She could barely think to prevaricate, to stall and try to imagine what it would mean to agree to go off with him. She found herself thinking not about a future in another part of India with Prakash, but about Lalita Amma and her distress at losing her son in such a way. Parvati's heart ached for Lalita Amma and the pain Parvati knew the other woman was suffering. But things could not stay as they were. Parvati would have to make a decision.

Parvati looked down at the apple she had been chopping—it was turning brown along the edges. Had she been daydreaming so long that fruit was beginning to spoil in her hands? This was a luxury given by a neighbor, an act of kindness perhaps in return for many such acts by Lalita Amma in previous years, and the fruit would be ruined if Parvati were not more careful. She deftly trimmed the fruit wedges and set about her work again. Behind her came the quiet slapping sounds of Vengamma's feet on the polished cement floor.

Thirteen

Joseph stepped away from the bonnet he was polishing when he saw Anita coming up the lane from the village. He must be bored silly, Anita thought when she saw him.

Used to driving to the airport and tourist spots, unobtrusively shadowing foreigners on short day trips so they didn't get lost or worse, sleeping in the car so he could hurry off to meet a three a.m. arrival at the airport, listening to stories of adventures in other parts of India, mollifying unhappy foreigners and natives, and in general being in the thick of an unusual world, Joseph had little to do at Lalita Amma's house. He could garden, if it were the season for gardening; he could mend things, if Lalita Amma had mechanical things that needed to be mended; he could run errands, if there was anywhere to go for an errand; he could, well, Anita thought, all the things he could do weren't in demand right now. Except driving, of course. Perhaps she should take a trip into Chengannur.

Yes, thought Anita, now might be the time for that. She had a few questions she wanted answered, and it would give Joseph a needed break from the tedium of his days here.

"They are having elevenses," Joseph said when Anita was within earshot.

"Just what I need." She drew level with the driver. "I'll be going into Chengannur later in the day. But it shouldn't take long."

The syncopated conversation of her two aunts filled the downstairs rooms when Anita entered the house. She had forgotten how musical her relatives often sounded when they got together—their conversations interweaving and overlapping, interrupted by giggles and punctuated by laughter and bursts of delight or surprise. The women in her family were animated and strong, and those qualities showed in their conversations. Anita dropped her shopping bags in her room and joined her aunts.

"You are finding things you like?" Lalita Amma smiled with approval. "We are not so much in the backwater, isn't it?"

"The vendors selling to the men going to Sabarimala are doing a good business." Anita reached for her coffee and wrapped her fingers around the warm cup. Lalita Amma had brought out her fine china, which she hadn't used at their arrival. She must be feeling good about life, Anita mused. "There was a big lorry filling up and getting ready to depart, the first one from this village, someone said."

"No, not the first," Lalita Amma said. "The first has gone earlier, I am thinking."

"Why are you thinking another has gone earlier?"

"Thampi is going. Don't you remember, Anita?"

Unfortunately, Anita did remember. She was hoping she had got it wrong, but no, she hadn't. The trip to visit Lalita Amma and Valli was arranged in this manner because Thampi wouldn't be here for a week or so. Meena didn't like the idea of Lalita Amma being here alone, without her usual complement of staff and household members, and Meena felt compelled to jump in and provide them. Well, at least one. That was why Joseph had come with them. But when Anita had come upon the lorry scheduled to leave for Sabarimala, the man she questioned was clear—this was the first lorry to leave for Sabarimala, and Thampi wasn't going to be on it.

"Thampi wasn't on the lorry," Anita said. "And it looked like they were full up and ready to go."

"Ah, you are mistaken." Lalita waved away Anita's comment. "He is gone for a week or more. An old man who lives so close to Sabarimala and never able to go." Lalita clucked to herself. "I had to let him go."

"You are generous to send him." Meena patted the other woman's hand, and the two women immediately launched into their mutual compliments punctuated by stories of previous visits and bits of gossip randomly recalled.

* * * * *

"What are you looking at?" Valli strolled into the kitchen storeroom, relaxed and cheerful and smiling. It occurred to Anita that she hadn't seen her friend look like this since she arrived, no matter how much Valli insisted that everything was fine, all was well, and what was Anita going on about?

"Nothing much, a packet of coffee I picked up in the village." Anita dropped the package onto the table. "The aunts and I were chatting. Meena Elayamma doesn't get away nearly enough, I think. It is good to see her acting like her old self—criticizing me, wishing I were different, worrying about what my mother will think. The usual." Anita smiled and for a moment Valli didn't seem to know if she should offer condolences or laugh. Anita remembered that Valli could be literal and very serious, sometimes too serious.

"Let us go for a walk over to the neighbor's house. I am wanting to see them after so long." Valli nodded toward the door and turned, motioning Anita to follow.

"Which neighbors are these?" Anita knew most of the families who lived in this area, but Valli was so casual that she could be referring to anyone, including friends who lived in Chengannur.

"The old couple, well, now they're old. They didn't

used to be. When we were little, I wanted to be like them—to grow up and have such a wonderful friendship with my husband. Do you remember the Iyers?"

"He's a retired civil servant and she's a retired teacher?"

"Yes, that's them. You do remember! Their son moved to Delhi and an older daughter moved to Germany and has never come back."

"Most unusual." Anita found this hard to believe. Most of the NRIs she knew, the nonresident Indians spread all over the world, tried to come back once a year or at least every two or three years. In some ways they never really left. "Why has she not come back?"

"She married a foreigner and he is not liking to travel, I think."

"She could come alone."

"Yes, so she could." Valli led the way to the door, and slipped her feet into a pair of sandals she had left on the veranda. "Does your mother come often to visit?"

Anita laughed. "You have made your point."

"No?"

"She spends as much money on telephoning as she would on a plane ticket." Anita found her sandals and slid into them. "She relies on me to keep her up to date on doings in Kerala, and on Auntie Meena for all the gossip."

"Lots of gossip there is, too, isn't it?" Valli led the way to a path and they set off through the jungle.

The deeper into the brush they went, the harder it was to carry on a conversation of any import. Words drifted back to Anita, and she filled in what seemed to be blanks in a sentence. She replied with fewer and fewer words, until the two fell silent. After a while the two women came to a clearing and Anita drew alongside Valli.

"Do you ever feel uncomfortable or wary walking through this area alone? It is very isolated." Anita looked deep into the trees and shrubs, but all was thick with greenery. If there was anyone out there, she wouldn't have been able to see him or her.

Valli gave her a quick glance and smiled. "Have I not spent almost my entire life running or walking through here? It is as known to me as my own home. These trees are my blankets and my furniture and my toys. This is my home too."

"That's a wonderful way to feel, Valli. You are fortunate. You must have done something wonderful to come to this life with such a good feeling about your world here."

Valli smiled. "We used to run through here all the time as children. You must have felt the same way, yes?"

"I suppose I did." Anita kept pace with her friend, but also kept her eye on the thick growth on either side of them. If she had indeed seen someone on previous nights, they might not be alone, but at least there were two of them. She had to wonder, though, if it were really possible for someone to stalk this neighborhood and not be found out at once by the villagers. This was a place where everything about everyone was known, recorded, kept on file in the minds of long-lived villagers, saved for the moment when it could be used to the best advantage. If a stranger was out there, still unrecognized, he had to be a first.

"Tell me about the new shops in the village," Anita said. "I saw lots of vendors selling things for the Sabarimala pilgrims, and a few new shops for general fancy goods."

"It's so much better, isn't it? We don't have to always go to Chengannur or even to Kochi to get what we need. So much better."

"I was thinking about the little coffee shop. He packages all the new types."

"We always have good coffee. And he knows what we like. He has provided to our family for years," Valli said. Anita hurried to come abreast of her as the path widened out.

"He seemed an interesting sort."

"I doubt he's at all interesting, Anita. He's making sure to make a sale to you."

"You surprise me, Valli," Anita said half to herself. "You sound very cynical."

The lane turned and opened onto a dirt road. Valli stepped onto the road. "I have listened often to Amma and Meena Elayamma discussing your peculiar interest in these sorts of people—the lower sorts—and I understand now what they mean. You mustn't let yourself be curious about them, Anita. It is unseemly and there is nothing to be gained from knowing them. They are small vendors, nothing more. If one of them wanted to make himself seem familiar to you, you must ignore this. It is nothing for you." Valli flicked her fingers to illustrate her disgust and pointed down the road. "And then if he persists, we shall report him and not let him do business here. Come. We shall go that way. This is a very nice family—you remember them. This is the sort you should be interested in."

* * * * *

For the next hour, Anita listened to Valli and a neighboring family share gossip and local news, all the while marveling at her cousin's ability to block out her current marital difficulties, Prakash's worsening circumstances, and Lalita Amma's declining situation. If it was one thing this woman is capable of, Anita mused, it's denial.

"What?" Anita came to attention when she realized Valli was nudging her with her bare foot. "So sorry." Anita smiled. "I seem to have lost myself in, ah, such a lovely painting."

The older couple turned around in their seats and looked at the oil painting hanging over the settee. Done in the western style, the painting depicted a voluptuous woman holding a pot on her hip as she crossed an old bridge. The background was lush, the once-bright colors beginning to fade beneath a veneer of dust and grime. The older woman glanced at her husband and sighed.

"Thank you," the hostess said, avoiding a second look at her husband. "It was painted in this area some years ago by a local artist. It is here more for sentiment."

"Your trip up from Trivandrum," the man said. "How was the journey?"

"Oh, that. Fine. Other than the rain slowing us down." Anita smiled, embarrassed at having been caught out daydreaming. She wasn't one for paying social calls and listening to pleasant chatter. It was a struggle to keep her mind focused, and it seemed this time she had failed. "Fine, not so much traffic. Except for the roadblock."

"What roadblock?" The older woman looked surprised.

"Ah, I wondered." The man smiled and nodded, apparently pleased to have his suspicions confirmed. "Yes. There is roadblock now, and inspection of all vehicles heading this way."

"You know about it?" Anita leaned forward, fully alert now. "Do you know who or what they are looking for?"

"It is some smuggling, isn't it?" Valli flicked away the idea of anything serious going on.

"Not this time, my dear." Mr. Iyer folded his arms across his chest.

"So you know what this is about?" Anita was afraid he wouldn't go any further with his story without a push. "What can you tell us?"

"It is nothing, Anita," Valli said.

"It is definitely not nothing, Valli." Anita turned to Mr. Iyer. "There was a man with a rifle—a very modern one—hiding off the side of the road."

"Ah." Mr. Iyer grew serious, no longer playful with his information. "Yes, it is serious."

"You have not told me this." Mrs. Iyer turned toward him, scowling. "An armed man concealed."

Anita waited. His eagerness to tell what he knew faltered in the face of his wife's disapproval. But as Anita watched him, she could see his concern was stronger than his wife's insistence on appropriate conversation with guests. Anita began to wonder what his career had been. Did he know something the rest of the village did not?

"I'm an old fool," he said, watching his wife out of the corner of his eye. "But sometimes my old friends in government remember me and they let me know if something will be happening in my area. Most are gone to retirement now, as I am, but some remain and they are privy to information. So I know a few things."

"You're not surprised that there was an armed guard, some military protection, out there." Anita tried to match her words to his expression, and noted that he didn't balk at the mention of the military. "They are looking for someone?"

"They are indeed." He glanced at his wife, apparently to quiet her. "Some sort of terrorist is said to be passing through the Chengannur area, perhaps to a training session or to launch an attack. We don't know. No one has found that out yet. Or if they have . . ."

"No, they couldn't tell you that." Anita leaned back, taking in his words.

"In this area?" Valli looked indignant.

"But there aren't any targets around here." Anita frowned. "He could be passing through, looking for a path through the mountains. The trains going onto the plains?"

Mr. Iyer shrugged. "We will know soon enough."

Anita's mind went back to the morning of their journey when Joseph had pulled up at the roadblock and the police had searched the car. Everyone was being stopped and checked—buses were unloaded, luggage taken down, car boots opened and backseats pulled apart.

"Which organization?" Anita asked.

"Ah," Mr. Iyer said, "that no one knows. There is only the chatter that the road out of Chengannur is the way. But the road goes different ways into the hills—old roads over the mountains, roads that lead to plantations, roads that go from village to village north or south. With so many old village roads, it is hard to know."

* * * * *

"I am certain it is nothing," Valli said after they left the Iyer home. "We must not make much out of gossip."

"It isn't gossip, Valli." Anita plodded along behind, deep in thought and sometimes tripping over tree roots and stumbling into ruts.

"But we don't know, Anita. We don't actually know." Valli planted herself in the middle of the road, arms akimbo, and scowled at Anita like a strict teacher taking to task a disobedient student.

"Valli, this reaction is what I have come to expect of most people, but must I now also expect it of you?" Anita stopped in front of her cousin. "There is a tendency in our family to push aside all unpleasantness, but that is perhaps not the best way to deal with reality. We must face facts."

"There are no facts to face." Valli glared. "It is not the terrorist you are talking about, is it? It is Kumar and Prakash and Amma. You want me to be a different person, with a different situation. But I can't, Anita, I can't."

"I'm sorry, Valli. I didn't mean to say that."

"What is there to embrace in my life now? My marriage is a disappointment, my brother is losing his job and his reputation and may even lose his freedom, and my mother finds herself old and widowed and poor. Why should I embrace this?"

"I didn't realize you felt so hopeless." Anita moved closer to her friend and slipped her arm through hers. "Perhaps there is something we can do."

Valli tried to laugh but instead sounded like a strangled goat. "Will you marry your Anand?"

"Oh, my," Anita said. "Where did that come from?"

"Meena Elayamma has been telling us about her—" Valli stopped and glanced at Anita, unable to conceal her guilty look.

Anita sighed. "—her efforts to find a suitable mate for me? Yes, I know. It's no secret my aunt is looking everywhere for a husband for me—even at Prakash!"

"Oh, Anita!" Valli clapped her hands across her mouth. "That would be wonderful. We'd be together all the time. But wrong! Absolutely wrong!"

"Don't worry, Valli. It will not happen, I assure you." Anita shook her head and tried not to laugh. "My aunt is doing every possible investigation into Anand's background. She is sure if she digs deep enough she will uncover something to prove that he is not suitable for me. She has great confidence in her power to uncover what she needs to find." They walked along, taking the road into the village instead of the lane back to the house. "But that is far in the future—very far. Right now, Anand and I are"— Anita paused to choose her words—"close friends."

"You like your freedom."

They walked on in companionable silence, taking note of the sounds of birds released from hiding with the ending of the rains, the horns of lorries in the distance, the occasional cry of a traveling paper vendor.

"Tell me again about Kumar," Anita said. She remembered Valli's wedding and the announcement months earlier that Valli had found her soul mate, as she called him. Anita had been skeptical but still happy for her, skeptical because she didn't believe in soul mates and wasn't the least bit romantic when it came to big decisions in life, but happy because Valli was someone who could decide how she would see her world and simply go forward with that. Valli was in some ways willfully blind, but this weakness had always served her well. Until now. Kumar apparently hadn't been willing to go along with her vision of life.

"It is embarrassing. I am ashamed."

Anita held her friend tighter while a scooter passed.

"I can't fancy him anymore." Valli sighed. "All he talks about is money, money for this and money for that and why is my mother so obsessed and why have I not spoken to her about it."

"Does he expect her to give him money?" Anita tried to hold this thought. In the Nayar families she knew, the groom's family provided the required goods at marriage—gold saris and jewelry and whatever else was negotiated. The groom's family provided the dowry, not the bride's.

Valli nodded and began to weep silently. "It's so unjust."

"Your mother already gave him money, didn't she?"

"It was a donation to the temple, so Prakash would get the job."

"But it didn't go to the temple."

Valli shook her head.

"I think the term is extortion."

Valli gasped. "No, Anita, he is not like that. It isn't like that."

"Valli, you must accept that perhaps Kumar is not being honest with you. He knew Prakash would be fired and investigated, and he sent you home to prepare your mother. Did he also suggest you ask her for some sort of donation for the temple, to perhaps persuade them to go gently on your brother?"

Valli's little beep of surprise answered Anita.

Anita tried to comfort Valli. "Perhaps it is not too late. Perhaps it is still possible to do something." Anita put her arm around Valli and gently urged her forward. "This afternoon I will drive into Chengannur and see what I can find out." Anita pulled Valli closer and quickened her pace.

Fourteen

"It's not that bad, Joseph." Anita sat in the backseat directing the hotel driver as he made his way through the narrow lanes of a nearby village.

"Ah, Amma. It is worse than you can imagine." Joseph swung the large steering wheel, and the car bounced around a muddy pothole. "It is not a friendly kitchen."

"Ah, is that the problem." Anita tried to keep the smile out of her voice. "Not enough snacks, eh? Portions are too small at mealtime?"

"You are making fun of me." Joseph began to pout and sank down in his seat, steering with his hands on the lower half of the steering wheel. Normally a good driver, he grew careless when unhappy. Anita kicked herself for not keeping her thoughts on the driving instead of Joseph's sullen complaints.

"Turn in here." She pointed to a narrow lane. Joseph glanced back at her, shrugged, and turned in, working the car slowly down the lane, dodging pots sitting outside doors, bird cages hanging from eaves, and a cat fleeing a marauding chicken. The lane widened, and Joseph sped up. "The last house but one, as I recall."

"Whose house is this?"

"Thampi's."

"But he has gone to Sabarimala."

"So I have heard. I will say hello to his family, and

133

then we will go on to Chengannur." Anita left him to turn the car around while she went in search of someone connected to Thampi and his home. After climbing over a low fence and wandering around the front yard, peering in the open front door, she heard a voice calling out. "I am here," Anita replied.

A woman approximately in her fifties came around the corner drying her hands on a towel draped over her left shoulder. When she was finished, she tucked one end of the towel into her waist and tugged her mundu into place. It was the simple dress of a woman working at home—the simple wraparound mundu and the towel in place of the nerid, which would have given the appearance of a sari if worn together. The woman studied her.

"You are Thampi's wife?"

"I am."

Anita introduced herself, and the wife looked past her at Joseph and the car.

"Yes, he told me guests were coming, and the driver would do his work while he was away. You are regretting this arrangement?" She was a matter-of-fact woman. A change in someone's plans would be one more inconvenience for her to manage in a long line of troubles and challenges. She wasn't going to complain; she wanted to know, one way or the other, what to plan for. When Anita said no, there was no change in plans, the other woman's face broke into a warm smile and her eyes softened.

"You take coffee?"

Anita said no but the other woman insisted, and Anita sat down on a small stool on the veranda. The coffee came quickly, so Anita suspected it was prepared for the woman and whoever else was waiting out back—a mother-in-law or another relative.

"I am sorry that Thampi was already gone before we arrived," Anita began. "It is years since I have seen him."

"Time passes." Thampi's wife sat on a stool nearby and waited. She was a practical woman, one who would wait for the real business and not get distracted by social niceties.

"When did he leave?"

"He was to leave tomorrow, I think, but at the last minute he decided to leave earlier."

"Ah. Did he tell you why?"

Thampi's wife shook her head. "I awake five mornings ago and he is gone." She waved her hand, as if to indicate that he simply flew away on a gust of wind. Anita sipped her coffee. The village woman was like a student in a classroom, waiting for the next question, patient and expectant.

"And he had everything ready to go? His *irumudi* and his clothing?"

The wife stared hard. She leaned forward, resting her forearms on her drawn-up legs and frowned, then looked at the house, as though she were walking through it in her mind, checking each room and her conversation with her husband. "He must have. His black lungi and shirt were gone, and he said he was purchasing his offerings that very day. He is telling me this the night before, as he is taking to his bed for the night." She tipped her head to one side, apparently satisfied with her memory of recent events.

"I thought he might have left earlier than planned for some reason, that he might have told you this," Anita said. Somehow the woman's explanation didn't feel right. Thampi had wanted to make this journey for years and had planned it carefully, including the group he would go with, and yet at the last minute he had departed suddenly, without a word to his family.

The wife smiled. "You think this is strange?" She shook her head and chuckled. "He is a man surrounded by women—a wife and daughters and mother and my sister and employer and employer's daughter and friend and friend's daughter and cook and maidservant. Then he has an opportunity to escape us—to be with his own kind—and you are surprised that he leaves sooner rather than later, that he finds a way to go as soon as he is ready to depart." She slapped both palms lightly on her thighs. "Can you blame him?"

"I suppose not." Anita had to laugh, when she considered how Thampi's wife described his situation. "I hope he is not unhappy at Lalita Amma's house."

Thampi's wife clucked her tongue and flicked her fingers at Anita's suggestion. "Has he not known Vengamma for years and years? Lalita Amma is good to him, and Valli appreciates him too. Parvati?" She shrugged.

"What about Parvati?" The offhand comment was all the more surprising because it was unexpected. Anita was used to the usual complaints staff made against each other—more like the bickering of children than the serious complaints of employees who know someone is stealing or cheating or endangering the household. But there was something different here; a sort of resignation, an awkwardness at the mere mention of the name that suggested lack of malice and deeper concern.

Thampi's wife pulled a face and hunched over, then, perhaps coming to a decision, sat bolt upright. "She is secretive, always keeping to herself. She does her work, she is obedient, but she is not present when she works. I don't know how to explain it," the wife said, struggling for the right words. "She is not part of the household. I think she is only passing through, but still, I wonder how she has ended up here."

"She is not from around here, is she?" Anita said.

"No." Thampi's wife grew thoughtful. "I am thinking she is shifty at first, but no, she is honest and careful. I have seen this."

"But?" Anita was caught by the tone in the other

woman's voice.

"But one morning I am going there to deliver chilies for Amma and I meet Parvati in the yard. She is searching for the chicken for the day's meal. We speak like women in passing do—we like each other—and I go into the house. I hear the chicken squawk and turn around. She has picked up the animal, holding it out in front of her. Then all at once she breaks its neck and rips off its head—so quick, so easy for her."

In the long silence that followed Anita heard only a dripping from an outside spigot.

"I use a knife," Thampi's wife said.

"So do we," Anita said after a pause.

"It is not an easy place to get to, Lalita Amma's estate," Thampi's wife said. "A good place for hiding."

"It's not likely she was walking by one day or heard that a servant was needed and decided to drop by and ask," Anita said. "No one else seems to know her outside the household." Anita looked up to find the other woman watching her, nodding at her thinking out loud. "I may ask Lalita Amma when I get back."

* * * * *

Anita timed her visit to the Thiruvadnagar Devi Temple for late afternoon, when the priests would be opening up for the evening puja and devotees would be arriving. Joseph pulled into the sandy lot surrounding the temple and parked under a tree. As a Catholic, he had never entered a Hindu temple, but he had taken his family to festivals, watched a Hindu cousin married on an abutting park, and ferried Anita and her school friends to programs at both temples and churches. He calculated a good hour's nap for this visit.

Anita kicked off her sandals at the gate and stepped over the threshold. Inside the devotees had already begun to gather, and Anita noted clusters of women lounging along the outer walls, some singing hymns to Devi or Shiva, others chatting and watching young children gambol about.

The tall and thin blackboard on which was written the price list was leaning against the wall by the main office door, and Anita strolled over to look at it. The trustees had made such a point of raising the fees that Anita wondered if they were inordinately high or uneven for the various pujas or other rites.

She scanned the list, noting the simple pujas or worships, the abhishekhams or bathing of the deity, the homas or pujas using a sacred fire pit, and more. The prices seemed reasonable, comparable to those of other temples she visited, and she made a mental note of them and moved on. She circumambulated the main shrine and ended up at a cluster of women singing a particularly poignant hymn to Devi. Anita joined them, sitting on the ground and soaking in the music.

An older woman, perhaps older than Lalita Amma, seemed to be the leader, with a strong voice and determined expression on her face. She picked up the pace as she felt necessary, urging the other women to catch up with her, then slowed as the emotion in her grew. This was her group, her chorus, and she led and shaped and guided them according to her interpretation of the song. Her clear voice rose, vibrated, then swung down and curled around one note, then another, rising, dipping, vibrating and widening, then sinking low again. In her mouth, sounds became elastic and long, thin or sharp, round like candy or thick like storm clouds.

Anita didn't try to join in the song. She was grateful for the opportunity to feel it envelop her, to become part of it even if only for a moment. She closed her eyes and listened, letting the thrill of devotion throb throughout her limbs. Gradually, the music slowed and came to an end, and Anita felt an unexpected sadness, as if something irreplaceable and invaluable had been lost, or taken from her. She opened her eyes to see the other women nodding as the final notes faded into the air, and the lead singer, the old woman, swaying as if in a trance, hypnotized by her own music and her own devotion.

In the silence that followed no one spoke. The sounds of the other devotees in the temple moved around them as though distant and barely audible. The music had removed them, separated them, and rewarded these women for their full engagement with a moment of otherworldliness.

Anita opened her eyes to find the old woman looking her over, sizing her up.

"You have come for the homa for well-being?" the old woman asked.

"I have come for whatever is here." Anita was thinking less about her original purpose than how well she felt at that moment.

The woman smiled and nodded. "It is tonight, a *mrithyunjaya homa.* I myself have done this and at the end I felt very well indeed—it has a good effect on health and happiness." Her smile faded and she turned back to her friends, who were by now getting to their feet and wandering off.

"And will you do this one today?" Anita was too comfortable to move. She had hoped the singing would continue, but when the other women rose to leave, Anita realized that the lead singer would not sing on her own. She pulled the group with her, but she would not take the journey into song alone.

The old woman shook her head at Anita's question. "No, not for me anymore."

Anita lifted her eyebrow in query. The old woman nodded to the price list.

"Too costly?" Anita asked.

"One rise and now another. It is too much." The lead singer grabbed hold of her pallu and her skirt and pushed herself up, then rearranged her sari, pulling the pallu around her shoulders and tucking the end into her waist. "We are poor folk in this temple." She glanced at the gate where more devotees were entering—a group of young women in modern saris, their young children in the blue-and-white uniforms of private schools. They didn't look like poor folk to Anita. The old woman must have understood what Anita was thinking by her expression.

"Not them," the old singer said. "They are new to our part of town. A new colony with new homes. Another rise is not a trouble for them." She didn't sound angry, just resigned and perhaps saddened. "I give to Devi what only I have to give." She patted her throat, flicked her palm up in a sign of resignation, and gave a nod of departure. Anita watched her go.

Devotees passed close by the price list, taking note, and finding their way to the main shrine. Anita joined them, taking a second look at the list and wondering if others felt like the old woman. The young ones glanced at the blackboard without interrupting their conversations, and went about their devotions. Occasionally, an older devotee stopped to read through the list carefully, reading some items aloud, before turning away.

"You are confused?" A young man in a dhoti came up behind Anita with an expression of helpfulness on his face. He looked like he worked here, perhaps as an assistant in the office or for one of the other priests, or perhaps he even assisted Prakash at one time. He seemed barely old enough to be employed in a responsible position. While Anita tried to decide how to approach him, he offered some advice to another devotee, answered a question about pricing, and directed another woman to a shrine located in an outer wall.

"You have no questions?" He turned back to Anita.

"Is this new pricing?" Anita asked.

"Yes." He seemed embarrassed, as though he had perhaps made a mistake. "Do you think it is too high? Are you forgoing a puja because of this?"

For a moment Anita wondered if he'd return to the earlier prices if she said yes, but instead she said no, the prices were reasonable. It was a nice temple, she added, well taken care of.

"We are proud of our temple," he said, blushing.

"Your trustees must be very involved, coming often to see how things are."

This idea seemed strange to him, and he thought about it. "I suppose this is so."

"Do they come often?"

He opened his mouth to speak, paused, then thought about her question. "I myself have not seen them or met them, but I hear they are very good people." This conclusion cheered him and he gave Anita a big smile, waggled his head, and moved on to help someone else.

* * * * *

Over the temple roof the sky was turning a pale rose, signaling the coming of dusk, the moment of danger, when the world moved from one state to another. The priests at their pujas offered praise and promise for a safe transition, and music and flame rose into the sky. A ragged cluster of bats stirred in the air above and sounds of auto traffic soared over the temple walls. The courtyard was filling up with devotees—this was the busy time—and Anita took advantage of the crowds to step into the temple office.

In the center of the notice board hung a list of employees and their schedules. Anita ran her eye down the list of names. Prakash's wasn't there. The list was neatly typed, clearly new, not an old one with his name crossed off. This was a new list of names, with two signatures at the bottom, making the list and timings official. She tried to read the signatures, but as was more common than not these days, all she could see were squiggly lines. But underneath each name was typed the word Trustee. The document was official.

"You are needing help?" The young assistant was

back, and although his offer was one of help, he didn't seem as friendly as before.

"Who is the priest who is officiating this evening?"

The young man recited the name and Anita noted it on the list. "Is this everyone who works here?"

"Everyone." He glanced behind him, then again at Anita. "You know of the one who has left, isn't it?"

Surprised that he would be so blunt, Anita nodded. "I had heard that someone I knew was no longer here." The boy nodded, and Anita continued. "I was surprised. I have never known anyone to leave such a job before—unless, of course, he got a better one."

"He did not get a better one."

"Why did he leave?"

The young man twisted away from Anita in embarrassment, and he seemed then to be only a boy; certainly he was not yet versed in diplomacy or prevarication. "The trustees are not happy with him. They are the authority. We must obey them."

"That's all?"

The boy looked up at her with large brown eyes. She thought he might be ready to tell her more, but in the end he grew formal and asked if she needed anything. He ushered her from the office, and she thanked him for his help. Even if he wouldn't tell her, she knew why the trustees had fired Prakash. The investigation was a formality—his career here was over.

Fifteen

Auntie Meena smiled lazily at Anita as she came up the walk. In the late evening, long past twilight, families were emerging onto their verandas and into their courtyards to enjoy the first rainless evening in weeks. A light breeze moved the thick air and brought the smell of fresh greenery and rust-red dirt and air so sharply clean it felt like a new substance against the body.

"And how was your little journey into Chengannur?"

"Very nice." Anita told Joseph to leave the shopping bags inside the door to her room, and pulled up a chair to sit with the two aunts. "Have you had a quiet afternoon here?"

"Of course." Lalita Amma winked at her and laid her head back. It wasn't often she got to enjoy this kind of leisure, nor did Meena Elayamma, and the two women were making the most of their time together. "Where did you go?"

"Oh, here and there." Anita thanked Joseph as he emerged from the house, and watched him as he drove the car around to the back. He was entitled to a bed in the kitchen or another room near it, but he chose to stretch out and sleep in the backseat of the car. This wasn't unusual for him on long trips—he was loathe to take the chance of anyone getting near his car without his being there to

143

protect it—but Anita thought, in this instance, his sleeping in the car was a sign of being unhappy with the visit.

"If I were not so relaxed, Anita, I would worry that you have been up to no good." Meena smiled again and glanced at Lalita, as though they were sharing a private joke. And indeed, Lalita winked at Meena and smiled at Anita.

"You seem singularly unworried this evening, Auntie. So unlike earlier."

"Kumar has called this very evening." Lalita tilted her head as if to say, See, I knew all would be well. "Valli spoke with him."

"Really?" Anita considered this, and filed it away for later. She checked the landline in the house regularly and it hadn't been working earlier, nor had she heard it ring. No mobile reception but a restored landline? "I was actually wondering how things were left with the trustees. I came into the meeting late, and I missed some particulars, so I know I haven't a complete understanding of how things are being arranged."

"Arranged?" Lalita lifted her head, then pulled herself up into a sitting position. She lowered the footrest of her teak chair and swung her feet to the ground. She glanced at Meena, who caught her eye, then seemed to go back to snoozing. "The trustees insist on this investigation, but it is nothing. A mere formality."

"And what exactly is the formality?" Anita thought she knew the answer, but she waited for it anyway.

"Only that particular puja. You know, it is for Devi's permission to raise the costs of certain things." Lalita rubbed her feet over the cement. "Meena, are you feeling a chill? All that rain has cooled off the land so much and now we shall all be chilled through the winter months. Meena? A shawl?"

"Perhaps." Meena sat up and gave Anita a warning look. "Perhaps it is too chilly now to sit out any longer. We shall be more comfortable inside, isn't it?"

"Yes, yes, you mustn't get a chill. I shall not have such a thing while you are visiting here. I would be a terrible hostess to let such a thing happen." Lalita pushed herself up, and reached out to offer her hand to help Meena stand up. "There will be supper soon."

"Yes, time to go in, I think." Meena stood and the two women walked into the house arm in arm, leaving Anita alone on the veranda.

Just how many nerves had she jangled? Anita wondered. How many lies had they told, how many secret arrangements had they concealed, how many deceptions had they fallen prey to? Anita wasn't looking forward to confronting either woman with the truth.

* * * * *

Anita listened for the low murmur of mantras being chanted while offerings were made to the household deities. She sat outside the puja room listening to Prakash's sonorous voice, wondering once again that he had chosen such a small temple so near to home when he could have earned a reputation as a priest throughout the area. He had once been ambitious, not in a greedy, grasping way, but with a sense of what was possible and how well he could serve in his chosen role.

He brought to each temple he visited with his family a deep appreciation for its history and unique features, the role of the devotees and donors in its maintenance, and its relation to the surrounding community. Each temple was to him a unique experience, almost like meeting a new person with his or her own character and personality. As a child he knew more about the temples of Kerala than most adults and entertained Valli and Anita with stories of the rare *pushpanjali,* or flower puja, at a Krishna temple and the places where the five Pandava brothers worshipped during their twelve-year exile, according to the great epic the *Mahabharata.*

The more Anita thought about it, the stranger it seemed that Prakash's life should have arrived at this point.

"Anita!" Prakash stood before her as he pulled the door to the puja room shut. He grinned at her, and she had to admit she probably looked a bit ridiculous, sitting on the floor, leaning against the wall, in a hallway with no furniture and nothing apparently occupying her time or her mind. "You have found a strange place to rest."

Anita clambered to her feet. "I got lost in my own thoughts." She pulled her sari back into order. "Could we speak in private?"

At first she thought he was going to say no, but he hesitated only for a few seconds, then said yes, and led her to the new wing. He pulled out his keys, opened the heavy door and motioned her to go through.

"This is about the only place where we can talk without someone coming along and wanting to know what we are talking about and why are we talking about that and should we be talking about that and how about talking about this?"

Anita chuckled. He was right, of course. Prakash switched on an overhead light and pulled two sheets off a pair of upholstered chairs. The dust spurted upward and swirled in the dim light, changing the colors from bright to hazy. Anita sneezed, then coughed. She wasn't used to dust. Some years back a housekeeper at Hotel Delite was feeling lazy, so she opened up the doors and windows on the side facing the ocean, and let the wind blow the dust around. It didn't quite work, but Anita did come to appreciate how breezy the oceanfront rooms were.

"I understand there's some good news." Anita watched Prakash for a reaction. He made a show of removing the sheets from their immediate presence, laying them carefully on the floor by the wall, and returning to his chair. He settled himself and smiled across at her, exuding confidence, but Anita didn't miss the twitch in his eyebrow

and the wary look in his eye. He was wondering how much
Anita knew and what she thought. I know enough, thought
Anita. I know enough. "The good news?"

For a moment Prakash looked blank.

"The aunts said Kumar called." Anita wasn't
surprised to see this startled Prakash, but he quickly
composed himself and formulated a reply. "Kumar is most
influential," Prakash offered, as though this explained
everything.

"So he is going to get you your job back?"

Prakash spread his hands in the universal display of
uncertainty and shrugged. "Who knows what I will do?"

That wasn't my question, thought Anita. "Does
another temple beckon?"

He smiled the smile of a satisfied man. "There are
many paths open to me."

Anita thought of the old woman singing in the
temple compound, the passion and love in her voice for her
deity, the sadness and resignation in her words over the
changes at the temple. Anita remembered her limping away
into the crowd.

"There will still be an investigation, of course,"
Anita said.

Prakash looked puzzled, then frowned. Slowly his
face changed into that of the younger cousin brother she
had known most of her life, indulged by the family but
obedient to expectations for the most part, the little one
who trailed after his big sister and her friends, accompanied
them on their errands and chased them in their adventures.

"But you said—" he began.

"You know they have to investigate, don't you?"

"I think this is being resolved."

"You have agreed to let them make a rise in certain
prices."

Prakash lowered his head and picked at a loose
thread in his mundu. "The trustees have ordered this. I

cannot argue. It will be done."

"And then the investigation."

He glowered at her. "I don't see why you are talking like this."

"Yes, you do. My only real question for you is: Are you ready for what the trustees will find?" She was gratified to see him flinch.

* * * * *

"It won't work." Anita's voice carried across the sitting room to a far corner where Meena was shaking her mobile phone, as if that would get it to work. The women had been quietly engaged in their evening activities, reading or mending or a card game. As Meena went on shaking her mobile, Anita felt a twinge of guilty pleasure at seeing her caught in her own trap. If Anita couldn't call Anand, it was rough justice that Meena would have to worry about Hotel Delite. "There's no reception out here yet. Remember?"

"Oh, dear. How will I know what is happening at the hotel?"

"You won't," Anita said. "You won't know the staff have stolen the receipts, let broke and drugged tourists sleep for free in all the best rooms, taken all the food home, and run a lorry down the lane and into the reception area, smashing the front door and leaving the upper stories to dangle dangerously over the parking area. You'll have to wait till we get home." Anita wasn't surprised to see a look of horror on both Lalita Amma's and Meena's faces.

"Meena?" Lalita Amma began to rise from her chair.

Meena sputtered, gripping her mobile phone so tightly that Anita feared she'd break it. Meena spat out her words in red-hot whispers. "You should not mock my feelings."

"Okay." Anita raised the newspaper to cover her face, then peeked out behind it. "Sorry. You know everything is running perfectly smoothly at Hotel Delite.

The staff adore you and no one would dare do anything wrong. They love their jobs." And fear for their lives when you're angry, Anita added to herself. She rustled the newspaper and began to read.

"You are terrible to Auntie Meena," Valli whispered. She raised her book to cover her words and the smile she could barely contain. "Where did you learn to say such things? Shh, don't say anything more." She lowered her book to her lap and began to read, peeking out from lowered brows to see how her mother and aunt were taking this encounter.

"Ah, this is interesting." Anita read out a short item on a new investigation into an old murder that had taken place in a dairy.

"Must you be interested in such things?" Meena returned to her seat, having given up on her mobile. Lalita offered sincere sympathies and promises of better reception tomorrow, although how she was going to accomplish that, she did not say.

"Perhaps you will like this one better," Anita said. "Oh, thank you, Parvati." Anita interrupted her reading to take the proffered cup of tea and set it on a nearby table. "The rains have disturbed the animals in Periyar Wildlife Sanctuary, and villagers are complaining the animals are moving into their areas and stealing food from their storage and pawing at their doors."

"Oh, villagers. They are so simple. They are exaggerating—no animal comes to the door." Meena took the tea from Parvati and rested the cup and saucer in her lap. Supper had been a simple meal, and the women had eaten without Prakash and were now taking tea in the sitting room. The hour was advancing, and even though all of them were tired, they were too comfortable to leave the room and end the evening. "The newspapers are making it up."

"Quite so, Meena," Lalita said. "Except for the

cobra. The stories we hear make me uneasy."

"Do you think we should move back to the city?" Valli asked. The doors to the veranda stood open, and a cooling breeze nudged through the curtains but barely reached the center of the room. With the decline of the wild monsoon rains, things were returning to normal, but the talk of animals being pushed out of Periyar Wildlife Sanctuary reminded them that what was happening now was not really what they considered normal. The animals were crossing a boundary and advancing into other territory, people's territory.

"The city is so noisy and so many people asking for things." Lalita looked exhausted with the thought.

"Oh, this is interesting," Anita said from behind the paper. "We shall have an easier trip back, Meena Elayamma." She lowered the paper and leaned forward to read. "The police have found a man they were searching for. Listen. 'A district-wide manhunt has been called off after the police found the body of a suspected terrorist outside Trichuvalla. The man is believed to be from Tamilnad with designs on installations in Kochi Harbor."

"No, no, Parvati. That is too much."

Anita lowered the newspaper, surprised at the sharpness in Lalita's tone. Rarely did Lalita Amma speak sharply to anyone, even a servant. Parvati pulled a cloth from her waist and began mopping up the tea spilling from the saucer onto the floor. She wiped down the table and picked up both cup and saucer.

"Where is Trichuvalla?" Anita asked.

"Soon coming," Parvati said to Lalita, and hurried from the room.

"It is a long stretch of land below here, below our village, farther west," Lalita explained. "Where that body washed up."

"So, Anita, it means you will not be searched on your way home, isn't it?" Valli said.

"I am very glad to hear it," Meena said. "Police have no business taking innocent people like ourselves and making us stand in the road while they search our property. This is very good news—the end of the manhunt. But now they must add additional security to the harbor in anticipation of others wanting to do the same thing as this dead man."

"Perhaps," said Anita. "Perhaps." She reached for her tea, then thought better of it, and pushed it farther away.

"Fresh, Amma." Parvati carried in a tray with a full cup of tea and placed it on a small table, which she lifted and carried closer to Lalita Amma. "As you like it, Amma."

"Do you think we should write to Chief Minister and tell him all these armed men are not appropriate," Meena said. "It is not suitable for a man with a rifle to suspect someone like me, even if Anita is unruly. She never does things that are illegal. Do you, Anita. Anita?" A note of alarm sounded in Meena's voice.

"What? Oh, no, never, never, Meena Elayamma."

"How do they know he was coming to attack Kochi Harbor? He wasn't even there." Valli shut her book with a clap and laid it in her lap. "There is much too much suspicion in this world."

Anita scanned the article. Meena had gone back to fidgeting with her mobile phone, Lalita was tasting her tea, and Valli was watching Anita read, waiting for an answer.

"It says he had a certain tattoo and they have identified its meaning. Ah, here it is. They had a tip from someone that in Trichuvalla they would find the suspect. And here is a description of the tattoo." Anita read it out, then lowered the newspaper and turned to Valli. Before she could tell anyone that she had seen that tattoo before, Valli burst out with her opinion.

"I'm glad they caught him. It is a terrible thing to go to a place to injure and damage. What sort of life is that? Who does that sort of thing? I am glad he is dead." Valli picked up her tea.

Surprised by Valli's harsh reaction to the news story, Anita reread the story, looking for the trigger. "He must have given himself away," she said after a while, returning to her own thoughts. "He must have thought he could trust someone and now he's dead." She picked up the paper again, looking for some deeper truth hiding behind the matter-of-fact sentences.

Sixteen

Parvati was a strong woman—she knew that about herself, and tonight she needed to know that more than ever before. She repeated this to herself like a mantra for the final hours of the evening, through all the clearing up after supper, while washing dishes and pans, and tidying up the sitting room, and while taking fresh blankets to the bedrooms, in case anyone was still chilled by the cooler air.

She repeated her faith in her own strength as she closed windows, put on the latch and tested, following Lalita Amma from room to room, making sure all was done as the old woman preferred. And Parvati said it again and again as she made her way to the sink, hearing the key turn in the lock behind her, shutting her into the kitchen rooms for the night, following the rules that Valli said should govern the housekeeping, despite Amma's arguments. The maidservant made it to the stone sink where she watched the cup and saucer clatter and rattle in her trembling hands before they tumbled into the sink.

The trembling and shaking spread through her body, reaching the end of every limb, until she slipped to the floor, her body folding up into a pocket of pain in a world that knew nothing of her and cared nothing for her. She rocked and rocked, her arms wrapped around her chest, the tears streaming down her face, soaking her mundu, washing away the sweat of a day's labor.

153

The half-foreign guest read out the story in the newspaper with no more than mild curiosity, finding no name to announce, and for that Parvati was grateful. She wasn't sure she could stand hearing the name called out to strangers, as though it meant nothing, as though it were only the name of a man found dead. But she couldn't stand either that he was not given the dignity of his name, his full and wonderful and great identity. His name was Rajan, she wanted to scream at them. Rajan. This is Rajan you are talking about. He is not any man, someone no one cares about. His name is Rajan.

Found dead. That was all. Was there a tip to the police to tell who he was? All she heard was that a man was found dead and a manhunt ended. He wasn't simply found dead. Parvati knew that. He didn't have a heart attack and lie down and die alone. He didn't eat something and discover he was allergic and die of anaphylactic shock. He didn't fall and hit his head and die alone in his room because no one knew he was injured. He didn't die suddenly of old age or a burst appendix. He didn't turn and see a lorry rushing toward him. He didn't slip into the river and drown. The police might have killed him when they found him—they might have. But Parvati knew they didn't. Someone else did that for them. Someone else made it possible for the police to find Rajan. Someone else made sure he was dead when he was found. The police would not have found him otherwise. Rajan was an expert. He could only be found by betrayal.

The betrayed and the betrayer.

There had been two of them out there, and she hadn't known. Now there was only one.

The tears came more quietly, and fewer, the wet streaks down her cheeks drying hard and fast. After a while she sat in silence and stillness, listening to the night around her. The goat was tied in another room on a long tether so it could sleep and move about if desired. Parvati turned around and saw the goat staring at her, its big golden yellow eyes curious about the sadness in the room. Parvati turned and slid across the floor, dragging herself over to the rough-haired animal. She crawled to its side and stroked its forehead, then lay down on the floor and rested her head against its warm stomach. The goat bleated softly, as though asking what is this, who are you to lie on me? But Parvati buried her head into the goat's stomach and drew in the earthy animal smell, taking comfort in the familiar odor and feel of the small animal.

The world shrank to the two of them alone in this room with straw and old rags for the goat and its warm body as comfort for her. For this moment she felt fear and sorrow recede as the goat's heart beat beneath her head, and the rough hair chafed against her cheek.

She awoke in the dark. She must have fallen asleep. She sat up, stiff and sweaty, and looked around to learn what might have awakened her. The room was dark, the candle she had left burning on the stone counter sputtering as it neared its end. A bit of wax had dripped onto the floor; she would have to clean it up before morning, before Vengamma came in and saw it.

That would be the beginning of it—the work that would consume her for the rest of her life, the drug that would keep her from thinking about Rajan. She would scour everything that came into her hands, search out the hardest tasks that would exhaust her by the end of the day, and even find more to keep her working through the night. She would work so long and so hard that she would forget her own name, forget anything about herself worth knowing—there would be nothing worth knowing, and she would have nothing left to tell. She would erase her own identity from her own soul. And that way she would be able to live—without Rajan, with knowing that he was nowhere on this earth.

She wouldn't think about all he had given her—

love, safety, guidance, escape, and finally his own life. He was the last, the very last one of her family. They were all gone now, every one of them—husband, father, mother, grandfather, grandmother, three brothers, four sisters, nieces and nephews, cousins, aunts and uncles. Every branch had been cut from the tree, every leaf raked up and burned; even the trunk had been cut down and chopped up. Even as she lay on the cement floor in this foreign place, she felt in her gut someone far away wrenching the stump and its roots from the ground.

Rajan had promised to protect her, and he had. She had no doubt of that. No soldier would come for her in the middle of the night; no soldier would block her path as she walked to a village; no soldier would raise a bayonet to her when she turned around at the sound of her name. Rajan had promised her that would never happen; he would protect her from it all. And he had. Whoever had found him had not found her. Rajan had protected her till the end. She was sure of it. But the knowledge didn't ease her pain. Parvati lay her cheek down again and watched the shadows dance along the wall and ceiling as the candle sputtered to its end, and the light vanished.

Seventeen

Anita was worn out from the long day of investigating Prakash and then Thampi. She knew her weariness was more emotional than physical, but as much as she wanted to lie down and give in to sleep, she was still on her feet. As soon as her eyes adjusted to the dark, the candle snuffed out, the electric light switch in the off position in case the power came back on, Anita moved to the veranda doors and pulled open one side.

She was relieved to read the news report of the discovery of the terrorist who was the object of the manhunt, but this did not answer her questions. She still did not know whom she had seen moving about the house late at night. It seemed odd that someone would be drawn here at that hour, but she didn't think it would be a terrorist. It was likely to be something much more pedestrian—a local thief, or a farmer or laborer on his way home, taking a shortcut.

Whoever it was seemed to be someone who wanted to remain concealed. At first she had thought this might be the person Parvati was meeting in the new wing, but when he gave no sign that he knew about the meeting place on the other side of the house, Anita dismissed that idea. Whoever Parvati was waiting for in the privacy of the new wing was not the man Anita had seen skulking about the house, and now there would be little chance of the maidservant meeting anyone while she was locked inside the cooking rooms.

The man Anita had seen had come soon after midnight—he had not stopped, had not approached the house, at least from the front, and had not reappeared later in the night. She had no idea where he had gone, or if he had gone. She stared into the darkness, no longer deafened by the rain. Tonight she was serenaded by the creatures of the night—the snakes moving across the yard, the bandicoots snuffling for food, the wild boars trotting down the dirt road squealing in surprise to each other. The only danger to her, however, was her weariness. If she fell asleep, she'd miss any chance of answering her own question.

Her thoughts drifted to her conversation with Prakash.

He was in trouble. She tried to understand how he had reached this point, violating important agreements with the temple, hiding his behavior from his family, refusing to back down even when confronted by the trustees and then by Anita. He certainly wasn't the Prakash she had known for so many years. He was more than a stranger—he was someone she would never want to meet, never be willing to associate with, if she encountered him now for the first time.

Somewhere in the house a door creaked, furniture settled as the damp continued to evaporate; a breeze sent papers skidding across the floor. Anita stood up to stretch and shake off her sleepiness. She stretched her arms above her head and then out to her sides. As her arms fell, shadows outside began to leap and change; a swatch of light crawled over shrubbery and storm debris and ran up the tree trunks. A torch. Someone was carrying a torch. Anita pulled back into the shadows of her room.

A few feet behind the shifting light came a dark figure—the man holding the torch. He crept along cautiously, stopping to point the torch to the ground, where the circle of light shrank as darkness closed in around it. He waited, listening for any other sound before moving on. He passed in front of the yard, staying well away from the open courtyard. She could see part of his back as he waited, the light hidden behind the tree.

"What was he looking for? What did he want?" she whispered to herself.

As she heard her own words, the light grew still and disappeared. She could see he was still there, but feared he had heard her. No, she told herself, he couldn't have. She held her breath, kept herself in check, and was relieved to see the light start to move once again. He seemed on track to reach the side of the house. Whose room would he be passing now?

Auntie Meena had a suite over the kitchen rooms.

Anita looked around her, grabbed a shawl, and hurried down the corridor, past the stairs, to the other side of the house. In the hotel, Meena always slept with her door locked, but here she never had. Anita knew that because as a girl she had often wandered into Meena's room late at night and got into bed with her, curling her little body against Meena's long one.

Those were the nights when she especially missed her parents, when her mother was traveling around India with her father and Anita wished she could be with them. She had once told her mother she would give up anything to go with them, but her mother had said no. They were almost camping out, she said, and her father insisted he could only worry about one female at a time. And since Anita's mother conveniently spoke so many languages, well, Anita stayed home. Meena took her in whenever Anita showed up, looking forlorn and lonely and sometimes little-girl scared. Anita prayed Meena still slept with her door unlocked, as though the aunt once again might be called on to ease the sadness of a little girl.

Anita crept along the passage and came to Meena's door. Anita lifted the latch and the door gave. She sighed, surprised to find she had been holding her breath, and entered, pushing the door shut behind her as quietly as possible. In front of her, Meena snored and whistled in her sleep. Anita moved to the window and opened the shutter enough to get a glimpse of the grounds. The unknown intruder had to be somewhere below her—he couldn't have hurried through the night, not if he wanted to be sure no one discovered him.

Almost directly below, at the corner of the house, the man emerged. The flashlight had been dimmed to a single thin line of light, a spotlight on the earth that wavered as it covered a puddle, a rock, a branch. He moved closer to the back of the house, working his way through a cut in the garden wall.

She had to get a look at his face, but how? Anita watched the light. He would reach the back of the house soon, where there was no balcony overlooking the yard, but there were windows there too, in Meena's second room. Anita moved to the other room, pulling the door shut behind her. This room had been renovated after an earlier monsoon had damaged the interior, destroying wood-framed windows, furniture and carpeting, and art hanging on the walls. The casement windows were never used, however, because the room was rarely occupied. Meena had recommended them, admired them when they were installed, and promptly moved into the other room, where only wood shutters hung in the windows.

Anita unlatched the window and waited for a breeze to spring up again. As the man moved closer to the back door—a common thief?—Anita saw signs of a breeze moving down the hill, waited, and rattled the window enough to make sound that would travel. Pulled back into the darkness, she expected him to look up, to see what made the noise, but instead he dropped to his knees and pressed his body against the wall. The flashlight cut off. She heard a rustling, and looked out. He had rounded the corner of the house and disappeared. Anita ran into Meena's room, pulled open the shutter, and saw only the end of a dark lungi as the stranger crossed the edge of the courtyard. Anita latched the shutter and turned around to leave. She still might be able to get a look at him if he moved to the other side of the house. If he was a common thief, he would be easy enough to scare away.

"Anita!" Meena was sitting upright in bed, a perplexed look on her face, her hair tousled, her blanket askew. "What are you doing?" She reached out and wrapped her hard bony fingers around Anita's wrist.

Anita swung the shawl from around her shoulders. "I wanted you to have this." She tossed it to her aunt and tried to pull away, but Meena held tight.

"Ah, you are missing your mother." Meena patted the bed with her other hand. "Come. Sit here."

"Actually, Meena Elayamma . . ." Anita worked to pry Meena's fingers from her wrist, but Meena was holding on even as she was being dragged from the bed.

"No, I will not be put off. I insist. I am not insensitive to your heart. Sit. Your aunt orders you."

With a sigh, rationalizing that the stranger had already gotten away, Anita sat.

* * * * *

At five thirty in the morning, Anita unlocked the kitchen area and found Parvati still asleep in the room set aside for the goat. Startled, Parvati sat up and took in her surroundings and the time. She scrambled to her feet, muttering apologies and promises to have coffee ready in a minute. It took Anita more than a minute to calm the maidservant and point out that she, Anita, was the early one disrupting the schedule. That barely slowed Parvati down.

Anita unlocked the back door and stepped outside. Night was waning, but it was still dark. She turned on her

161

torch and ran the light over the area. She moved along the back of the house to the corner where she'd seen the man earlier in the night, then into the shrubbery and trees where she had first seen him. She found nothing of use. He had moved carefully through the yard and along the undergrowth, leaving a single footprint here or there, but nothing else. He wore sandals, chappals from the looks of it, as did almost everyone else around here.

By the time Anita returned to the kitchen, Parvati had brought out the goat and tethered the animal to the old well. The goat bleated. Anita went to look for Joseph. She found him and the hotel car near the far back of the house, in a small clearing probably meant for furniture or tool mending. When she peered into the rear window, she saw him sprawled across the backseat with his feet dangling over the front. He looked far too uncomfortable to sleep, but asleep he was. Anita rapped on the window. Joseph awoke with a start and tumbled into the well in the backseat.

"Nothing, I am telling you, Amma, nothing." He sighed and rubbed his head where he had hit it on the door handle. "No one is coming. Am I not a guard? Do I not see everything?"

No, thought Anita, you don't. But aloud she said, "I was sure I saw someone moving around the house, some time past midnight."

"No, no, you are mistaken. A farmer going home. No thief is coming so early in the nighttime. People are still awake and doing things. What thief comes to a house where people are awake?"

"But no one was awake, Joseph. No one is ever awake here at that hour. This household always retires before midnight, well before midnight."

"No one is coming last night. I am certain. I am here, isn't it?" He grew indignant at the implied challenge to his integrity. "No one." He waggled his head in emphasis and crawled out of the backseat, disheveled, sore, and now irritated.

"I think someone tried to get in through the kitchen wing," Anita said. "And he has tried before, so he'll try again."

"Why would a thief come to the kitchen? In these old houses the kitchen is always locked away. He is a stupid thief," Joseph said. "Not from around here. Outsider and stupid. And why does he think an old house like this, with no man at home and such unkempt grounds, will have something to steal? So, he is stupid and a fool. You should not waste your time on him." Still grumbling about his sore head, Joseph went off to make his morning ablutions and get some breakfast. He loved his car, but he did not like sleeping in it.

He's right, thought Anita. This house is unkempt.

She began to make a circuit around the house, passing the closed wing, with its windows shuttered, the vines crawling up to the roof, the shrubbery pressing against the rain-streaked walls. The black lines of mold were thick and tapered like flames; the ground was covered with debris from years of neglect.

When she reached the front, the courtyard seemed especially sad. Instead of the pots and pots of flowering plants and greenery that usually filled a courtyard, and had filled this one in past years, Anita found only a few broken pots tucked away near the corner of the veranda, the shards left to crumble. The covered veranda with its chairs and small tables was inviting, but nothing said this was a home with the furnishings normally found in such a large house of a once-prominent family. No plants on the veranda, no framed photographs of deceased relatives or deities hanging high up under the eaves announcing that this was an important family—nothing that would attract a thief. Here was nothing that said this is a house worth investigating, worth studying, worth the risk of capture or injury or imprisonment.

And Joseph was right about the kitchen door, too. A thief could not know if a kitchen door would lead to anything more than a cooking room—even the larder would probably be locked up. And certainly he knew that staff sometimes slept inside the kitchen, especially if they were longtime family workers.

No, this was not an ordinary thief. Joseph was right about that.

* * * * *

Breakfast was a trial for Anita. It was all she could do to keep from blurting out what she was really doing last night when Meena awoke and found Anita in her room after midnight.

"And a shawl was her excuse," Meena said, smiling at Anita. The older woman was positively besotted with her niece now, and could barely contain herself. Meena began the morning with a whispered conversation with Lalita Amma as the two women sat down for breakfast. They barely noticed Vengamma as she doled out the food, idlies, those lightly steamed rice and lentil cakes, served with sambar and chutney. When Lalita began giggling like a girl, Anita closed her eyes and clenched her teeth.

"Really, Meena Elayamma, it was only a shawl." Anita was still furious with herself for having let the midnight stalker get away without at least getting a good look at him.

"I remember when you used to do that." Valli tried to suppress a grin, but failed. "I thought you were so silly."

"I was ten years old." Anita's teeth were still clenched.

"But you were so loving," Lalita Amma added. "And you still are. It is good, isn't it?" She grew serious as she identified a topic on which she felt strongly but rarely had an opportunity to discuss. "So many of the younger ones do not appreciate the love that is required to raise a child to adulthood, to be ready to enter the world and achieve great things."

"Or small things." Meena was besotted but not blind. This was Anita they were talking about, she of the no future on the horizon because she refused to take her aunt's advice.

"Or small." Lalita patted Meena's hand. Lalita Amma seemed to have been waiting for this opportunity, and she launched into a list of the young people in this area and in Kochi who had failed to honor their families' contributions to their success in life. How could this be, when she herself knew these families intimately? Only Meena remained fully engrossed in Lalita's laments, her psychologizing about the families and her despair for the future of the entire country. It was no wonder Prakash didn't come to breakfast and Valli finished in record time.

"Come, I must show you the letters I have received from another cousin sister. She is recently returned from Canada—so many years I haven't seen her, and now she is living in Bangaluru." Lalita led Meena from the room and left Anita to finish her breakfast. When she looked down at her plate she was appalled to see that she had been tearing up her idly but not eating any of it. Before she could call out to Vengamma, the cook was standing in front of her, leaning over with a large spoon on which balanced two more steaming idlies. She dropped those down onto the plate and a moment later returned with more chutney and sambar.

"She does get to you, doesn't she?" Valli said as Anita began breakfast all over again.

"And you didn't offer a word of defense," Anita said with her mouth full.

"Well, I can't really, can I?" Valli stretched out her legs and leaned back against the wall to drink her coffee. "I think Amma goes off on her tirades not thinking that any of her words are real. She doesn't think she could ever be talking about us, me and Prakash or you or anyone else she's related to. She's parroting all the sad stories she hears from her friends about others—you know, friends of friends of friends. The stories grow in the telling, don't they?"

Anita had to admit this was true. It had to be so much easier for Lalita Amma to rant about children she didn't know than face the trouble coming into this home because of her own two children. Lalita Amma was going to have to have one of those talks with her own son and daughter, sooner rather than later. Anita reached for another idly. She felt sorry for all of them—Lalita Amma, Prakash, Valli, but mostly for Valli.

"I shouldn't have laughed at Meena Elayamma's story," Valli said in a soft voice when Vengamma was out of the room.

"She misses having a family, and her own daughter is so far away—in so many ways." Anita paused, dropping the topic. Meena's daughter, and her only child, went away young and had stayed away, preferring life overseas to life in India. Not for her the running of a hotel and catering to foreigners.

"And you don't really miss your mother that much, do you?"

Anita looked up at Valli's sly expression.

"So why were you in Meena Elayamma's room at that hour?" Valli leaned closer to Anita, eyes gleaming. "What have you found?"

Anita stuffed her mouth with more idly, giving herself time to think. There was no reason not to tell Valli, but then, there was no reason Anita should tell her. It was possible Valli had some idea about who the stalker might be—perhaps she had heard something in the village and had not mentioned it. Or perhaps she knew who the stalker was because she knew him, knew he was coming here looking for something. Maybe he was even coming to see her, though why he would come through the kitchen, Anita did not know.

"You can tell me, Anita. Didn't we always tell each other everything?" Valli set aside her coffee and pulled closer to Anita, crossing her legs and waiting with her hands clasped in her lap.

"Well, if you must know." Anita calculated what she might get from Valli, and decided to gamble. "I thought I saw someone going around the side of the house while I was closing up the shutters." Anita watched Valli to see how she reacted. It wasn't what Anita expected. Valli's face paled and she pushed herself away along the floor.

"You mustn't tease me, Anita. I am your friend, and this is how you treat me?"

"You're hurt!" Anita said. "Why?"

"You make up this story so you won't have to tell me the truth. Why shouldn't I be hurt?" Valli crossed her arms over her chest and looked ready to cry; instead, she began to pout, repeating again and again that friends should tell each other the truth. "Haven't I told you the truth—as painful and as embarrassing as it is. This is a humiliation for me, my husband not protecting my brother in his position and asking for more money and my mother, who is now poor, not knowing what to do. And you brush me away with such a story. Really, Anita, you are cruel. You have become as silly as you seem now—I always thought it was a way to tweak Meena Elayamma, but it is more than that. You are unkind to me."

Anita was brought up short by this reaction. "Valli, I am telling you the truth. I really did think I saw someone. I know I did. I saw him go around the house to the kitchen, but I couldn't see his face."

"Why would he go to the kitchen? Do you think our little Parvati has a secret lover?" Valli glared at her. "Ah! You do! I can see it in your eyes. You think she has a lover! Oh, Anita!" Valli jumped to her feet. "This is too much. The ideas you get into your head and here in this house! The stories you tell. Auntie Meena is right. Your family must get you married and settled down. You are becoming much too strange and foolish to be left to your own devices any longer." Valli brushed her hair away from her face with both hands, closed her eyes tight, and shook her head. Then she marched out of the room, leaving Anita to finish her breakfast in solitude and confusion.

* * * * *

Thinking about Valli and her tirade left Anita with a headache, and she decided to let time resolve that minor volcano. Instead, she'd give her brain a rest by considering a few of the other lingering problems.

Anita had an idea about the goat and decided to test her theory. She wasn't convinced that a wild animal was after the goat. It could as easily be someone trying to steal it. A household of women (and Prakash wasn't generally known to be living here) was an easy and inviting target. The goat sleeping outside throughout the night was an easy steal. She walked through the kitchen, noting that Parvati was hard at work scrubbing pans and Vengamma was taking inventory in the larder.

The goat was wandering on its tether, as much as it could, and showed no sign of wanting to go any further, no tugging on the line, no struggling for grass a bit out of reach. The ground seemed clear also, no signs of any other footprints than Anita's and Parvati's and Vengamma's, the small prints of women.

Anita crossed the yard and began to walk along the low compound wall, not meant as a deterrent so much as a container for chickens and goats and small children. The ground was still more mud than soil though the greenery was drying fast even in this humid air, and Anita hoped for tracks of anyone who had come close. She came to the end of the compound wall and turned back and walked the wall in the other direction, toward the front of the house.

As she reached the farthest corner she found what she had not really expected to find. When the goat had sounded terrified in the storm, her first thought was only that it was afraid of the wild weather. Later she thought the goat was calling out to the stranger stalking the house. But now, as Anita bent down to study the unexpected paw print, she had to dismiss these suppositions. She spread her hand and fingers above the paw print to get a rough estimate of its size—it was not small. It had to be the print of an adult cat—a leopard, probably. That's what lived in the Periyar Wildlife Sanctuary. That's the animal that would have been driven by the storm down the mountains to the nearest villages, where food and water were more easily available. But now that the monsoon was ending, the weather calmer, would the animal find its way back?

Anita retrieved her camera from the house and took a few photos of the paw prints, walked deeper into the underbrush and took a few more shots. She would take them to the constable in the village and see what he could do. Perhaps someone would come down from Periyar and track the animal.

Anita looked over the low wall. The goat munched as though nothing else in the world existed except that small clump of hay on the ground. The animal raised its head and turned to gaze at Anita, its big golden yellow eyes friendly and amused and slightly bored. At the moment it was content, well fed and safe. But that could change in an instant, and the animal would be lost. The creature was helpless on a tether and helpless off it.

Eighteen

Anita was only too eager to get away from the aunts by taking a trip into the village. She had a few questions for the constable. She found him with his feet propped up on his desk reading the newspaper. He didn't move when she walked into the station; he didn't even look out from behind the paper. She sat down in the first chair in a row of them set against the wall for petitioners, and prepared to wait.

"I have some business, but not serious. No crime or anything like that." She took the end of her dupatta, the long shawl worn with a salwar khameez set, and wiped her face. After listening to Meena Elayamma gushing through breakfast about knowing Anita's real needs, Anita had decided she'd had enough of wearing saris to please her aunts, and pulled out a salwar khameez with a blue-and-yellow-print overblouse and solid-blue pants. The dupatta hung limp in the humidity, and Anita was beginning to sweat in the midmorning heat. She patted her throat with the light fabric.

"If there is no crime, why are you here?"

Anita recognized the voice, the ennui, and the challenge. Really, she thought, do we have to go through something like this every time there is a small matter to deal with? Instead, she said, "I found paw prints outside the compound wall, where the goat is kept, this morning—they

170

are large. A couple of days ago we had to bring the goat inside at night because we thought there was an animal outside stalking it and now we know there is."

"Hmm."

Anita sighed. This could be a long interview.

"This is what you have come about?"

"I am thinking the monsoon pushed the animal out of Periyar and now it is lost down here among the villages. Perhaps someone from Periyar can come and reclaim the animal and return it to the sanctuary. They must know how to capture such things, yes?"

This idea seemed to interest him, and he lowered his feet to the floor and rested the newspaper on the desk. He went to stand in the front door, squinting into the sharpening sunshine that turned everything white outside. Apparently satisfied the animal in question wasn't outside at that moment, he returned to his desk. "We are having this difficulty before, some years back."

"Did they send anyone to trap the animal?"

"Someone is coming but the animal is disappearing. We are thinking so many searching for the animal is driving it back into the mountains. No one is seeing it again, and workers at the sanctuary are not noticing any creatures missing, at least not among those they see often."

"And will they come a second time?"

He shrugged. "Who knows?" He watched the foot traffic outside the door from his desk and then sat down again. Anita leaned around the doorjamb to take a look, in case something interesting was happening outside. There was no use trying to hold this man's attention if he was only going to ignore her in favor of something more exciting. She looked. Nothing; only the usual shoppers passing by. Anita was beginning to find the exchange tedious.

"Can you send a message to them at Periyar? Is there some authority I can notify? If the animal doesn't find enough food, it will starve, and as a protected animal, this could be bad for the village. But if it does find enough to eat, it may come to like it here, and that means it will be living on livestock and perhaps even tormenting families with young children."

The constable blinked at her and frowned. He shook out the newspaper and folded it neatly, checking the alignment of each page and the creases and placing the folded paper on a nearby chair. "Authorities will be informed."

"Well, I hope so." Fed up, Anita leaned over to pick up her bag, ready to leave, but instead of doing so she pretended to rummage in it for something, to give herself time to think.

"Is that all? Is that what you have come for?"

Anita was about to dismiss his query as one more sign that he was relieved to have her gone, but something in his voice—the surprise, and yes the relief—caught her attention. She thought she had heard more than the usual relief at avoiding work. She sat up again, leaving her bag on the floor, and looked at him expectantly.

"I thought you have perhaps come on another matter," he said.

"Well, yes." And I hope you're going to tell me what it is, she added to herself.

He looked so uncomfortable that Anita wondered what she could possibly have done or said to bring this about. He placed a hand on his wooden desk as if to make sure he was where he thought he was, to get his bearings before plunging further into something that clearly disturbed him. "It is the matter of the dead body found in the river."

"Yes. You know more about him?" Anita almost leapt out of her chair.

"No, no more. Only he is known to the police. We are fortunate the river got him."

Anita gaped at him. "The river did not get him, as you put it." She clenched her teeth. "He had marks on his wrists and his neck."

"No, no, you are mistaken."

Anita stood up and walked over to his desk, leaning over it. "I am not mistaken, sar. I know what I saw."

"Madam," he said, avoiding her eye, "in the heat of the moment, in the extreme stress of such an experience, you perhaps imagined things that were not there. And this is understandable. A man falls into the river during a dangerous flood and we see the danger manifest in the body, but it is no more than that. All else is in our imagination, the imagination of a good heart."

"It was not a good heart that saw his body torn to shreds." She leaned on the desk and pushed her face close to his, abandoning all decorum.

"Madam, you are having a good heart. I know this. You are coming here with concern for the animals that might have been driven from their safe home in Periyar, isn't it? This is such a fine sentiment. And there are many who admire this. Indeed, we are having here in our village a fine young man who is superb at discerning the truth of these matters. If a leopard or other animal has been driven here to its detriment, this young man will find it and assist in its return to Periyar. No finer tracker exists in our village."

He handed her a slip of paper on which was written a name and address. Anita snatched it from his hand, her teeth still clenched, not daring to look at the little glass paperweight on his desk for fear she wouldn't be able to control the impulse to pick it up and heave it at him.

* * * * *

It took Anita the walk across the full length of the village before she was calm enough to understand what the constable had done for her. She pulled out the slip of paper and studied it. A few minutes later she had located the young man and persuaded him to help her, which consisted of opening her mouth and mentioning the jungle. He was already ten feet ahead of her before she caught up to him mentally.

Nagesh was only fifteen, but he already knew almost everything the older guides could teach to young men who wanted to know about making their way safely through the forest. The remainder of his education came from walking with the tribals who lived deeper in the jungle, following the forest guides, and learning by observing and doing. For a young man with ambitions, there was little work in the village, and he was eager to explore the forests around Lalita Amma's estate.

Thin and lanky though not yet at his full height, Nagesh moved through the forest with practiced skill and native instincts. Even if his parents insisted he had no bloodlines going back to any tribals, Nagesh must have thought secretly of previous existences in other families with other lives outside cities and villages with rows of shops and buses careening through several times a day.

"Go carefully there." He pointed to a hole barely covered by twigs, but one that Anita might have missed had she been alone and more worried about the branches that threatened to slap her in the face at every other step.

After some time Anita and Nagesh came to the spot where the man's body had been found, washed up against flood debris and caught in the cleft of a trunk stripped of bark. Nagesh knew the dangers of floods firsthand and nodded solemnly when Anita told him her intent to track back along the river and try to locate the spot where the man had been washed into the water. She didn't believe the police claim that the man had fallen in only a few feet from where he was found, and she was pretty sure the constable didn't believe it either. It was a crazy idea, perhaps, she added, but Nagesh continued to nod with a serious expression. Everyone in the village had heard the story of the body and its discovery, he said, and a hush of fear fell over conversations when the topic came up. He was eager to help her.

"This way." Nagesh led her deeper into the forest, and after a while Anita thought she could smell the river.

"Have you heard anything about animals pushed out of the sanctuary because of the rains?" Anita hated to admit it, but she had a gnawing fear of running into something large and hungry. At this, Nagesh turned around, holding a branch aside for her, with a slight smile but definitely sparkling eyes. "You think I'm silly, yes?"

"We will not meet one." His smile faded, and Anita thought he looked disappointed. Good, she thought; that's the way I want it.

The two walked on, clambering over downed trees and torn-up shrubs, making a path where there might have been one but now certainly was not. The canopy above seemed to press the heat down onto them, deflecting any breeze and hoarding all the humidity lest any of it evaporate and the village cool off. Every now and then Anita found herself wondering if this was a dumb idea; after all, there was so much unsettled land along the river— the man could have been attacked anywhere. But her gut told her that the body had taken a beating, not only from nature but also from a human.

"Look!" Nagesh called. Before Anita could respond, Nagesh plunged into the forest and thrashed his way deeper than Anita could see. She looked, but saw only the jungle, nothing else, and had no idea what he had seen. She waited, listened, and heard his sounds of surprise. "I have something." He made his way back to her, and she saw his discovery before he emerged—the bright-orange cloth that signaled a first-time pilgrim's *irumudi*. Anita gave a little gasp of air and held her breath. She reached out for the bag Nagesh held out to her.

Anita pulled open the front pocket and saw that it

was not yet filled with the traditional offerings—no coconuts with ghee for the abhishekham, or bathing of the deity; no jaggery or spices, no rice or dhal for offerings. The pocket held only a few betel leaves and some coins. She poked around inside the bag, but there was nothing in the second pocket that would identify the owner—not even a toothbrush or headscarf. She thought back to the lorry filling up with pilgrims. She had seen a few bags like this.

"This is not good, to find an *irumudi* abandoned here." Nagesh was firm about this. "It is not easy to move through here—there are only so many paths."

Anita hadn't noticed any path at all for some time, and tried to see what Nagesh was seeing.

"We go on." He motioned her forward, and went ahead. When they came to a spot in the river where a tree had fallen across, he noted the buildup of debris and told Anita he would report it; otherwise, the river would overflow its banks and more damage would be done. "It is a bad thing to leave it."

Nagesh was now confident there was something to find, and he was reciting the various sites he had come across during his many explorations. "There is a bridge up here. No one uses it now—it is old and the villagers go another way. We will look. After this there is an old house where a family lived but they are all gone now. There are places for us to search."

"Do you think he came this far east, into the hills?" she asked.

Anita followed him, pulling her sandals out of the muck with a smacking sound, reclaiming her dupatta from a clawing branch, picking leaves out of her hair. She felt a twig snag her pants and heard fabric rip—they were moving deeper and deeper into the jungle, and also moving uphill. Anita felt the sweat dripping down her chest and back, and the warm glow of perspiration on her face.

"There."

Anita emerged from the trees and looked where Nagesh was pointing. Ahead, along the river, where it was only a few feet wide, stood a pillar that had once been one half of a bridge. On the other side stood its twin. The boards that had once allowed pedestrians to cross over the river were gone, and much of the ground into which the pillars had been sunk had been washed away.

"Very old!" Nagesh flicked his fingers and squinted to indicate the great age of the now-ruined bridge. "No one is using this now, but once it was very important. I have seen this before it was taken by the storms."

Anita climbed as close to the bank as she dared and studied the pillar on this side. She ran her hand over the iron rings set into the stone and looked across the river. There seemed to be iron rings in the pillar on the opposite bank also. "Can we get across?" She studied the river, uncertain of its depth and flow.

"Yes, we will cross." Nagesh began to look around him, and disappeared into the undergrowth. He returned dragging a downed tree. He managed to get this upright, and then gave it a gentle shove. The tree fell across the river, its broken peak landing on the other bank. The storm had driven a lot of water over the riverbank, but the waters had already begun receding, and the river ran at a slower pace. He stepped into the river and moved through the water, holding onto the tree trunk for safety, reached the other side, and turned back. "Yes, it is good."

With one hand holding the tree trunk and her other clapped onto Nagesh's shoulder as he walked in front of her, Anita crossed the river and climbed out on the other bank. She clambered over to the stone pillar and reached for the iron rings. So much damage had been done by the flooding that she dared not make much of anything she found, but she couldn't conceal her excitement when she pulled the muck of grass and leaves from one iron ring and found threads of coir rope underneath, still wound around

177

the iron. Her breathing quickened. This could be the spot, she realized, where the man had been tied up and left, left to the mercy of the storm and the river.

"You are finding something?" Nagesh moved closer.

Anita showed him what she'd found.

"Amma!" Nagesh called to her. Anita looked where he pointed.

"Oh!" Deeper in among the bushes was something that looked like yellow fabric caught on a branch. Anita struggled closer and ran her fingers over it. "Oh no. Nagesh . . . This is fur."

"Yes, I know it. Leopard from the sanctuary has been here." He held the clump of fur in his fingers. "Some days ago, in the rains."

The picture of the body she had found flashed across Anita's memory. She recalled clearly the gash and torn flesh that seemed too violent even for this storm. That poor man, she thought. Whoever he was, he had been tied up here and abandoned to his fate, with the river rising and a leopard stalking.

* * * * *

Anita ran her hands over the stone pillar and its iron rings, then closed her eyes, imagining how it must have felt to be tied here, seeing waves of muddy water churning closer and closer, and the storm building. What she really wanted to know, however, was what sort of man had been behind this cruel act—tying someone up and leaving him to the mercies of the jungle and the weather. She wasn't quite sure how it had been managed logistically, and recalled the fragments of coir rope on the man's wrists and neck. She looked about her for other fixtures that might have been used. In the ground seared away by the rushing water she saw only sleek red soil. The deep gashes in the riverbank were being gradually smoothed out by muddy green water.

Anita couldn't have said how long she spent

speculating on what might have happened, but when she next looked up, Nagesh was nowhere in sight. She peered into the thick growth for a sign of him. She called out his name, but the sound was quickly absorbed by the dense leaves and branches; she called again, louder this time. Surprised and curious about what could have drawn him away, she climbed the bank to higher ground, finding a foothold near where the ramp to the bridge might have begun. She found little evidence of the ramp now, but enough to tell her that this bridge at one time must have been a more elaborate structure.

More curious than worried, Anita began walking along the river, a few feet in one direction, then backtracking and going a few feet in the other. She expanded her path a few feet each time, so as not to become lost in the jungle.

"Amma! Amma!"

Anita heard his voice as Nagesh broke into view.

"Come. You must see this."

Anita followed him into the undergrowth, struck by his childlike excitement. She thrashed through the jungle, trying to keep him in view. He seemed to know exactly where he was going, and halted on his path every few feet to let Anita catch up. He pulled back branches, pointed out dangerous spots in the ground, found a way around downed trees and snagging undergrowth. After they had gone some distance and Anita was beginning to tire, he stepped into a small clearing and turned to her with an expression that was a mixture of perplexity and hopeful delight.

It took Anita a moment to understand what he was showing her, so fully part of the jungle was the little lean-to of woven palm leaves. Someone had made himself a half hut, more like a hunter's hide, in the middle of the jungle, on a gentle slope. She couldn't tell exactly where the hut was in relation to the river, only that they hadn't crossed it and had done some climbing. It was hard to tell with the land so wild and thick.

Anita ran her fingers over the fronds. "It's not very old, is it?"

"A few weeks, no more."

She peered inside. The ground was littered with old banana leaves but not a scrap of food—the ants would have seen to that; a dirty white vest and a faded plaid lungi hung from a fold in the weaving. Stuck into the side wall was a toothbrush. Was someone living here? She looked up at Nagesh and gestured. He shrugged.

"It is not meant to be lived in, I think," Nagesh said. "But it is good for those going to Sabarimala for the first time. They can keep their austerity vows as first-time pilgrims more easily if they are sometimes able to get away from others."

"Of course." Anita thought back to Thampi's crowded home. "No meat, fish, sex, alcohol, or abusive language for sixty days, isn't it?" Could Thampi have stayed here?

"It is forty-five to sixty days." Nagesh nodded. "My brother and uncles and I went last year and we lived two months in a warehouse where my uncle worked in Chengannur. Very long time."

Curious, Anita studied the hut and its meager contents. A few items sat on a small wooden shelf hung on a bamboo crosspiece—nothing more than soap and a washcloth. She lifted a half woven mat on the ground with her toe and shifted it aside, then used a branch to rummage through the debris underneath. She pushed aside dirt, a few scraps of coir rope and strips of palm frond.

"There." Nagesh pointed, and Anita looked, but all she could see was dirt. He took the stick from her and poked the ground with it.

"Oh." Loosened dirt.

Nagesh began to dig. It didn't take long for them to learn why the soil was so loose. The teenager understood first, and turned to look up at Anita. "Do you want me to continue?"

"Of course," she said, moving closer, too involved to pick up on his hesitation. "Oh." The word came out softly, as she exhaled.

First, the arm, then the shoulder emerged. When the boy looked up at her again, she paused before nodding. He kept on digging, but carefully. She was tied to the spot by curiosity and fear. She wanted to know who it was, but she was afraid of finding out who it might be. When Anita saw the earlobe and jaw emerge from the soil, she put a hand on Nagesh's shoulder and he stopped digging.

"Oh, Shiva! Namah shivaya, shivaya namah." She closed her eyes and prayed. Nagesh rested the little spade he'd created from twigs and a branch, and leaned back.

"I'll go for the constable," he said.

"Yes."

"Who is it? Do you recognize him?" he asked.

Anita stared down at the decomposing body, and her eyes blurred. The outline of a familiar face transformed the discovery in front of her. "Yes, I think I know him. He works for Lalita Amma. You probably know him too." She watched Nagesh turn to look, but he only frowned and shook his head. "It's Thampi," she said. "I've known him all my life. He was supposed to go to Sabarimala this year. His heart's desire."

* * * * *

Anita continued to lean on Nagesh as she tried to absorb this new tragedy. "How did you find this place?" she asked Nagesh.

"I followed little breaks in the branches, little torn grass where there is no grass, coming on feet or sandals."

"How long since someone has been here?"

Nagesh walked around the hut, along the edge of the jungle, studied the soil. "Days."

"How long has Thampi been dead?"

Nagesh shrugged. "More days."

Anita turned around. The jungle would fill in the clearing in a matter of weeks if not sooner; the monsoon would make it unlivable. It was a long walk from any shop or village. "I can understand his wanting a quiet place for his austerity vows, but why would he come all the way up here when he only lives in the village?"

"It is solitary, good for a man seeking spiritual life. And closer, more convenient for him." Nagesh waggled his head and lifted his eyebrows, as if to say didn't she understand that.

"Closer?" Anita stepped back in surprise. "Closer to what?"

"Your house."

"This is closer to Lalita Amma's house than the village?"

"Yes, yes. Amma's house is not far, just over there." He pointed into the forest, behind the back wall of the little hut. Anita looked in the direction he indicated and tried to orient herself.

"Show me." Anita spoke so sharply that Nagesh blinked and looked hurt. But he plunged into the forest, and Anita again struggled to keep up with him. She could tell they were moving more downhill than up this time, and it was a much shorter walk than the one from the river. Although she saw no homes or pathways that she could use to get her bearings, Nagesh seemed to know exactly where he was going, where in the darkness of green and branches and vines that seemed desperate to capture them there was a path straight to Lalita Amma's front door—or back door, as it turned out. They walked in silence, Anita listening for Nagesh's call to keep her from turning in the wrong direction.

A moment before they broke through the last patch of undergrowth, Anita heard Parvati singing to herself as she hung out the wash. The line was strung from tree to tree to tree to tree, looping back on itself and creating a labyrinth of laundry. The maidservant didn't hear them emerge into the clearing.

"I am here, Parvati." Anita walked up behind her.

The maidservant looked over her shoulder as she draped a hand towel onto the line. "Ah." She lowered her hands and wiped them on her mundu. "You are wanting something?" She looked puzzled but not alarmed, and quickly glanced at Nagesh, but seemed to find nothing of interest there.

"We are coming through the forest," Anita said. "We found a hideout there, like a meditation hut, and it is situated toward this house." She tried to block out the image of Thampi's body—she wanted to catch Parvati off guard—and she did. The color in Parvati's face drained away, her eyes widened in fear, and her facial muscles twitched. A hard look flickered in her eyes, and Anita suddenly recalled Thampi's wife's story of the chicken and its beheading. Parvati looked down at the ground, and spoke in a quiet meek voice.

"I am never going so far into the jungle, Amma. Only here to do my work. You are wanting something? I am getting?"

The transformation unnerved Anita. Behind her, Thampi lay buried in a shallow grave, and in front of her a maidservant had turned from terror to obedience right before her eyes.

Anita drew Nagesh aside and ordered him to say nothing of what he had found; he was to go directly to the constable and report. Then he was to go to the village crossroads, and stay there, keeping track of who left the village in a direction that would lead them to the hut. The little hut could not be known to anyone other than the one who had built it, Thampi—and the one who had used it to hide Thampi's body. That could have been the man whose body she had found earlier, or the man she had seen stalking Lalita Amma's house last night.

"And the last thing is very important, Nagesh." Anita lowered her voice and moved closer. "When the men volunteer to remove the body, take them a long way around to the hut, away from Lalita Amma's house, and back to the village the same way. Don't let them come near or know how close it is to this house. It is up to you to make them think the hut is remote in another direction." When Nagesh looked doubtful, Anita repeated the order. "Do you understand?" she asked. He nodded slowly, then more enthusiastically. "I'm counting on you, Nagesh."

She thanked him again and reiterated the importance of her instructions. He sensed her urgency, and she could see the change in him as he nodded, absorbing the idea of an important mission. She watched him run off, a mere boy who didn't flinch at the sight of a corpse buried where it shouldn't have been but was confused by a ruse to protect a family.

Anita turned away from the jungle. The sun that had warmed her body seemed to disappear, and she felt a chill. In a hut nearby she had found a corpse, and not far away she had found a stone pillar that had imprisoned another man until his death. She pulled her dupatta tight around her shoulders as though she could squeeze the ugly images out of her mind and soul.

* * * * *

Anita let herself into the house through the front door and listened for voices. Someone was humming, a cupboard door opened and closed, Lalita Amma was giving orders to Vengamma—it was the normal business of family life. But someone here was the object of a man set on murder. Anita's thoughts ran through the members of the family, and wondered what each of them could have done to attract such notice.

Lalita Amma was growing poor, but she was a wily sort. Anita half imagined when she first understood the old woman's plight that her aunt had secretly stashed away a portion of her wealth for such an eventuality. Anita wouldn't put it past Lalita Amma to have buried the family silver, so to speak, in this instance the family antique murtis and other bronze items. Lalita Amma had always been a formidable woman. It was possible the stalker was a professional thief, and Thampi was sacrificed on the altar of greed.

Prakash in his new role of priest may have let the position go to his head and implied that his family was richer than it was, inviting such attentions. Or perhaps he had done something well beyond what the trustees had implied, and the price of temple rites was only a ruse to get at him for something else. He seemed so young and eager to Anita, but in truth how well did she know him as an adult? He wasn't a boy, and she had to admit that she really didn't know him at all anymore.

Thinking of Valli simply made Anita sad. Valli was regressing to her younger self, a child who wanted to be indulged while she sulked about a lost boyfriend. It seemed to Anita that Valli's marriage was little more than an ongoing business negotiation, with Valli making endless excuses for her husband's greed and her mother's poverty. She loved her husband too much to stand up for herself, and he took advantage of her immaturity to keep pressing for more money. She made him sound like a controlling man who made unreasonable demands that Valli simply accepted and tried to accommodate. Was he behind the stalker here, someone sent to spy on Valli? Was her husband a jealous man making sure she did nothing improper while she was out of his sight? Was he so jealous as to be irrational, murdering in order to possess her absolutely?

Anita found the idea of any of the members of this family being the object of the stranger's stalking close to ludicrous. But the servants didn't seem any more compelling. Anita had known Vengamma almost her entire life, and couldn't imagine a more innocent woman anywhere. The cook was fussy, often overbearing, sometimes a scold, but she was devoted and honest, and Anita hadn't heard of anything occurring in the old woman's life that would have changed her character. And since she didn't live in, why would anyone seek her here instead of at her own home, where she would certainly be more vulnerable? Anita cringed at the thought.

Parvati was a cipher—sweet, endearing to Lalita Amma, hardworking—but definitely holding something back. And the story about the chicken suggested a hidden side to her. Yet Parvati appeared to be exactly what she said she was: a servant and nothing more. If she were someone in disguise, in hiding, she would have given something away by now, some little clue that she had known another life—a flash of indignation or resentment at being piled with duties, a moment too familiar or too knowledgeable. But no, she seemed to be exactly what she claimed to be, a maidservant.

An unwelcome thought struck Anita. Auntie Meena? Meena Elayamma? Could she be the object of this stranger's interest? Anita felt her sweat go cold, icy on her back. Not Meena. Surely no one could mean harm to Auntie Meena. What could she possibly know? What danger could she pose? But that wasn't the real question. No. The real question, Anita realized, was whether she could see this family not as relatives but as individuals who could be in danger—or could be the danger. Could either Prakash or Kumar be the one responsible for Thampi's death?

"Oh, there you are." Meena swept into the room with a broad smile. "You are missing your meal. Foolish girl. It is not good to be so cavalier with your health. A good diet is so important." She stopped and stared at Anita. "Anita, you are having asthma attack? You need air?"

"No, no, I'm fine, really."

Anguished from her recent thoughts that Meena could be the one in danger, Anita went to her aunt, wrapping her arms around her. She held the older woman tight, then stepped away.

Meena frowned and eyed her niece. "Are you up to something I would disapprove of?"

Anita laughed. "I'm always up to something you disapprove of, so I won't tell you anything."

"What is it?" Meena whispered, pulling Anita closer. "I am worried."

"No, no, don't be worried." Anita slipped her arm through her aunt's. "Come with me to the kitchen and let me ask you things, and then I must go into the village—an errand." That was all it took, Anita realized, for her to go weak in the knees and think only about her aunt's safety. Rationally, she might be able to make herself believe that Auntie Meena was in no danger, that the threat lay elsewhere, but beneath that layer of reason and sturdy faith wriggled the fear that if she, Anita, were wrong, something horrible would happen to Auntie Meena. Anita couldn't bear the thought. She had to get her aunt out of the house, out of the village, out of the district. She had to think of a way to send Auntie Meena back to Hotel Delite. Anita gripped her aunt's arm tighter on the way to the kitchen. This would require some of her best creative lying.

"Ask me what things?" If Auntie Meena had learned nothing else, it was to be alert and suspicious where Anita was concerned.

* * * * *

Joseph drove into the parking area and pulled up under a banyan tree. The half dozen men lounging on the stone base surrounding it barely wasted a blink of an eye on him, and continued chatting desultorily among themselves.

"This will do," Anita said as she climbed out of the backseat. She didn't bother waiting for Joseph to agree or argue or even ask what they were doing there. He had scowled when she told him they would be heading back to Hotel Delite at once after an errand. He tried to argue, but she cut him off. He was to do as she told him and not argue, so he hunched over the steering wheel and pouted.

Anita headed for the entrance to the Thiruvadnagar Devi Temple. While Prakash was in hiding, and in disgrace, the temple was still functioning, and Anita wanted to know who was fulfilling the duties that had been Prakash's. After all, Devi wasn't going to wait patiently while mere mortals figured out their problems; she expected attention on schedule.

The evening puja was already in progress. The program had included a flower puja, rare but always attracting a large audience. The quantity of flowers to be offered to the deity in a blissful, fragrant shower was determined by the weight of a member of the sponsor's family. Apparently the member of the sponsor's family that had been weighed, in the antique wooden scales now hanging in front of the inner sanctum, for Devi to observe and, everyone hoped, approve, was an infant, Anita reckoned this by the small number of bags of flowers now waiting at the foot of the steps leading into the inner sanctum. The priest, a young man of no more than thirty, perhaps, was busy with the offerings of milk and ghee and water, and the devotees were standing quietly outside, watching and praying. Anita joined a group of women and tried to get a good look at the priest. She hadn't seen this pujari before, but he didn't look like he was new to his duties.

Anita turned away and began to circumambulate the shrine, stopping for brief prayers at smaller shrines to Ganapati and some local deities. Children ran about, devotees came and went, and Anita continued to make her circuit. At a small shrine to a local figure who protected the villagers against a plague some centuries ago, an older man leaning on a cane tossed flowers at the image. He muttered his prayers in a raspy voice, like a needle skipping on an old record; Anita heard the threatening sounds of inelastic lungs. When he was finished he stepped back and bowed.

"A beautiful puja," Anita said. "The pushpanjali puja," she added.

"Not done often enough." He had courtly manners as he leaned on his cane and inclined his head. He moved slowly, probably from pain, but it gave her the impression he was an old-fashioned gentleman who would listen politely, make diplomatic comments, and never be disagreeable no matter how strongly he disagreed.

"He performs the puja with grace," Anita said. "I haven't seen him before. Is he new?"

"Just so." The man nodded once. "Recently come to the position. He inherited from his great-uncle. That is the line for the pujaris here—uncle to nephew."

"He is the main one? Does he have assistants?" To soften her questioning, Anita motioned to the temple walls and buildings around them. "It seems small with many duties, and it is hard to see one man managing everything by himself."

"Indeed. There is a young man who comes for early-morning puja and is a great help. He has asked to take on more responsibility, and it has been given to him. He is proving himself."

"That's the best kind of pujari," Anita said, not knowing if it was true or not; she would have said almost anything to move the conversation along, to keep it going while she whittled her way deeper into the workings of the temple. "Still, it leaves the pujari with a lot of work, managing the women who clean and assist, making sure the prasadam is made properly, all of it."

Again, the man inclined his head. "Temple is adding helpers—so many want to assist. It is service, is it not, to give to Devi?"

189

"Indeed." Anita was the one to nod this time. "You seem to know a great deal about how the temple functions. I was never able to quite grasp the intricacies, but then I never met anyone I could ask." At least that part was the truth, sort of.

"I am not usually here. I live on the other side of the village and there is a small temple nearby. Because of this"—he indicated his infirm leg—"it is easier for me."

"So you have come for the pushpanjali puja."

"In part. Another reason is to see that this pujari gets off to a good start." He offered a thin smile, and the single layer of skin still containing his bones and brain strained with the effort. "We have had some difficulties but all is resolved."

"Ah! There are always difficulties."

"There are lessons here for all of us."

"You sound like you are more closely involved with the temple than as a devotee."

He nodded, this time with an old-world charm at having been identified as someone important. His lack of modesty, instead of offending Anita, as it might have, was in fact charming. His smile warmed, and his eyes softened. "As one of the trustees I am charged with correct administration. It is the lesson for all of us. Do not deviate from the given rules. They have guided us successfully for hundreds of years, and to abandon them now only leads to difficulties. Devi will remind us of our lapses no matter how we rationalize what we have done."

"So the pujari is a correction for an earlier error," Anita said, making sure she got it right. He wasn't going to come right out and tell her what had stained their linen, but he seemed to enjoy pointing obtusely to the guilty items.

"The pujari cannot be anyone but the one in line from the uncle. Choosing another line does not please Devi. And we are not here to please ourselves." He pursed his lips in disapproval of the thought, and dipped his shoulders in emphasis. Apparently finished with the conversation, he began the hard work of turning his body to continue on his circumambulation to the next site of devotion. Anita watched him go, his words about the pujari shouting in her head.

Clearly, there were a few things both Lalita Amma and Valli had neglected to tell her.

Nineteen

Parvati moved through the cooking rooms with a silence that surprised even her. This was done in part for the sake of Vengamma, who fell into deep grief and wailing when she learned late in the day from the guest, the niece to Lalita Amma, that the dead man found in the jungle was Thampi, a man Vengamma had worked with almost her entire life. Her face puckered and pulled, until she could no longer control herself, and she fell into wailing and swinging her arms and rubbing her face with her hands. Even when she calmed herself, pulling the end of her sari over her face again and again, she sounded like she was choking, sputtering, and might even collapse.

Parvati ached for her. She knew how the cook felt, and that only made her feel worse. Every wail from Vengamma echoed in Parvati, and so strong were her feelings that they frightened her. Parvati feared if she fell into despair, she might not come back, might not escape the grip of the real thing, and that would crush her.

He was a good man, Thampi, and Parvati would mourn him also if she could find her feelings, wherever she had buried them. But for the moment, she moved almost stealthily to spare Vengamma the pain of having to notice something outside her own world.

The guest, Anita Amma, was kind in the telling, bringing Parvati to the doorway to help when the time

came, as the guest knew it would, while she spoke with
Lalita Amma and Meena Amma. But pain breaks through
no matter the kindness. It was the rest of it that at first
confused Parvati—the guest's lies. Parvati could see the
surprise in Joseph's face as he listened to Anita Amma, but
he was good at concealing his feelings, and Parvati was
certain she was the only one who caught it. Anita Amma
consoled Lalita Amma and Meena Amma for the loss of
dear Thampi, sitting and listening and comforting. And
then the guest went on.

Anita Amma told the news of trouble elsewhere
only now discovered. But these were lies. There was no
phone call made during their trip to Chengannur, no frantic
tale of trouble at Hotel Delite that required Meena Amma
and Joseph to return at once. Parvati knew it, Joseph knew
it, but Meena Amma and Lalita Amma did not. They were
far too distraught over Thampi's death to catch the shift in
Anita Amma's voice. Only Joseph knew because he had
been with her, and he alone muttered as soon as they
returned how dull a trip it was. Parvati was ordered to
prepare their things for the trip home.

Parvati often knew more than she was expected to.
That was the nature of a servant's life. The visit by the
trustees about Prakash's position at the temple was
supposed to be secret, but she could hear them through the
half-open doors, and though a servant, she still had ears,
she still had a mind, she still could think. Prakash was in
trouble.

He came to her later that night and she probed, but
he wouldn't tell her anything. They are not important, he
insisted. I am entitled to this position—my uncle was once
pujari there—a distant relation, yes, but of the correct
family line. It is a family temple and my family is
connected. It is correct that I am priest there. All this
nonsense about fees and not obeying orders is meaningless.

She listened to him talk, saying the same thing

again, telling her, it's all politics. He insisted it did not matter because he loved her and he had enough money to take them away, far away, to the North, where no one would find her or him, and they could live the life they really wanted. They would have a small house and she would have her garden, where she would grow flowers and vegetables, and lacy trees would shade their terrace where they would sit in the evenings and talk about their day. There would be children and neighbors who called to wish them well. It would be the joy that comes from the ordinary, from the two of them being together.

It scared her when he talked like this because she could feel him getting closer and closer to something deep within her, the little smoking ash of hope from the fire that once burned brightly and warmed her life because she had been a believer. She had offered up her life to Tamil Eelam and the fighters who would give the Tamils their own state within the nation of Sri Lanka. And even though she had not been called on to carry out the work of building a new nation, she had been ready and willing to undertake other work as preparation. She had trained and obeyed, fought and killed, and watched the patch of land that would be Tamil Eelam grow. All that was lost in a massive war to the death, where every person she knew and loved died, either by bullet or by starvation or by torture or by drowning while trying to swim to freedom. All were gone. And gone, too, were the old thoughts she had accepted and nurtured and husbanded for years, waiting to demonstrate once and for all her devotion. Back then she had the hope of a world for people like her, where they farmed and lived in safety.

But the hope turned shabby. One morning, in a moment of silence, perhaps for reloading, perhaps for a tea break, her only surviving family, Rajan, her youngest brother, whispered to her about the other life that was possible, the one they had thought they were building in Tamil Eelam and now knew they would never have. No, she said, she couldn't give up, but he argued. And eventually she felt herself falling, pieces of her drifting away, the beliefs that shackled her to hope loosening and breaking. But unlike Rajan, she saw nothing to fill the emptiness. He went on talking, and she barely listened.

"There is a way. We must take it. The real life for us is elsewhere. It is time to let all this go." His face was earnest, his mind sharper in his understanding of what the future held, though she had five years on him. He was only a teenager, still a boy. Sometimes Prakash seemed even younger than Rajan.

She wouldn't agree. She clung to the dream of Tamil Eelam, the promises they had made, and he countered her at every step. Still, it took him months to persuade her, and only then by taking her back in time to the day when their parents and siblings had walked to the beach to see a particular shaman who was passing through the area. She never knew if the rifle fire that killed her father after he rejected serving the Tamil Tigers was accidental or not, but after that, the Tigers claimed her family one by one, even standing within sight of the cremation of her mother, waiting for them as they left the cremation ground. She and her siblings took up arms, and she learned to believe.

When she at last agreed to Rajan's plan, she half hoped she had taken too long, that it was too late and they would have to stay here. Instead, she found herself on a boat the next night.

She had that same feeling now, the feeling that she had to make a decision about Prakash. Instead of feeling exhilarated at the prospect of once again traveling to safety and a new life, she felt a gnawing fear. To place her trust in anyone frightened her—trusting someone else to save her, guard her, protect her, seemed beyond her emotional capability, and even worse, beyond what was possible. She knew Prakash was lying to her about the temple trustees, that there was something he was not telling her. It was true his family belonged to the same family as the last priest and it was true that fees could be raised only in certain ways at that temple—she had figured those things out over the months here—but there was something he was hiding, and it worried her.

But what worried her most was what she saw in him. He was weak. She could see it in his face, the way he tried to cajole her into seeing things his way, the way he made big promises that were nothing like what he had achieved so far; they were the promises of a small boy fantasizing about his future. His dreams weren't even realistic or honest. When he spoke to her about what they would have together, he spoke for himself. He didn't know her well enough to know that all she wanted was to be able to walk down a lane and not worry about who was coming around the corner, who might push away from the wall at a bus stand and start following her. How could he know what it meant to live knowing that someone would always be looking for you, to claim a life in exchange for a vow that was broken? He was a boy, weak, unknowing, selfish.

The household was full of secret conversations now: the death of Thampi and speculation over how he died, none of which was entirely clear yet to Parvati; the whispered comments about Prakash and his future; the hut Anita Amma found in the woods. That was the one that scared Parvati most of all. Perhaps it wasn't a leopard or a wild dog that had startled the goat outside at night. Perhaps it had been a person.

Parvati sat down on a stool, the dirty dishes in the sink, water dripping from her hands. Rajan would not have told anyone where she was, but he did come here at least once. It was possible someone had followed Rajan—he was stealthy, cautious, well trained, but he was not perfect. He was still young, a long way from combat, perhaps too confident in his new life. It was possible he had grown careless. She would never know. But she did know one thing.

She would have to leave soon. She wasn't safe here.

Twenty

Anita thought hard, worried she had missed something and would be caught out, but everything seemed to be going according to her plan. Auntie Meena was easy to convince to return to Hotel Delite. All Anita had to do was mention Ravi's distant relation showing up and moving into a room, thereby displacing a Dutch family due to arrive the following day, to get Meena revved up to dangerous levels. She would not tolerate the staff's relatives behaving as badly as her own. It was one thing for relations she barely knew she had showing up and demanding free accommodations and then expecting to be waited on hand and foot, but to have the staff's relations doing the same thing! Well, it could not be tolerated.

Auntie Meena treated Anita and the rest of the family to one of her best displays of histrionics entangled with tears for Thampi and her cousin Lalita's sorrow. It was all too much for poor Auntie Meena—almost. She snapped her fingers for the maidservant, ordering Parvati to pack and telling her how to pack. Meena let everyone know that as sad as she was for Thampi and as angry as she was about Ravi's relations, she was still sound and fully in control. Anita hoped Ravi could cope with Meena when she arrived unexpected and unannounced. The unreliable mobile reception out here was turning out to be a blessing in disguise, in Anita's view.

198

Anita was clear in her own mind about her
duplicity, and indeed felt a twinge of guilt that she had
chosen to send Auntie Meena and Joseph away from
danger. Intellectually, Anita knew she should inform
everyone about her suspicions, but her gut told her that in
Lalita Amma's household, there were no innocent parties.
And for that reason alone, Anita would lie to Meena about
why she had to leave Lalita Amma's house. When Anita
thought about what might happen to Auntie Meena, there
was no ambivalence—Meena had to be removed from
danger. Whatever Lalita's family had brought down onto
their heads, Meena was not part of it and Anita would not
let her be harmed.

Anita watched her aunt take leave of Lalita Amma
to go upstairs and supervise Parvati's packing. Anita had to
look away from the disappointment that plainly plagued
both of them. Neither Prakash nor Valli exhibited the same
depth of feeling, even though they had known Thampi all
their lives, been tended and comforted and cared for by him
from birth to adulthood. He had taken them swimming,
made toys for them, taught them to climb palm trees when
no adults were looking, though he wouldn't let them go so
high as to hurt themselves in a fall; he told them stories
about the gods and goddesses, warned them about snakes
and worms that could sting and make you sick and leave
you wracked with pain, and furry worms no bigger than
your little finger that could do the same. He had watched
over them, worried about them, loved them.

Anita couldn't understand the family's reactions to
the news of Thampi's death. They were sad but not grieved.
Valli wept and wiped away the tears, declaring that she'd
miss him. She sighed, wept some more, and wandered over
to her mother, sitting beside her and patting her knee. She
called softly, "Amma, Amma, such sorrow." Valli put her
arm around her mother, offered words of comfort, and after
a while, said she was going to make sure Parvati was

packing correctly. Prakash seemed to find his mother's grief disturbing, worried for her as though she might suddenly split apart and scatter all over the terrazzo floor, but he didn't look particularly sad himself. He shook his head, clucked in sympathy, and sighed heavily.

How was it they had lived with Thampi for so long and this was all that came out of them at the unexpected end of his life? Their reactions took Anita aback, and she knew she'd been right to send Auntie Meena home. Anita was glad she hadn't told anyone in the household how she had found Thampi and what she suspected had been his end.

* * * * *

Anita did not relax until she saw the old Ambassasdor disappear around a corner the following morning, with Auntie Meena in the backseat undoubtedly telling Joseph to watch out for branches, note the bus coming straight at them, miss that puddle. It would be a long and torturous ride for both of them, for different reasons, but Anita felt like an old woman who has learned her last unmarried daughter finally has a suitor. Relief, almost giddy, swept through Anita.

She leaned against the doorjamb savoring the feeling of relief, watching the breeze lift branches of a kadamba tree and the trunk of a coconut palm sway. She didn't want to move, to break the spell of the moment, but she had much to do. A man on a bicycle came slowly up the lane and stopped at the end of the walkway. He climbed off the seat, shifted the bike onto the metal stand, and straightened his mundu. From the basket hanging on the handlebars he pulled a black plastic briefcase and tucked it under his arm. Then he turned and walked straight toward Anita. She greeted him.

"Ah, you are the young one of the household?"

Anita nodded.

"I am sent from the postal office with telegram." He

200

unzipped his case, reached inside, and pulled out a flimsy piece of paper. He handed it to Anita, bowed, and turned around.

"Wait! We are not used to writing letters. When do you think telephone service will be restored?"

"Soon, soon. We all hope it will be soon." He shuffled back to his bicycle. He turned the machine around, retied his white mundu so that it covered the bottom of his pressed white shirt turning yellow with years of washing, and climbed onto the red plastic seat. He gave her one glance, nodded, and let the brakes go. Anita could hear them squeaking as he neared the first turn, holding his bicycle at a sedate pace.

"The young one," he had said. Not a name, just the young one. That would be either Valli or Prakash. Anita held the telegram in her hand, running her fingers along the folded edge, sensing the dampness in the paper that made it feel almost like a piece of fabric. She'd have to give it to one or the other of her cousins, and she would do so as soon as she knew the intended recipient. The delivery man didn't say exactly who that was. It could be for Anita, and indeed it might be for her, something from Hotel Delite sent by a guest frustrated by the lack of phone service out here. Yes, it could very well be something for her from Hotel Delite.

It was a good enough lie, Anita decided. And that's really all she needed. Someday she would work out in her own mind to her own satisfaction the relationship between intent and deed, lying to protect someone and lying to get something one didn't deserve. There was good lying and bad lying, and Anita liked to think the impulse in her to lie always came when she was concerned about someone else, such as Meena or Lalita. It made things seem so much more benign. No, Anita could not hand over this telegram without taking a peek at it.

Anita slipped her nail under the flap, worked it free,

and unfolded the telegram. She read it quickly, then again. She pondered this new information, but as she did so, she had to admit that it fit—it made perfect sense. In time, one or two days from now, she probably would have drawn the conclusion prompted by the information contained here. She reread the simple statement:

"I will come to you. I will do all I can for your brother, but some things even I cannot do. We have been happy. We will be so again. Please. Kumar."

Anita thought back to her first conversation with Valli about what had gone wrong with her marriage. At first Valli's talk was all innuendos. Overt complaints that Kumar had only wanted money from her and her family came later. She made him sound mercenary, calculating and manipulative, and yet here was evidence to the contrary—a love telegram promising a better life. Valli had been lying, but so had Lalita Amma.

Anita folded the telegram and slipped it into her pocket. In a few short hours she had lied to Auntie Meena, lied to Lalita Amma, intercepted a telegram for Valli, and set the remnants of this once-grand family on the path to its reckoning.

* * * * *

Lalita Amma was surrounded by piles of laundry, white sheets and pillowcases sorted into little mounds whose reasons for being Anita could only surmise—some to mend, some to discard, some to bleach, some to give away as still usable but not in this household—she had seen these piles at Hotel Delite, though not so high. Lalita Amma seemed to have emptied every linen cupboard in the estate, pulled sheets off every piece of furniture in the closed wing, stripped every bed.

Parvati squatted on the edge of this puffy white

circle, awaiting further instructions. She watched Amma's eyes move from pile to pile, and seemed to anticipate where the old woman would point next. At the moment that Lalita Amma spoke, Parvati jumped up and grabbed the offending sheet.

This was what Valli was born for—managing an estate, making much of small tasks in order to have no larger ones surprise her or anyone else in the household, overseeing a constantly expanding staff, winning loyalty and duty from people who were once strangers and had now linked their lives to hers, making her husband proud with her ever-increasing competence. This was what Anita had not been born for, and unconsciously Anita had known that even when she and Valli were little girls. And yet, ironically, Anita had come closer to this birthright than Valli had. Anita and some of her duties at Hotel Delite mimicked Lalita Amma's duties on the estate, but Valli had somehow not managed to create the world suited to Anita, the one of the professional woman making her parents proud and marrying late in life.

"It is a dull task," Lalita Amma said when she noticed Anita sizing up the piles of sheets. "But it is a task that must be done." Lalita shrugged and pointed to another pile. After a few more minutes, she directed Parvati to take one pile out to the laundry, and pushed apart several of the remaining piles with her foot. "So much to be done."

"It is good to have Parvati here to help," Anita said. "You were lucky to find her."

Lalita Amma smiled, but not without interest in Anita's comment. "Do you find fault with her? A compliment of a servant usually precedes a complaint." Lalita returned to pushing white mounds apart.

"I didn't mean anything like that, Lalita Amma. I did mean you were fortunate to have someone who fits so well into the household. I know how hard it is when we have to hire someone new at Hotel Delite. Sometimes we get someone who only wants to stir things up." Anita moved to the edge of the room and sat down on the floor. She stretched out her legs and tipped her toes toward her body, then stretched out her arms to her toes. She was feeling lazy these days and neglectful, so when she remembered she hadn't done her yoga she sometimes fell into an asana. "I know you are fond of her, Lalita Amma. I was paying her a compliment."

Lalita Amma grunted and pulled a chair away from a closet door, which she opened; she ran her hands over the empty shelves, perhaps to reassure herself that she hadn't missed anything.

"What happened to Bhogamma? She was here so long, but she is younger than Vengamma, isn't she? I thought she was someone who would stay forever." Anita moved into another yoga position.

"Her daughter married and moved away and Bhogamma could not bear to be parted from her. Her son-in-law is a good man and he was glad to have her come. She lives there now. Somewhere in Idukki." Lalita Amma closed the closet door and opened the next one. The closet was a deep niche cut into the wall, with a wood frame attached to the surrounding plaster; it made the doors and frame seem like a window opening inward, into the room.

"I missed her when we got here." Anita stretched out her legs again and raised her arms straight upward, closing her eyes. She could hear other doors opening, drawers being pulled out, pushed back in. "I remember her being especially fond of Prakash when we were children."

"Ah, yes." Lalita Amma turned to Anita, a khadi sheet hanging from her hands. "She did indulge him, didn't she?" She shook her head and seemed lost in a memory.

"Too bad she couldn't stay." Anita watched the old woman fold the sheet.

"Nothing stays the same. We are given something to use, to learn, then we are to move on. Nothing is static."

Lalita Amma tucked her pallu, the end of her sari, into her waistband, and leaned over to count the sheets in a pile.

"How did Parvati come to be here? Is she related to Bhogamma? I remember your telling me a long time ago how to find servants—relatives and friends, tracing along a line that was known and verifiable." Anita opened her eyes when the silence lengthened. Lalita Amma was standing up staring at her.

"Why do you want to know this?"

Anita recognized the choices facing her. She could respond to the tone in Lalita Amma's voice and back off, apologize in some awkward way for prying, let the other woman think her inept and nosy, or she could lay more of her cards on the table and say, Look, this is what I have— the king is not really a king, the queen is a cypher, and the jack could be dangerous. One choice would put the cards back into the deck, a complete deck of fifty-two cards, nothing missing, all in order; the other would point to the little pinholes in the aces, the torn corner on the kings, all the little marks that said this was not an honest deck of cards.

"Valli doesn't trust her but you do," Anita said.

Lalita Amma snorted—that was how she felt about Anita's observation. "It doesn't matter where she came from. I hired her because I needed her and I liked her. That is enough."

Anita watched her aunt a few more minutes, absorbing the strange realization that her aunt knew exactly what that deck of cards really held.

* * * * *

Anita didn't need any more evidence of Lalita Amma's character and her choices. She was a hard woman because she had to be. But there was something more. Anita thought back to all the seasons she had spent here as a child, the massive freedom she and Valli had enjoyed to follow their curiosity and their own devices. For Anita it was a thrill, all that freedom, but as she watched Lalita Amma and listened to her reminiscences, Anita knew it wasn't an adult who understood the heart of a child—it was a parent who couldn't be bothered with a daughter because the mother was too besotted with her son, Prakash. Lalita Amma gave him everything—her time, her heart, her parental guidance, her devotion. He could do no wrong, and he would always be the only one who mattered.

Lalita Amma cared for little else in this world beyond her son. The times she spent bemoaning her lot in life were only meant as an interlude for entertainment, something to fill the time, and because all good Nayar ladies had offered the same laments for thousands of years. It was part of the culture—the feckless husband, the unexpected poverty thanks to an unkind fate, the child lost to premature death, the war that wrecked the crops and killed the men. This was a woman's lot in life and she could at least make a beautiful lament out of it.

But beneath this, when the song was packed away and the time for play was past, Lalita Amma got down to business. Anita knew this about her aunt: she was a determined, persistent woman, one who set her sights on a particular goal and kept at it until she got it. She picked her battles to win, not to make a point. She meant to restore Prakash to what she regarded as his rightful place.

"I'm curious how much you know about Parvati," Anita said. "I'm used to hearing maidservants spill out their life stories, but Parvati doesn't do that."

Lalita Amma continued to count linens, confident in the belief that her choices were always the right ones; she wouldn't be wrong. If by some strange trick of fate she found she had made a mistake, she could right it.

Twenty-one

"My mother is in one of her moods." Valli leaned across the table and plucked a grape from the cluster sitting in a bowl. Anita had collected them in the kitchen and then gone in search of her cousin, but had not found her in any of the usual places—in her rooms, in one of the upstairs sitting rooms, or on the veranda. Anita stood outside on the stone in her bare feet trying to imagine what she had overlooked when one of the upstairs windows in the closed-off wing flew open. Valli looked out and waved to her.

"What are you doing up there?" Anita called out.

Anita headed for the new wing. A moment later she put the fruit bowl on a low table and looked around the room. She sneezed when Valli blew dust from the marble top of an old Victorian side table. "Are you hiding out up here?"

"Dusty, isn't it? Do you think it's ugly?" Valli studied the table, tipped her head to one side, then the other, as if trying to make up her mind whether or not to keep it, or get rid of it. Apparently bored with the whole thing, she looked around for somewhere to sit, glancing enviously at the settee where Anita reclined, her arms draped over the ornate carved back and her legs stretched out in front.

"Oh," Anita said, sitting up as though she had

remembered something. "This came for you." She reached into her pocket and extracted the telegram. She had managed to reseal it, and then had spent an hour or so idly thinking up an excuse for not delivering it at once. She couldn't find Valli (this was true, but she hadn't looked very hard), got caught up with Valli's mother (this was not really true, since Anita was the one who entangled Lalita Amma), forgot after being distracted by something (what could be that distracting that she'd forget about a telegram?). Anita decided to shrug if Valli asked about the delay, but her cousin sister surprised her by not asking her anything. "Aren't you going to open it?"

"I am sure it isn't important." Valli reached for another grape.

"It came from your husband's town."

"Yes, I see that."

Anita waited while the woody vines were denuded of fruit. She recalled a man who had stayed at Hotel Delite for three months while he underwent various health regimens, including a quit-smoking program. That was the first month, and during the first week she had been told what foods he could eat; the list included grapes. She brought him a bowl of fruit with bananas, papaya, oranges, and grapes the first morning, thinking he would take it to his room and have a piece every now and then throughout the day. Instead, he began to ask her questions about the village nearby, the fishermen whose lights he had seen on the horizon the night before, the other hotels and recommended restaurants. He had Anita working hard to come up with appropriate answers, and when she caught her breath and looked down at the bowl, a single denuded stalk, remnant of the grape cluster, dangled over the other fruit, like a spider claiming the bowl and all its contents. Now Valli was doing the same thing.

"Why did you come home, Valli?" Anita couldn't bring herself to eat any more fruit.

"Didn't I tell you?" Valli looked surprised. "Yes, we talked, didn't we?"

"I think there is more." Anita shifted on the settee, so she could look at Valli directly. "Does it have to do with Prakash?"

"Of course not." Valli pushed away the fruit bowl, and something flashed in her eyes—a warning, perhaps?

"You sounded sad when we first talked, as though you felt your husband had abandoned you, ended the marriage, because he wanted more money from your family." Anita recalled how sorry she felt for Valli, as she would for any woman who discovered that after two years of marriage, of getting to know each other and help each other and be together, her husband didn't really care and never would. Women are told to adapt to what marriage is after the honeymoon, assuming there is one, but how does anyone adapt to a life without regard, without consideration and kindness and, in time, love?

"And I was sad. Of course I was."

"But he didn't send you away, did he?"

"Didn't I say? I'm sure I told you."

"Valli!"

Valli glared, the facade of the sad little wife crawling home for comfort slowly fading, and in its place emerged the crusty look of a woman who had always managed to get what she wanted. She was very much like her mother, though her mother was stronger and more subtle. "All right, if you insist." Valli reached for the telegram and opened it, tearing the flap. She struggled to get the telegram opened, tearing the bottom almost in half. She glanced at it, and instead of rereading it to be sure she understood it, as Anita thought she would, she grunted, folded it once, and crushed it in her hand. "So?"

"We can never know what goes on inside someone else's marriage, and I keep that in mind, especially for my friends and family," Anita said. "I want to think they are happy, that the little tiffs people have are never important, that the marriage is a good one." Anita paused, marveling at her own willed naïveté.

"Yes, well, it doesn't always happen like that, does it?"

"When I met Kumar at the engagement party, I was impressed with him. Something in me said he would be a good husband for whoever he married. I forgot that he would have to have someone who would be a good wife, otherwise how would anyone know what he was capable of?"

"Perhaps to someone else," Valli said, deciding to close the subject.

"He loves you, Valli." The change in Anita's voice caught the other woman's attention. "You were the one who abandoned the marriage, not Kumar."

"And why would I do that?" Valli leaned back and crossed her arms over her chest.

Anita swung her feet to the floor and leaned forward, as though about to engage in a passionate exchange, a discussion on the meaning of life or the newest political movement that would change their circumstances forever. "I have asked myself that question over and over again."

"Really, Anita, I thought you were my friend. I thought your visit would be a comfort to me."

"It would be if you needed comfort."

"Really, Anita!"

"I suppose the question is not why did you leave him but why did you marry him in the first place?" Anita was gratified to hear a little gasp from Valli.

"Amma chose this man."

"I know, so the question is why this man, and why you agreed?"

"Really, Anita. This is too much. You are offending." Valli started to get up.

"Sit, Valli." Anita waited while Valli lowered herself into her chair, her expression that of a child who feared she was going to be scolded. "Kumar was a good catch for anyone," Anita said, "but he was a man who knew whom he wanted to marry. He wasn't someone who would go along with whatever his parents wanted. He knew what he wanted. I could see that at the wedding."

"So? Really, Anita, you make too much of this." Valli flicked away a curl dipping over her right eye, then sniffed.

"You knew each other long before Lalita Amma starting looking for a marriage partner, didn't you?" It was so plain to Anita now that she wondered how she had missed it. The speed with which the negotiations were concluded, the giddy look on Lalita Amma's face when she told Auntie Meena and Anita, the undercurrent of there being more to tell but a smug satisfaction in Lalita Amma that was never explained—till now.

"We met in college and around at various people's homes. We were in the same circle." Valli shrugged, not looking at Anita while she spoke. "There is nothing out of the ordinary in any of it." The word *petulant* came into Anita's mind.

"He was already a trustee of the Thiruvadnagar Devi Temple, wasn't he?"

Valli shrugged, but without much force this time. She was wary now, moving closer to the edge of her seat, as though she had to be ready to jump up and flee when given the opportunity. "For many years."

"With much influence," Anita said.

"I told you that. He extracted donations from us."

Anita shook her head. "Ah, the fatal lie."

The color drained from Valli's face, leaving the whites of her eyes even whiter, her skin gray. "What are you saying?"

"You know what I'm saying." Anita waited. "Will

you say it or shall I?"

"There is nothing to say."

Anita shook her head. She was at that moment when she knew she had the information she wanted and needed, but it came at a cost of her respect for someone she loved. There was that instant when she thought about pulling back, saying to herself that it wasn't her business, let someone else deal with it. But in a nanosecond, the moment passed and she pressed on. It was always the same with her.

She shook her head and sighed. "Oh, Valli, Valli. He was so besotted with you that he would do anything for you, anything, and Lalita Amma knew that. She used it; she extracted from him a guarantee that if she let you marry him, Prakash would take the hereditary place of the pujari at the temple. Kumar knew what that meant, and he swallowed it and said for you he would do it. He didn't ask for money—he merely told Amma how much it would cost in a donation to the temple, and she gladly paid it."

"It is required in our community for the man to provide the marriage gifts, the dowry." Valli was adamant, resentment and entitlement rising in her like bile as she spoke through clenched teeth.

"The gift your family sought was a great violation, Valli." Anita waited, hoping for some sign of remorse from Valli. "But you insisted."

"We are of the same family as the pujaris' line. We have as much right as the others." Valli lifted her chin and avoided looking at Anita as she delivered her statement.

"And when you learned Prakash was in danger of losing his position for some behavior not explained by him to anyone, you left Kumar. What did you tell him? He had not lived up to his half of the bargain?"

Valli jumped up, her hands balled into fists. She closed her eyes and took a deep breath. Anita could see the color flashing across her face, the red of anger, embarrassment, shock and distress. Her face went from

For the Love of Parvati

gray to red to white to red again. She was controlling herself, but just barely. "The temple took our money, and now they are throwing out Prakash. Kumar is a trustee—he is knowing this is coming and he is doing nothing about it!"

"Maybe there's nothing he can do." Anita knew the limits of influence and friendship and connections. Even someone like Kumar would have to bow to public pressure and whatever else the trustees had learned, and they had learned of Prakash's violation of his most basic duties and responsibilities—Valli's brother would be lucky to avoid being arrested for embezzlement.

"What husband abandons his wife's family? It is terrible what he has done to me." Valli trembled with anger, glaring at Anita, who could only look on with amazement at a facet of Valli's character she had never seen before.

* * * * *

Anita listened to Valli banging down the stairs in her bare feet, too worked up to run safely down them and too angry to pay attention to what she was doing; hence the stomping and the odd banging of her fist against a wall as she worked out her anger at each step. Anita leaned back on the settee and looked up at the old ceiling fan that dipped a little too low, cobwebs dangling from each blade.

It was pointless, she knew, to wonder why she hadn't seen this side of Valli before, pointless because Anita knew the answer and hated it. She had loved Valli, a true cousin sister who had used her imagination and great wheedling skills to get whatever she wanted from her parents to make Anita's visits some of the most fun and memorable of her young life. Valli's father took them hither and yon to festivals and cinemas and processions and picnics, ordered servants to make toys that the girls destroyed in a single afternoon, hired jugglers and snake charmers and boys with flutes to entertain them on quiet afternoons. Her visits were more than idyllic—they were

213

privileged and special. But in the end the difference was that Anita knew they were special, out of the ordinary, and would end with adulthood. Valli didn't. She still wanted everything to go her way. She wanted to be special all her life, to live by a different set of rules.

What is wrong with me? Anita thought as she pushed herself off the settee. Here I am visiting a dearly beloved family and ferreting out secrets that will destroy them one by one. Lalita Amma put her son's future ahead of any sense of fairness and honesty, corrupted her daughter's prospective marriage by requiring what was essentially a bribe, and then her son repays her and his sister by violating the trust of the temple and its devotees. Devi will not be happy, that's for sure.

Anita peered out the same window where Valli had leaned out and waved her up to the second floor. It was dark now, dusk long settled into night, pujas begun and completed, cooking fires fading. Supper with the family was going to be uncomfortable at best and downright hostile and unpleasant if anyone said anything.

* * * * *

The night couldn't come fast enough for Anita. She listened to the sounds of Lalita Amma shutting up the house, Parvati at her heels, occasionally Valli calling out to the maidservant about some minor detail, a choli blouse to have mended, a new salwar that needed washing. To an outsider it might have sounded normal, but to Anita, Valli's voice was arch and her words contrived. The sound of their voices engaged in normal activities brought the women a comfort that, however false, must have been desperately needed.

Throughout the entire meal that evening Lalita Amma had looked up from her plate only to glare at Anita. Valli appeared smug, as though she knew something no one else did, as though she really did have command of the situation and Anita was going to be the one who was embarrassed and humiliated. Once again Prakash did not appear.

In her room, in the darkness, Anita drew her legs up and wrapped her arms around her knees; she leaned against the doorjamb, her feet on the cool stone of the balcony. Above her clouds drifted across the waning moon, like rude young men marching in front of an old woman once beautiful who now had to struggle to get a seat on the bus. Anita was glad for the silence, for the softening sounds of a village settling in for the night. But she worried the peace wouldn't last.

When she had passed Prakash in the sitting room earlier in the evening, he had also worn a look of concealing something. She tried to engage him in conversation, but he slipped away, polite but elusive. She had wanted to ask him if he knew anything about the hut she found in the forest. Perhaps he could confirm that Thampi had built it for his period of austerity. But she didn't get the chance.

She had shut off the lights in her room; matches and a candle stood nearby. But she wasn't ready to light the candle yet. If there was someone out there, still interested in this house, Anita wanted to catch a glimpse of him. She half regretted sending Joseph off to Hotel Delite with Auntie Meena until she admitted he would have been of little help. He was getting old, and since he knew a friend's son in the police department, his first reaction to everything was to call him. Unfortunately, the friend's son worked in Ernakulam in a police supplies office.

Anita stood up, locked the door to the veranda, and moved to a window. She wasn't very good at keeping a vigil, since she tended to get bored and fall asleep. She pinched her cheeks, took a few deep breaths, and rubbed her hands over her face. In a few minutes, she thought, she'd be banging her head against the window to keep herself awake. Behind her the windup wall clock ticked, and she heard the spring grind its way to the quarter hour and deliver a wretched tearing to announce fifteen minutes past the hour. It was a wonder these clocks kept going—they all sounded like they were ready to spring their coils and pop their gears right through the glass face. An hour later the same series of sounds had her wondering if she'd been awakened from a sleep or from daydreaming. She stopped wondering and pressed her face against the window, to better see the man moving through the undergrowth.

There was no way for her to be certain it was the same man as on the previous nights, but she couldn't come up with a reason for two different men to be skulking around Lalita Amma's house at this hour. The family didn't have any night guards, something of an oversight Anita now thought.

Anita hurried down the hallway and into the room Auntie Meena had used. She pushed open the door, then the window, and looked down. Where were the village dogs when you needed them? The man didn't seem to notice her, and she couldn't figure out what he was doing. As quietly as possible, she leaned out. To her surprise he was running his fingers and hands over the wooden windows, not the joints. She was about to call out to him when she heard a low growl. She froze. A thousand inchoate thoughts flashed through her mind.

Where was Amma's goat? Where was the animal growling? Nearby? Was this a man we should fear, but what if he's attacked? Do we help anyway? The thoughts rattled on. But the man below wasn't rattled. He pulled from his waist a bag, crouched low, and waited. Anita was mesmerized. When he heard the sound again, he stopped and looked around; she didn't know what he saw or heard down there, but he stopped whatever he had been doing and ran. Where had he gone? What did he want?

Twenty-two

Anita spent a fitful night watching through windows, checking out sounds she had heard all her life that suddenly seemed ominous. But no matter how much she chided herself for overreacting, she kept her vigil, moving from room to room, seeking out creaks and sudden slaps of tree branches against the house, waiting for the telltale crack that told her where to go next. It was the sounds of Prakash's footsteps that awakened her where she lay, on the settee in the front sitting room, her feet resting on a footstool. She didn't know how long she'd been asleep.

"You are either very early or very late." Prakash stood in front of her, his arms akimbo. "Is there a man who has just left?" His eyes twinkled with the prospect of a scandal, and he looked about the room for some evidence he was on the right track.

Anita pushed herself upright and yawned, wiping the strands of hair away from her face, rubbing her cheeks to wake herself up. "No man, Prakash. You know better than that."

"No competition for Anand?" He leaned over and almost leered at her, but he was still too much of the younger brother to go that far.

"You have heard?"

"Poor Meena Amma!" He sat on a nearby low table, pushing aside the old newspapers and a small bowl. "She

217

has so set her heart on choosing the man for you, and now you are throwing spanners and screwdrivers and all manner of tools into her wheels. She ails, but does not dare weep openly." Her sorrow seemed to encourage him. "It is the subject of many conversations with Amma."

Anita could image the two aunts thinking frantically how to thwart Anita's deepening friendship with Anand, trying out strategies on each other and rejecting them for one reason or another. Meena wouldn't risk failure—the plan had to be perfect. "She is checking out his background."

"They all say that." Prakash leaned back and smiled, his hands resting on his thighs as though he was about to stand up. "So it is true? You have chosen him, yes?" His eyes softened, and he looked like the sad-eyed does Anita had seen in the forest as a girl, the soft brown spotted coats glimpsed among the trees, the long neck and graceful turn of the head, with the look of sweet longing in their eyes. They needed to be protected if for no other reason than as a reminder of gentleness in a world that seemed inured to violence.

"You seem to like the idea," Anita said.

"Is not the heart our best guide to the deepest devotion to Devi?" He seemed to be appealing to her to agree with him. This was no longer bantering. Anita smiled as she rearranged her salwar.

"It is a voice that must be heard," she said. Prakash nodded enthusiastically, and for her unexpectedly. "But the heart says many things." She wasn't surprised to see the light dim in his eyes.

"Yes, many things." He started to move away.

"Prakash, wait. I am wondering something. Only a small question, but it has been bothering me."

"Yes, yes, ask. You are my cousin sister." He began to look like the Prakash she had always known.

"The trustees seem very angry about what you have

done." She wasn't surprised to see him stiffen. "But that is not the real question, so please let me continue."

"You are my cousin sister," he said, looking down at the floor. He would stay, against his own desires.

"It seems to me, after visiting your Devi temple, that what they are angry about is your refusal to raise the rates for certain pujas. And you have refused because you already raised the rates without telling anyone, and you were pocketing the extra money." She saw a small shudder, but immediately Prakash stiffened and lifted his chin, perhaps in defiance, perhaps in fear. She had been right. One rise and then another, the devotee had said to her in the temple compound. The trustees hadn't caught on that Prakash was fighting to hide his theft, not protect his independence.

"Why are you saying these things? They are insulting!"

"Stop it, Prakash. You are not a politician. It is me, Anita, you are talking to."

He looked up at her from beneath his thick black eyebrows, and Anita immediately thought of his sister's pout—they were the same, nearly twins in their reactions to bad news or a scolding. "You should not be saying these things." He was starting to whisper.

"But it is true, isn't it?"

"I am a good pujari," he finally said.

"Yes, you were a good pujari, until you got greedy."

"I am not greedy!" He straightened up and repeated this assertion.

Hmm, Anita thought, surprised at the contrast. Yes, he raised the puja prices, but no, he was not greedy. Somewhere in his mind, he was not breaking the rules for money. She mulled the problem over while he glared at her. "How angry are the trustees, Prakash?"

"Angry," he said. "They are taking my position."

Anita restrained herself from pointing out that it

hadn't really been his position to begin with, only something that Valli's besotted suitor and husband had managed to wangle for him, cutting out the rightful candidate. No one was going to emerge from this fiasco untainted.

"Are they so angry they would send a goonda to threaten you or your family?"

"A goonda? From the temple trustees?" Poor Prakash was shocked, and then perplexed. "I am not making enemies in my position. I am having good terms with everyone. Only after the order to raise the prices is there trouble." He sighed. "Then quickly I am sent away to think about this." He paused. "But they are not hating me, I know this."

Yes, Anita thought, as she recalled the trustees' visit. As awkward and uncomfortable as the whole thing was, she recognized the trustees' visit as the usual effort to win concessions, renegotiate positions, save face. She had been surprised at Prakash's intractable positions and his refusal to accept the peace offering. But whether he knew it or not, he had been dismissed.

"I was very surprised," Anita said, "when I realized what you had done. I wondered if the trustees were much more upset than they let on, but truly I don't think so."

"Why did you ask?"

Anita leaned against the settee—it was a hard upholstered piece of furniture, with no cushions to ease her now stiff and sore back. Things were not adding up in the way she thought they would. "I have seen something."

"Yes?" Prakash was curious.

"Three nights I have seen a man, late at night, in the dark, circling the house."

"Here?" Prakash was increasingly perplexed.

"Here. Last night he seemed to be checking the kitchen windows and doors, studying them but not trying to break into them." She paused. "After finding that hut in the woods, and Thampi, well . . ." She was still going over this when she looked up at Prakash. Before her eyes, the curiosity in his expression changed to consternation, thoughtfulness, then abject fear—a transition so clear, it was like watching someone channel surfing through a series of television shows, fragments of emotion flashing through him till his mind settled on terror.

"Three nights since you arrived?" he whispered.

Anita nodded. "You recognize something. I can see it in your eyes. What does it mean to you?"

"Nothing, it means nothing. Why are you mentioning Thampi?"

"Because of the way he died. He was strangled and buried in a hut not far from here." She waited. Prakash's eyes widened. "In the hut we found the same rope that was tied around the wrists of the man who was drowned and washed up farther downstream."

"In the hut?" Prakash was stunned. He repeated her words robotically. He leaned forward, clasping his hands in front of him as he sank into his own private thoughts. All this means something to him, Anita realized.

"Shall I show you?"

* * * * *

Anita led the way through the front door, across the courtyard and onto the narrow path that led into the forest and then to the village. It would be daylight soon—she could hear the temple music in the distance. She flicked on her torch; they veered off the lane and made their way deeper and deeper into the jungle. Every now and then Anita looked over her shoulder to make sure Prakash was still behind her. He had grown moodily, eerily silent, his eyes peering deep into his own thoughts and feelings, glancing up at her when he sensed her looking at him, but otherwise his body moved behind hers while his thoughts wandered elsewhere.

Nagesh had left markings along the trail they had

made on their awkward, stumbling way from the hut to the house the first time, and Anita was relieved to see each one come into view, a reassurance that she could find her way back. As a child, she and Valli had played in the forests, but they had never gone far from the house and servants who watched out for them. The girls had followed paths to the river, another home, a wider path to the village, another to a small, family temple. But she didn't recall veering off into the jungle that clung to the mountains and disappeared up into the sky.

Before the mouth of the opening for the clearing, Anita paused. Prakash came up behind her and lifted his eyebrow in query.

"I am thinking that someone might be here, and we don't know what sort of person this might be." Anita looked to Prakash for a reaction. He had remained somber throughout their walk, and now seemed grim. He took a deep breath.

"Let us go forward." He pushed ahead of Anita and stepped into the clearing. There was the sound of birds startled in the trees seeking safety higher up, fluttering through the leaves, and the echoing of that sound by animals closer to the ground, rustling out of sight among ground cover. But no person emerged, or was sighted fleeing. Anita followed Prakash to the open side of the hut, and watched him as he made the same discoveries she and Nagesh had made.

The villagers had taken Thampi's body away but left the rest of the site intact. No one had rummaged through the meager possessions left behind, but someone had partially filled in the hole that had been Thampi's grave, which meant that Prakash was seeing almost the same site that Anita and Nagesh had come upon. There was very little change. It made Anita shiver, as though she were going to go through the whole horrible experience all over again. Prakash fingered the old clothes, kicked away the rotting banana leaves, glanced at the toothbrush. But then he surprised her.

Prakash crept deeper into the hut and felt along the edges of the leaves sitting on the dirt. He examined each bamboo corner pole, running his fingers over each one, top to bottom. After thinking hard, he went back and dug his hands into the base of each pole.

"We were not quiet coming here," he said.

He was right. They had all but announced their approach with throbbing drums and nagaswarams blaring. Suddenly she felt vulnerable and reckless. She tried to focus on what Prakash was doing, but instead found herself looking over her shoulder, wondering if someone even then was planning an attack on the two of them. She glanced back at Prakash, but he didn't seem worried. After probing the bottom of one of the bamboo poles, he lifted the pole and drew out a small piece of wire from the hollow interior. Satisfied there was nothing more hidden therein, he stood up and showed the wire to Anita.

"What's that for?"

Prakash stared at it, holding it between thumb and forefinger, as though it were precious, a special match to light the lamps for an aarti for the deity. When he again looked at Anita, his face was grave. "I think we should go back now."

* * * * *

If Anita hadn't been so caught up by her own feelings, as she later told Auntie Meena, she might have realized that Prakash's reaction wasn't the least bit normal. He said nothing, offered no speculation, no wondering, no questions to Anita about how she found the hut, why she was looking for it, what she thought it meant. He said nothing. He held the piece of wire tightly as he led the way back to the house.

When she looked back over his behavior and hers, she tried not to believe she could have changed the outcome. That was the only rational way to look at a crisis that had been building for years. But to learn only too late something that might have made a difference in a deadly time would always leave her aching for a second chance, ruing the moment she didn't pay attention and, because of that, lives were lost.

At the time, as they pulled out of the hut and took the path back to the house Anita thought only that Prakash was as unsettled as she was. She tried not to use the word *fearful,* but that's what it was. She assumed he felt as unnerved as she did because they were vulnerable and unprotected out in the forest. If something happened to them at that moment, no one would know. It would be hours before anyone started searching for them, and this wouldn't be the first place they looked.

* * * * *

"I want you to tell me what you know about that hut." Anita confronted Prakash as soon as they came through the front door. "I sent Auntie Meena home because I was worried about her. I didn't want her to be part of some terrible act of revenge against your family by a goonda. I don't know who sent that man, the one stalking the house, but when I saw someone three nights running and then I found the hut and Thampi's body, well, I had to get her away from here. You must tell me what is going on."

Prakash let her speak, staring at her with blank eyes, occasionally turning aside, as though he were a child undergoing a scolding and wanted to get away.

"I don't know who that man is." Prakash spoke simply, without intonation. "But he won't stay here, I can tell you that."

"That's not an answer, Prakash. This man, whoever he is, is a danger to your family. Do you think you can ignore this?"

"No. My family is not in danger from anyone out there. I assure you of that."

Oddly enough, Anita had the feeling that Prakash believed he was telling the truth.

Twenty-three

It took Anita most of the morning to arrange what she wanted in the village. The police constable had been visibly suspicious, and she could hardly blame him. Even to her own ears, she sounded like a hysterical woman seeking male reassurance. But he pursed his lips, gave her his usual long-suffering look, and pointed her to an agent who supplied Gurkhas and others as guards.

The trend for buying and keeping dogs to roam one's walled property at night had not yet reached here, mostly because many of the village homes and estates had no compound walls, or had walls so scattered and broken that the dog couldn't be relied upon to stay nearby and do his duty. Anita thought the idea of hired guards was a good idea, at least in the short term, and sought out the agent.

Anita returned to her aunt Lalita's estate with a man willing to guard the house during the day, and remain at his post until his relief arrived near dusk. Between the two of them, Anita felt, the household would be amply warned if the unidentified man approached. The guards were armed with lathis and whistles, and even though Anita sometimes thought this charmingly naive, she didn't question their bravery.

They were Gurkhas, down from Nepal, making a living as best they could as security guards here and there. Despite their short stature and sweet open faces, the

Gurkhas were famous for having met the British as equals
on the battlefield; they were renowned fighters. Anita
hoped that was still true. After much bowing and nodding
and examining the house, the first Gurkha settled in on the
veranda, turning his head this way and that, like a turret,
and occasionally rising to walk the perimeter of the house
and get to know the area. She saw his wide brown eyes
peering up at the second floor, his lathi checking doors and
windows, his keen hearing at work all the time.

"Who is that man?" Lalita Amma grabbed Anita in
the entryway, her strong bony fingers belying her age and
apparent frailty. "What is he doing here?" The old woman
repeated the question at least six times before Anita could
maneuver her into the living room. "Tell me now. What has
happened to you, Anita? You were such a sweet girl."

It was the inevitable lament—how had Anita gone
so wrong when she had started out as such a sweet girl?
Poor Auntie Meena, what she had to put up with. Anita had
heard it all. It was right up there with the buzzing of
mosquitoes and constant whooshing of the ceiling fan.

"I hired him to watch over the house and someone
else to be here for the night shift. It is necessary, Lalita
Amma." Anita managed to pull her aunt to the settee and
nudge her to sit down.

"This is nonsense."

"I believe it is a serious matter. I have three times
seen a man at night skulking about the house, and I think I
have seen him in the village also. I think it is the same man.
He is living there but not working. No one knows what he
is doing. He says he is looking for work, but he has turned
down work that is suitable for him."

"It is nonsense. Why would such a man come
here?"

"He is a goonda. I don't know who has sent him. I
thought perhaps one of the trustees, but Prakash says no,
they are not that angry with him. I asked if Kumar might be

the one."

Lalita Amma gasped and at once covered her mouth with her hands. "No, never. He worships Valli."

"Yes, I know." Anita tried not to pull a face, but the lies that Valli had told about Kumar and her marital situation still rankled. Anita had been grossly misled and wouldn't easily forget it. "So, not the temple, not Kumar." Anita studied Lalita Amma, and knew the kind of outrage she was capable of. "Is there something you have not told me?" Uh-oh, Anita thought, here it comes.

"You are not the child of my cousin sister! You are not a true Nayar. You are acting like a foreigner! What sort of girl talks this way to her elders. You have the tongue of a cobra and the morals of politician, and the—" Anita cut her off in mid flow, knowing that next came a diatribe against her father being "foreign" and a kidnapper for taking her mother away to America.

"So, there is nothing you want to tell me?" Anita slipped in her question while her aunt was catching her breath.

"I forbid you to do any more of this. I will call your aunt to send the car for you." Lalita Amma managed to get to her feet, shaking and flushed with rage, and marched out of the room. Anita forbore from pointing out that there was no telephone service out here at the moment, and Joseph was unlikely to leave the hotel at the drop of a hat, since he was almost always engaged in driving guests around southern Kerala.

"Well, that was a bust." Anita leaned back in the settee, draping her arms over the back and side, stretching out her legs. So, no one in the household can possibly imagine a reason for any of this, but when asked, Prakash went dead silent and Lalita Amma exploded in rage. Both know something, Anita concluded, but did they know the same thing? Were they reacting for the same reasons? I would hate to have to abandon Occam's Razor, Anita thought; complications are so, well, complicated.

A cup of tea seemed in order after all that emotion, and Anita headed for the kitchen.

* * * * *

"Parvati! Ivite undoo?" Anita poked through the cooking rooms, calling for the maidservant. "Aar illa?"

Vengamma had headed into the village for her morning shopping some time ago and had not yet returned. Anita had seen her haggling with a man over the cost of a cabbage, her cloth bag already filled with small onions, carrots, ladies' fingers, and ginger. Lunch would probably include carrot and cabbage thoren, a favorite of Anita's (and probably the last time Anita would get to eat anything she liked if Vengamma heard about Lalita Amma's flare-up).

Anita stepped out into the backyard and caught sight of Parvati coming around the corner. "Ah! Parvati!"

The maidservant seemed surprised to see Anita, but recovered herself, smiled, and offered to make tea at once. Anita looked down at the other woman's hands held a few inches away from her mundu. Parvati's fingers were covered in clumps of dirt, and her nails were especially dirty as though she had been digging in the dirt with her hands.

The first thought that came into Anita's mind was that Parvati had been working in the vegetable garden, but Anita recalled at once that the garden had been destroyed by the monsoon. It would be some weeks before anything started to break through the soil again there. Had Parvati been at the hut? Was she the reason Anita felt someone watching her and the young guide, waiting for them to leave? Had Parvati buried something out there? Was she the reason Prakash knew to search the bamboo poles? And what about Thampi? Had he come upon her out there and asked too many questions? Parvati passed Anita and hurried into the kitchen.

The tea was soon steeping in a pot, and Parvati arranged a tea tray with cup and saucer, sugar and creamer, and added a plate of biscuits. Parvati had made the tea as a foreigner would have it—each element separate, leaving it to Anita to mix it as she preferred. Anita glanced up at the clock. Time for elevenses. Parvati took the tray into the sitting room and Anita followed. The little sound the two of them made echoed in the room, and reminded Anita that after less than a week, she had managed to alienate everyone in this once-loving family—Lalita, Prakash, Valli, and probably Vengamma too. The cook was very loyal to her employer. Parvati placed the tray on a table and backed away.

"Thank you, Parvati." Anita turned the tray to her and sat down. "Did you see the Gurkha outside?"

Parvati waggled her head to say, yes, she had.

"I think there is danger to someone in the household." Anita picked up the teapot and poured the dark tea into the cup. She was pleased that nothing spilled. It was an old porcelain pot of many years' use and purchased because it would not spill or waste tea. "I have hired the Gurkhas to patrol here for our safety."

"Yes, Amma." Parvati's glance went again to the kitchen area, so Anita thanked her and watched her disappear. Since Vengamma hadn't yet returned, it was up to Parvati to begin the preparations for lunch—perhaps grinding rice for parathas or cleaning and boiling the rice.

Anita sipped her tea and worried about what she should do next. She had placed her trust in the Gurkhas and was having trouble letting go of her worries and trusting others. She sighed, closed her eyes, and offered a prayer to Shiva.

* * * * *

The cooling breeze lifted and fell and rose again. Anita felt it wafting over her body in distinctive waves, each one like a separate being caressing her in its own special way. She lay there getting hotter and hotter, the sweat forming on her brow, little beads of perspiration sliding down her back. Time to move, she decided. I have napped long enough. She opened her eyes and sat up.

"I was wondering when you'd notice." Lalita Amma stood over her, arms akimbo, a stern look on her face. Anita idly wondered if her aunt had always been like this and Anita simply hadn't had reason to notice before. Lalita Amma seemed to have become more than stern— more than curmudgeonly and demanding.

"Ah, Lalita Amma." Anita tried to offer the appropriate smile.

"Hah!"

Oh, dear, Anita thought. One of those days. "You are upset, isn't it?"

"About these Gurkhas. Why are you spending my money on this foolishness?"

"Do not worry, Lalita Amma. I am paying for this, for my peace of mind." Anita tried to be soothing with a wave of her hand and a genial look while she wondered where she'd get the money. She had conveniently ignored that question when she'd hired them, thinking more of safety than cost. Anita often made that mistake, since she had no money to speak of and couldn't bring herself to make an effort to get any. She sold a few photographs every now and then and earned a little for her assistance at Hotel Delite, but the desire to earn a lot of money failed to grow in her, much to the disgust of her relatives. "Not to worry, Amma."

"Why should I have such a team even if I don't have to pay for it?"

"Well, for one thing, Thampi is no longer here."

"Ah, Thampi." Lalita Amma sagged with sorrow, but soon recovered herself. "He wasn't much of a guard. A good worker, but I never thought of him as a guard. He did not think of himself as a guard."

231

That was probably true, Anita tacitly agreed. He was getting older and older, and while he might have been able to drive off a gaggle of mischievous boys and perhaps a pair of beggars, that was merely part of the play of village life. The boys expected to be driven off and enjoyed the game of annoying the old man. And the beggars were only doing their duty of asking at every house, knowing that one or two patrons would take care of them for the day and which householders those were.

Anita wondered if she should explain herself. Should she tell what she suspected, what she had seen and heard and now worried about? Or should she try to manage the situation as discreetly as possible, with Prakash's help, until she could enlist the police in the morning? Anita hated drama of any kind, and alarming Lalita Amma and Valli would certainly mean drama of an unpleasant sort. But if Anita didn't tell them, it might mean drama of an even worse kind later on. The whole atmosphere here felt so unsafe and unpredictable.

"Amma, please, come sit with me. I am wanting to talk." Anita patted the settee and moved to the side to make room.

Lalita Amma arched an eyebrow, made it clear that she was willing to indulge Anita for a moment but no longer, and sat down, her legs crossed at the ankles, and her hands clasped tightly in her lap. When the old woman was composed, she turned to Anita and gave a barely perceptible nod. Anita began her tale.

Lalita Amma's expressions were a map of Anita's discoveries of the last several days—Valli's duplicity about her marriage and its origins; Kumar's message of passion and devotion, Prakash's predicament at the temple, his mendacity and his strange reaction to the finding of the hut and its contents; Anita's own fears and concerns for Auntie Meena's safety; and now Anita's anxiousness to be through the night and off to the police in the morning when she knew the divisional inspector would visit, someone who would perhaps take her more seriously. Lalita Amma's expressions went through irritation, anger, embarrassment, hurt, surprise, shock, and shame. But she was Lalita Amma, and she had coped with as much over her long life.

"You may not believe me," Anita concluded. "But these are my thoughts after all I have found since my arrival. This person, whoever he is, is persistent. It may seem foolish, but I am hoping you and Valli will lock your bedroom doors when you retire tonight."

Lalita Amma gave no indication of her feelings about that suggestion, She rose, nodded to Anita, and left the room—but Anita was relieved later that night to hear the tumblers in the bedroom doors click and iron bolts slide into place.

* * * * *

At close to midnight, Anita was restless and edgy. She paced the upstairs hallway, jiggled the doorknob to the closed wing to make sure it was still locked, and wandered back to her own room. In the deep stillness, she listened and stared out the window into the darkness. Just as she was about to turn away from the window, she heard something in the jungle. A moment later she watched the muscular figure of the Gurkha in his khakis with his lathi swinging by his side circle the house. She listened to his footsteps as he crossed the veranda, turned the corner at the far end of the house, and approached the cooking wing. She heard a pebble skitter across the yard, pinging a clay pot or perhaps the stone wall. His footsteps faded.

She didn't know how long she stood there, listening, waiting, trying to stay awake. She had somehow gotten it into her head that if she could stay awake all night, she could get the help she needed in the morning, and that included persuading Lalita Amma, Valli, and Prakash that she was not a hysterical cousin with an overactive imagination. She would get them out of the house and into

Chengannur or some other place where they would be safe until she could figure this thing out or persuade the police to take over.

Whenever she told herself she was being hysterical and that the constable's skepticism was valid, the image of Thampi's body flashed in front of her. The sound of someone moving through the brush brought her back to the front of the house, where the Gurkha was once again passing. Shivayashivoo, she was glad he was here.

Anita yawned. Perhaps his being here was why she was having so much trouble staying awake. She was beginning to feel safe again. She raised her arms above her head and stretched, rising on her toes, reaching to the top of the doorjamb, then pressing her hands flat against the sides, pushing as hard as she could, relaxing, then pushing again. She reached her arms out in front of her, held them tight, then relaxed. She lowered her arms and took a few deep breaths.

The night air was cool. A blessing, really. The monsoon was winding down, and soon life would return to something more normal. She knew people down on the plains and farther south were suffering with the mugginess and the unseasonable heat. Kerala was changing along with the climate. Flowers like the konnapu that should bloom in the spring, in April and May, for the holiday Vishu popped out bright yellow and pink last year in the middle of January. She didn't know what people would do if they had no konnapu for Vishu; they'd have to use something else. But it wouldn't be the same. Vishu called for konnapu, not champaka blossoms or thetti or anything else. The world was out of whack, and the gods would grumble.

Anita braced her hands on her hips and stretched again. It was good to feel alive and energized. The morning would come soon, and with it safety. Everyone in the family was leaving—everyone, whether they wanted to or not. She peered down into the courtyard. Soon the Gurkha

would pass by, the mere sight of him, his cheerful face and
iron limbs, an inspiration for anyone who knew their
history. She waited.

Anita had timed his circuits. She knew how long
one took, what his variations were. He should be here by
now. Curious, she stepped out onto the balcony and walked
its length, looking down, listening, waiting. Nothing. The
night was still. More than still. Everything in the forest had
gone to ground. The night creatures were hiding. The
Gurkha was missing, and the other creatures knew it.

Anita backed away from the parapet and into her
room. She closed and locked all the windows and doors,
and stood in the blackness, trying to catch her breath. The
Gurkha was gone.

The downstairs inside shutters squeaked only once
before she lifted them to swing over the rusted spots and let
her peer out. Anita went from window to window like this,
until she reached the window in the storage room. She
looked out and saw a body sprawled in the dirt.
Thoughtlessly, stupidly she later admitted to herself, she
threw open the kitchen door and ran to him. She pressed
her fingers to his neck, feeling for a pulse, but yanked her
hand away—her fingers were wet and sticky. In the barest
of light from the open kitchen door she could see the line of
blood and crushed skin circling his neck like a ruby
necklace. Swallowing an inchoate protest, she fled back
into the kitchen.

Twenty-four

Anita leaned against the thick wooden door. She had to think fast. She looked around her, expecting to see Parvati come to see what was going on, but no one came. Anita pushed open the doors to the other kitchen rooms, but there was no sign of the maidservant. The straw for the goat was untouched, the bowl still full of water. Where was Parvati?

Anita ran through the house, through the sitting room and across the hall to the other wing. To her surprise, the door was unlocked. She ran up the stairs. Hadn't she heard the sound of what she thought were footsteps of the Gurkha? But they had been coming from the wrong place to match the moment she saw him. She thought there was something odd, but when she saw the guard, she felt reassured and put it out of her mind. Anita ran across the upstairs room to the window. It was open. The interior shutter moved slightly in the breeze. Anita leaned out the window. The vine hung loose from the wall and was torn away at the bottom. Someone had already come in or gone out—yes, gone out and down to the ground—by the vine. Anita locked the shutters and ran back to the main house.

Surely Parvati hadn't killed the guard, had she?

Prakash was the one who knew what was going on. Anita banged on his bedroom door and banged again till he opened it.

"The Gurkha has been murdered and Parvati is gone. Now you will tell me what is going on." Anita pushed him into the room and grabbed at his shirt. "We have no weapons and someone is out there meaning to do one of us harm. Who is it?"

"Parvati is gone?"

Anita was not prepared for the anguish on Prakash's face. "What is this about?" she pressed, but he ignored her and pushed past her. Anita followed him down to the kitchen rooms. His shouts to Parvati echoed through the house, getting louder and louder as he searched room after room and did not find her. He began to tremble, his eyes wild as he came to understand that she was gone.

"She's not here!" he said to no one in particular. "She's not here. She is gone." Helpless, he stumbled into the middle of the last kitchen room and stared at the counters and shelves and large water pots sitting on the floor. "Where has she gone?"

The sound of his voice died down and Anita touched his arm. But as she did so, a scratching sound came from outside the door. The goat, Anita thought, left out to fend for itself. It must be terrified alone out there, in the jungle at night.

"Parvati! She's come back!" Prakash pulled open the door.

It wasn't Parvati. It wasn't the goat.

Twenty-five

"Who's that man? What is he doing here?"

It was true, Anita thought. Time does slow down. The universe has unseen powers that manifest when we can do nothing—not think, not rationalize, not escape. It's like tumbling through the sky and landing on cloud after cloud, floating and falling and floating and falling, while the mind is outside watching, alarmed and impotent and swept along.

Anita turned around at the sound of Lalita Amma's voice. The old woman stood in the doorway with Valli clutching her arm and peeking out from behind her mother, only Valli was too old to be holding on like a six-year-old.

Yes, thought Anita, who is that man? She turned back to the open doorway and there he was, still there, his hands holding a bundle. Each movement of an arm, a finger had the slow-motion beauty of a ballet of lovers meeting and separating and searching and meeting once again. But his bundle lacked beauty.

Lalita Amma's voice came again, like a fading call from a train moving far away down the track. And there was Prakash, the train moving forward, he too with limbs too slow but graceful, purposeful, stretching and reaching. It was dark in the kitchen and the voices came out of the blackness.

"Parvati! Close that door!" Again, Lalita Amma's voice. It was always her voice, Anita thought, always through the years the old woman's voice calling them,

238

ordering them, cajoling, scolding, loving, laughing, managing them as they moved year to year into adulthood.

Parvati is gone, Anita thought. But no one seems to know that. Gone, out the window and down the vine, like a Rapunzel no longer willing to wait, taking her life into her own hands, waiting for no one. That was the sound Anita had heard, a sound out of sync with the guard and the house, the sound of Parvati escaping, fleeing the household that loved her. Why would she do such a thing?

But life can't drag forever. As soon as these thoughts clicked into place, the swirl of real time wrapped around Anita and she knew she was too late.

Prakash let out a howl of rage and anguish and with his hands like claws dove for the stranger.

"You!" he cried out. "You cannot have my Parvati!"

Anita couldn't reach the door in time—instinct, not reason, told her this—and she turned and threw herself onto Lalita Amma and Valli. Anita knocked them sideways onto the floor in the dining room, propelled in part by the blast, which knocked the kitchen door off its hinges and shattered the wood, ripped out the doorjamb and pulverized the sunbaked bricks lining the washing basin. The pots and pans rattled and spilled off the shelves; a jar shattered when it hit the floor, sending cardamom seeds everywhere.

* * * * *

Anita was the first to recover. Her head ached, her back hurt, her feet burned, and something was wrapped around her head blowing in her ears. She rolled over onto her back and looked up—a stain shaped like a tamarind pod hovered over her. She closed her eyes and lifted her hand to her head—she felt her hair, her forehead, lowered her hand to rest at her waist, then rolled over onto her side and pushed herself upright. Lalita Amma groaned. Valli lay on her back and stared up with vacant eyes—her head was resting in a pool of dark blood. Anita crawled over to her.

"Valli!" Anita called softly. Something flickered in her cousin's eyes. Anita called again, and Valli's eyes searched for the sound of the voice. Anita leaned over her cousin and called again. Valli's eyes filled with pain. "It's all right. We are going to hospital. Hold Amma's hand and stay with her."

Anita reached for Lalita Amma's hand, and watched the old woman turn on her side to face her daughter. Lalita stretched her hand out to rub her child's face and call Valli's name. Anita could hear them murmuring to each other as she crawled into the kitchen. She stopped in the middle of the room—glass and spices and pots and pans and old newspapers littered the floor. But there, in her path, was something else—a finger. No, a toe. No, she wasn't sure. A digit, yes.

Anita stopped crawling and sat back. She would have to wait. She stared at the floor wondering how the digit got there and thought only that she was waiting. Her thoughts would not come together. After a while, she couldn't think what she was waiting for, only that she was waiting. Later, she could not have said how long she sat there, listening to the quiet moaning and murmuring of the two women nearby, smelling the charred flesh in front of her, only that she sat and waited and forgot what she was waiting for.

Twenty-six

The screaming seemed to go on and on and on, swirling around Anita like a wind raising the warning of a storm, a flame reaching for the bit of cloth dangling nearby—the insane scream of mutilation and death. Anita saw a man and woman carrying Lalita Amma deeper into the house, and the screaming went also. Hands stroked Anita's face, and she felt herself lifted from the floor and carried into another room. She was laid down on a mat spread out on the floor. But she had seen them.

Through what was left of the back door dozens of men and women, villagers who must have heard the blast, gathered in the dark, their lanterns splashing bits of light over the nightmare scene—bodies torn in half, pools of blood and twisted limbs, splintered wood and bricks turned to dust again. They carried Anita, Lalita Amma, and Valli to safety and quiet, hovered while an ayurvedic doctor poked and prodded and pronounced the necessary. The screams and wails came and went, like cloudbursts, and beneath them the steady whimpering. Anita wasn't sure which woman was responsible for which sound.

Anita began to recognize faces. Each time she awoke, the same faced dipped closer to her. There were those faces again, smiling down at her, calling her name. "Can you hear me? Can you feel this?" Somewhere there was a sharp pain, but Anita wasn't sure if it was hers or

241

someone else's. Perhaps she was borrowing someone's body while her own slept. She couldn't resist the pull down into the dark blankness. And then there was that face again, and here was another one. Really, so many faces with so many questions, and random pain floating in the air around her, looking for a place to lodge. And then that jolting and swinging and the stars in the night sky. Why was she moving through the night?

Twenty-seven

"You have been concussed. You must be very careful." The doctor peered at Anita with a worried expression. She slid her feet into her sandals, thanked the doctor for all his assistance, and headed down the corridor. She would have to get a ride back to the house. She barely felt able to walk. As it happened, the police inspector found a driver to take her—after he quizzed her for at least an hour. She had never said "I don't know" so many times in her life—and actually meant it.

"And where is the maidservant Parvati?"

"I don't know. She wasn't there last night. She disappeared."

"When was the last time you are seeing her?"

Anita thought back to the previous afternoon, or was it the day before that? Parvati had been digging in the garden, but now that Anita thought about it again, there was no garden. What had Parvati been doing? "She made tea for me."

"Yes, yes."

Anita went over the previous day's events.

"Parvati is illegal. You are knowing this?" the inspector said.

Anita had to think—thinking was rather hard right now—she felt like she was slogging through a swamp, a very thick swamp. "I don't remember."

243

"Hmm. Well, she is illegal. From Sri Lanka. Tamil."

"Oh." Did she know that? She couldn't remember.

"Belonging to Tamil Eelam. Freedom fighter fleeing."

"Oh."

"I see you are not understanding."

Not understanding, thought Anita. What was it she wasn't understanding?

"Flight is not forgiven. Never. Not even after Tamil Eelam is no more."

"Tamil Eelam," Anita repeated. "I thought the Sri Lankan government finally wiped them out."

"Hmm." The inspector sighed and looked over at the constable, shook his head, and sighed again. "I am saying this. Never forgiven. This man who came here, the one with the bomb—he is a Tamil Tiger, one of a few left. We are knowing this. Did you know this man? His job is to hunt down anyone who abandons the cause of Tamil Eelam, the nation of Tamils within the nation of Sri Lanka. Where has this Parvati gone?"

"I don't know. She disappeared."

"Ah, I see."

They sat there in silence for what seemed a long time. Anita wondered if she had fallen asleep. The next thing she knew, the inspector had a car for her and someone to take her back to the house for a quick viewing, but not for staying.

* * * * *

It couldn't be real. Anita kept telling herself this. The minute she stepped onto the veranda, the smell, the feeling in the air was as strong as a glass wall, and she almost fell over backward as she sensed the deaths of last night pressing against her. She walked to the front door. It was still unlocked, and she looked around for the villager who had promised to stay and guard the house until the carpenters could show up. She found him asleep in a corner of the veranda, dossed down on a towel, his sandals strewn nearby. She didn't bother to wake him.

The front door fell open to her touch, and the smell of burnt wood and flesh greeted her. She thought she'd retch but she didn't. Instead, she walked directly to the kitchen rooms. To her surprise, they were as she remembered from the night before: the hole that was the doorway, the shattered wood and plaster and glass jars, the pots and pans and food spilled and thrown and ground into the floor where rescuers had walked.

The bodies of Prakash and the stranger were gone, but Anita knew what that meant. Someone or several someones had spent hours in the darkness with only kerosene lanterns picking through the damage to collect the limbs and remove them. But they would have missed some, and Anita braced herself for what was to come. She walked through the doorway, and the stench grew stronger. The cleared path through the doorway, across the yard, and into the jungle showed where the villagers had worked in the night, but in daylight Anita could see what they could see not in the near-total darkness.

She rummaged along the edge of the yard and salvaged an old kitchen cloth, its blue border unraveling with age. She tied the corners together to make a sack and slipped it over her arm, then she walked slowly among the trees and shrubs, looking and finding, looking and finding, pieces of flesh. She used leaves to pick up the small pieces, and sticks to chivvy larger ones along till she found a piece of wood to use. She wouldn't look at the collection growing and weighing down her arm. But she would not leave this job for anyone else, or the flesh for wild animals to find.

It couldn't be real. Anita kept telling herself this. A man had not come to the kitchen door with a bomb and blown her cousin brother to bits, killing both of them, and nearly destroying Anita, Lalita Amma, and Valli. But he had. And he had done so because of Parvati. So obvious now. A stranger looking for a stranger.

Parvati was gone. She knew what this man was about, and she had fled. No one had seen her, no one knew where she had gone, and no one knew why she had come here. But Prakash had thrown himself at the stranger in a deranged act of protection for a woman who wasn't even here.

Anita walked across the yard and lifted her eyes to the deepening blue of the sky and the setting sun. She heard something move in the undergrowth nearby and turned to track the sound—more rustling, a squawk or bleat or something. Anita moved closer to the undergrowth.

The goat broke cover and stumbled towards her, limping, bleating halfheartedly it seemed, until Anita saw its neck and flanks. She reached for the rope still dangling around its neck and drew the animal into the yard. Long thick claw marks ran along both sides of its round body, a thick gash ran beneath its neck, its chest was coated in blood.

"Ayoo." Anita knelt beside it and ran her hands over the gashes. The goat flinched and tried to jump away, then bleated louder.

"Ayoo, Amma!" The villager guarding the door, apparently awakened by the sound of the goat's bleating, hurried up behind Anita. He slapped his hands over his mouth and bent over to look at the woebegone creature. "Claw marks. Ayoo! Such a lucky animal—escaping a leopard. Ayoo!"

He was right. Those were claw marks, and the goat had escaped. Anita had wondered about the goat last night when she came into the kitchen. No Parvati and no goat. Anita knelt down again and the goat lowered its head, looking pathetic. She ran her hands gently over the claw marks. The only thing that could have saved the goat last

night was the explosion—terrifying everyone and
everything that heard it. The goat could not have been far
from the yard. The leopard would have felt the blast just as
Anita and the others had.

"You are here and you are safe." Anita rested her
forehead on the back of the animal; tears streamed down
her face.

* * * * *

A week later Anita found herself arguing again with Valli.
Valli didn't want to go, but Anita decided that now was the
time for Valli to grow up. Anita put her hands on her
cousin sister's shoulders and told her in no uncertain terms
that cousin sisters did not lie to each other, and a woman
lucky enough to have a husband who would sacrifice his
own good name for her should no longer get away with
being so foolish and playing on his devotion to her. Valli
didn't deserve Kumar, and if she continued to spoil her life,
he would figure out there were other ways to live, and other
people to live with.

Valli tried every excuse possible, but Anita would
have none of it. She pushed Valli into the back of Kumar's
car and sent her away. Lalita Amma was a different matter.
But Anita managed that too—a relative near Kochi begged
to care for Lalita Amma, and Anita was glad to have her
aunt go there after Prakash's cremation. Anita put her aunt
in a car and prayed no one would let Lalita Amma see a
newspaper or answer the telephone for at least three
months. By that time, some other scandal would take up
everyone's interest, and Lalita Amma would never know
what people were saying about the violent death of a
favored son, the whispered stories about the good family
ruined because one cheated Devi, the centuries of karma
taking over the present, and the disobedient Valli who
abandoned a good husband.

* * * * *

"A few words, madam." The young woman dogged Anita's

steps as she hurried back to the small homestay, the private home that occasionally rented rooms to tourists. She had remained behind long enough to close up the house, answer even more questions from the police, and arrange a car to take her back to Hotel Delite. The kitchen rooms were heavily damaged, but the rest of the house was untouched. But it hardly mattered. The family would never live there again.

"There are no more words." Anita was growing exasperated. The journalist had been following her around for over a week now and was persistent to the point of being annoying. She didn't know the proper name of the village and confused the panchayat leadership with the temple trustees.

"It is being said this was the only way he could bring an end to the scandal." The journalist stuck a microphone in Anita's face.

"That is nonsense."

"It is being said that funds are missing. Have you found them?"

"No one except you has said anything to me about funds going missing," Anita said. "And by now, if they were out there, someone would have found them. The entire village has been scouring the property looking for more terrorists and the missing maidservant, thinking she might be lying dead somewhere."

"And what have they found? The people have a right to know this."

"Nothing, they have found nothing." Only a little hole in the ground, Anita thought. She recalled the dismissive look on the worker's face when he showed it to her, telling her it was for a fence post that was never put in place. It didn't occur to him that no one would have any reason to put up a fence post at that spot. But there it was— a hole beside a tree, two feet down, deep and narrow and recent.

"What do you think happened to the money?" the journalist asked.

"I have no information about any money going missing." Anita spun around to face her. "I will tell you this." The young woman moved closer, signaling to her sound man to come up closer too. "We were standing in the kitchen. The door opened. And he was standing there. I think Prakash acted to save the lives of his family—his mother and sister and cousin sister. That is what I think."

"Ahha! You are saying you think he committed suicide."

Anita clenched her teeth and balled her fists, kept her arms stiff at her side, fearing there would soon be another murder if this woman didn't get away from her. A few minutes later, Anita heard the journalist reciting her news report on the disgraced pujari who committed suicide to save his family from the humiliation of his prosecution for theft from the temple.

It was all Anita could do to keep walking, walking as far away from that woman as possible.

Twenty-eight

As she drove away from Lalita Amma's village Anita kept
her eye on the baggage in the backseat as well as the driver.
This trip was costing her a fortune, but it would be well
worth it. The car reached Hotel Delite by noon. Anita
opened the door and climbed out. She was ready to stretch
her legs.

"Ah, you have come! At last!" Auntie Meena flew
out the front door and scampered to the parking lot. She
grabbed Anita by both arms. "How could you have stood it!
Those horrible people!"

"There was only one horrible person, Auntie."

"But such a horrible thing to have happen! And
poor Prakash! The things the newspapers and television
reporters are saying about him. The man is murdered in his
bed in the middle of the night and they say he hung
himself."

Anita fell back, trying to keep up with this spate of
gibberish. "They aren't saying such things."

"Yes, yes, I have heard it." Meena clapped her
hands against her cheeks. "Ayoo! If I had been there I too
might have been flung to my death."

"No one was flung to their death, Auntie." This was
all getting to be too much, and Anita slipped out of her
aunt's grasp and opened the car's back door. "I've brought
you something." She reached in and pulled, and the little

goat tumbled to the cement ground, then like a drunk scrambled to its feet and began to sway. It looked up at Auntie Meena and bleated.

"What is that?" Auntie Meena took a step back and pointed an accusatory finger at the animal.

"That's a goat. A very lucky goat. An amazingly lucky goat. One that stands first among goats as the luckiest of goats."

"Yes, yes, I am understanding. This is a lucky goat. But what has it to do with us? And why is it in the backseat of a taxi?" Auntie Meena eyed the goat with obvious dislike. She sniffed, recognized the smell, and took another step back. "This goat rode in the taxi?"

At that moment the taxi driver took it upon himself to request his fee. Auntie Meena gasped, looked at Anita, and stared stunned at the taxi driver. "How much?"

"That much, Auntie, that much." Anita dug out her purse and began counting out thousand-rupee notes. "It is a goat, after all, and it couldn't very well ride in the boot."

"Why not?" Auntie Meena all but wailed.

Anita handed over the notes. The driver pulled out the blanket covering the backseat, a tuft of straw, and bowl of water, and tossed them onto the ground. He nodded good-bye to Anita, climbed into his taxi, and backed out of the parking lot. The goat took a few more steps toward Auntie Meena.

"But what is it doing here?" Meena asked.

The staff came out to look at the forlorn creature, which continued to bleat and step this way and that, perhaps hoping someone would take notice of it and feed it.

"It is going to be our goat." Anita beamed at the animal.

"Is that blood?" Auntie Meena leaned over to get a closer look.

"It is. And those are the claw marks of a leopard. This little kid survived a leopard attack, the only one not injured by the terrorist and his bomb. This little kid is special."

No one had anything to say to this. A couple of the bearers seemed to find the kid amusing, and joked among themselves.

"It will live in the yard near the beach," Anita said.

"That's where the dhobi works. The clothes, they will never be clean, they will smell, the animal will eat them." Meena turned to Anita with eyes strikingly similar in their expression to those of the kid. "Couldn't we sell it? Give it away?"

"Oh, no, Auntie Meena." Anita leaned over and stroked the kid's snout. "This animal was meant to survive. It will bring us good luck," and remind me of how fortunate we are, she added to herself.

Twenty-nine

It was the sheer size of everything that struck Parvati at first. The train had so many cars that she felt she could walk through one and then another and on and on and never come to the end. The buildings seemed to go straight up and never stop, and get lost in the clouds. But the slums where she thought she could hide were the most terrifying because they were like villages where everyone knew everyone else, but so complicated she feared she'd become lost and never find her way out.

Parvati moved through a maze of alleys until she came to a little shop selling small brass puja objects—little pots and lamps, camphor pellets, incense and holders, and plates and bowls, whatever anyone could want. She had passed several of these shops, but at this one Parvati saw in the owner an approachable man, someone with kindness in his eyes, not yet hardened by life.

When Prakash had first told her they would move to Mumbai, where no one would find them, and make their way there as husband and wife, she had looked at him with an expression he thought meant affection and agreement. He did not see in her eyes the pity she held for him, pity that anyone could think escape was possible. Prakash saw only what he wanted, lived only the dream he believed was possible. He never stopped believing.

She remembered how it made her feel, as though a

253

little insect were flapping its wings inside her chest, and out of the blue she remembered running along the paddy fields with a tiffin carrier to deliver to her father in the midday sun, her younger brother calling for her to slow down, wait for him. She had forgotten that child, the person she had been. And now she was afraid to remember.

As she looked around her, passing lanes that went on to other lanes, stepping over bodies asleep on the sidewalk, or in a doorway, women stoking braziers along the side of the road, hawking their cooked corn, tea wallahs carrying their urns and cups on the backs of bicycles, fortune tellers, dhobis running along with piles of washed and ironed shirts on their heads, all this and more, she wondered if perhaps he had not been right. Perhaps it was possible to begin anew.

It had taken her days to find a shop with an owner she thought she could work on. At first she had been frightened of the noise and the speed and the roughness of the people. She had felt her body ache with the stiffness of her limbs, too frightened to walk freely, to let her arms leave her side lest someone rip one off and flee with it. But as she walked and walked, following this path and that road, dodging tuk-tuks and taxis and buses and bicycles and motorcycles and cars as large as a little house, she felt her limbs gradually relax. She reached deep inside herself and found once again the way of thinking that had kept her alive in the jungle in Sri Lanka, allowed her to work with other women to set up an ambush, kill everyone in the truck, and slip away into the darkness. But whenever someone smiled at her, she heard the voice of her little brother Rajan calling out to her, "Wait for me, Chechi! Wait for me! I want to come too!"

Even as she relaxed, she walked with one hand at her waist, resting on the knot tied into the end of her mundu, where she kept some of the money she had found in the cash box Prakash had buried near the house. He had shown his treasure to her one day as a way to convince her that he was serious about going away with her. He had enough money, he said, here, let me show you. And watch me now. I am adding more, just for us, he said, as he opened the small cloth bag and showed her the bills. Now you cannot doubt me, he said. No, she thought, I do not doubt you. The money was so much, all sorts of bills, large ones and small ones, and many. She counted it twice, divided it up and tucked it into three parts of her clothing.

On that last night in the hills Parvati heard the blast from a distance. She heard it, and she knew at once what it was and what it meant. In the early morning of that day she knew it was coming and did not wait. She knew she had been found. Prakash was not one to be persuaded, so she had to choose. The next morning, he'd said. But that would be too late, she told him. The Gurkhas were a provocation for a Tiger Eelam soldier, a direct invitation to act. Prakash dismissed her fears.

Parvati had to choose. She saw the guard, dug up the money, and was ready to go. The cousin sister visitor, Anita Amma, was the only one holding her back with little queries and requests, but Anita Amma was no one, too soft to know what was happening. Parvati knew it was time to go, and left. She heard the blast far away and knew Prakash was dead—she had no doubt.

With every step, Parvati studied the city Prakash had described to her—the buildings, the people, the traffic, the rich, the poor, the shouts and cries and laughter. All of it was familiar to her from his words. He had loved her, she realized, but she had not been able to believe it. His voice was erased by her fear, the certain knowledge that death was stalking her. But he had helped her. He had given her something precious—a way to begin again. And his mother too had loved her—a blanket on a chilly night, making sure her meals were good ones, offering a smile and a gentle word. Parvati was grateful for that. It had been a long time since anyone had shown her pure kindness.

Parvati walked up to the shop, and looked over the small brass pots for puja. She knew the owner was watching her, making sure she didn't steal anything. For the next few weeks, she would stop and evaluate and sometimes buy. After a few months, he would trust her, pass a few words with her, and even tell a joke or two. Shyly, she would admit that her Amma, a good employer, had gone away and left her with no job. It happens when the rich are suddenly taken with another place, another toy. They move on, leaving their servants to fend for themselves. Perhaps he knew of someone who needed a cook or a maidservant? In time he would tell her of a position, and she would go there.

In time, she would disappear into the millions of people living lives one day at a time, holding on with dirty fingernails and funny stories and threadbare sleeping mats. In time she would get used to it and forget about the estate in the hills and the old woman who took her in.

About the Author

Susan Oleksiw is the author of two earlier books featuring Anita Ray: *Under the Eye of Kali* (2010) and *The Wrath of Shiva* (2012). Oleksiw also writes the Mellingham series featuring Chief Joe Silva, who first appeared in *Murder in Mellingham* (1993).

Oleksiw compiled *A Reader's Guide to the Classic British Mystery* (1988), and was consulting editor for *The Oxford Companion to Crime and Mystery Writing* (1999). As a cofounder of The Larcom Press and of Level Best Books, she edited and published an annual anthology of the best New England crime fiction.

The Anita Ray mystery series grew out of Oleksiw's lifelong interest in India, where she lived and studied. She received a PhD in Sanskrit from the University of Pennsylvania.

Made in the USA
Middletown, DE
26 August 2020